THE
FAR SIDE
OF THE
DREAM

carla dietz

For Nicole, Fianna, and Alia

Never lose sight of your dreams.

CHAPTER 1

Miles To Go

I

Elsbeth scrunched up her eyes as tightly as she could to dim the blinding flashes scissoring across the western sky, but nothing could blot out the booming thunder that echoed in response. A quickening breeze, laden with the threat of rain, billowed the walls of canvas which had been her world for the last 33 days. A frypan rattled overhead on its wooden peg.

The gust of cool air raised gooseflesh on her arms, and she curled her knees to her chest for warmth. But it was more than the temperature which caused her to shiver.

Close by, a series of loud snorts punctuated the sound of raspy breathing. Captain Buehler rolled over in the cramped quarters, disturbing his sleeping wife, who then mumbled incoherently and shifted her weight. Another, more youthful voice sleepily protested in turn. Elsbeth pressed closer to the splintery side of the wagon, longing to make herself disappear into the cracks of the wood.

The harder she begged for the oblivion of sleep, the more vividly the memories of home swirled in her head. She felt if she reached out she could touch it—the snug parsonage nestled in the Ohio valley. It was that real...so far away, so long ago, yet so near at hand, so bittersweet.

Eight months. Had it only been eight months ago that her father had announced her birthday to the entire congregation?

"My daughter," said the Reverend Elsworth, his voice grown husky with pride and affection as he called on her to stand with him at the pulpit. "On this the occasion of her fifteenth birthday, I will honor Elsbeth by momentarily stepping aside and allowing her to read to you from the scriptures."

The young girl beamed as she ran her finger down the holy page and read the sacred passages. Silently she prayed she wouldn't stumble over difficult words such as *blasphemous* or *Armageddon*. She wanted her reading to be flawless, just as her father's recitations were without fault. Not until the final amen did she dare lift her eyes and then just to peek over the top of the Bible, searching the faces of family and neighbors for approval.

She thought she had done well. She hoped she had done well.

Among those filling the pews, nodding and smiling, were her mother and three older brothers with their wives, a bevy of cousins, and Martha, her best friend. When her father's hands settled warmly on her shoulders and his words "Excellent! Excellent!" rang in her ears, she experienced profound joy. But then he added, "Next time will be even better."

Elsbeth's smile faded by degrees. Her father's approval meant so much, but she had fallen short.

The next hour flew by. Had someone asked the meaning or even the subject of the sermon, she would have been at a loss. In her disappointment she forgot the most familiar of hymns and, lest she again embarrass her father as well as herself, took to mouthing the words.

At last the service was over and the congregation streamed out into the late September sunshine. A gesture from the reverend invited her to stand beside him as he bid the worshipers farewell. On other Sundays she would have assembled with the family, off to the side, while her father basked in the expected congratulations and well wishes of his flock. To join him on the lawn, smile and extend a neighborly handshake would have been a great honor if not for his earlier, veiled rebuke. Hesitantly she stepped to his side, heartened only marginally when he introduced her to a new parishioner.

"My daughter, Elsbeth," he said. "A promising student of the Bible, wouldn't you say?"

The man bowed, acknowledging her with a toothy grin then shuffled away.

Once again, she wondered at the true meaning of her father's words. Was what sounded like praise tainted ever so slightly with the hint she had not lived up to expectations?

Anxiously she looked down the line of people waiting to be recognized by their pastor. There was Mr. Strenger, a farmer from the county, looking uncomfortable in his Sunday best. Mr. Strenger, however, never said much. Indeed, this morning he said nothing at all, merely tipped his hat and moved along.

Elsbeth waited with singular focus for the next of the parishioners to step forward. These people were closer neighbors and perhaps she could glean from their remarks a more supportive interpretation of her performance at the pulpit. One was the postmaster's wife, Mrs. Lange, the other the widow Markham. At first, they chatted with her father about an upcoming parish potluck dinner. She listened intently. Not even the children's high-spirited laughter ringing from the church garden distracted her, nor the gaily-colored dash of leaves—the season's first—that blew against her feet.

Finally Mrs. Lange turned in Elsbeth's direction and gave her arm a gentle squeeze.

"Well done, my dear," she said.

"A fine reading," agreed Mrs. Markham. "Your father must be so proud."

Spirits buoyed by their comments, Elsbeth lifted her chin a little higher, stood a little straighter, smiled a little deeper. Before she could respond, though, Reverend Elsworth reached out and clasped the women's hands in his. "Thank you, ladies. It was an admirable first attempt."

The widow hesitated. "Remarkable presentation," she continued, directing her comments solely to Elsbeth. "You should consider preparing for the schoolteacher's position. Miss Hollowell will be leaving that post in the spring."

"Why, Mrs. Markham, I think I'd—"

"Ho, ho now," interrupted the reverend. "I've got better plans in the making for my daughter's future."

The woman lowered her voice. "Yes, well, dearie, you possess talent…and so good with the children."

"Thank you, Mrs. Markham, but Papa knows what's best for me."

The girl forced a broad smile at her father who smiled in return and said, "That's what I always tell you."

"And I trust you, Father."

"As well you should."

Come evening, when chores were done, Elsbeth happily responded to her father's ritual summons to the desk in his study. He trimmed the wicks in the lamp and propped open the Bible in front of him.

"Proverbs 13:24," he said.

Her answer came swiftly. "He that spareth the rod hateth his son."

"Good. Now Matthew 5:5."

"Blessed are the meek, for they shall inherit the land."

"Earth, Elsbeth. They shall inherit the earth."

"Earth. I'm sorry, Father. I meant earth."

"Psalms 34:14."

"Father, what plans did you mean?"

When Reverend Elsworth cast a quizzical look at her, she went on. "This morning after meeting you said you had plans for me."

"Ah. For your future, Elsbeth. For your future. But now, Psalms 34:14."

"Plans for what?"

"My dear child," said Elsworth, sighing heavily. "Don't you worry your head over such important decisions. I've taken care of it all."

Elsbeth puckered her face. "What decisions, Father?"

"When the time is right," he went on, "there'll be a young man for you in Columbus. I met his father at Revival last spring. A Mr. Coleman. We've been corresponding. The boy seems to have a calling. He ought to do nicely."

"Nicely for what?"

"Marriage, of course. You've proven yourself worthy."

At this, the girl's eyes lit up with interest. "*My* marriage? What's his name?"

"Of what import is a name if he has a true vocation?"

"Is he handsome?"

"'Vanity of vanities; all things are vanity.' Ecclesiastes 1:2."

"But is he handsome?"

5

"Elsbeth, how can you ever hope to make a proper minister's wife if you don't prepare yourself? Psalms 34:14."

A faraway look came over Elsbeth's face. A minister's wife, she thought. She answered, but a dreamy reverie replaced the crispness in her voice. "Keep thy tongue from evil and thy lips from speaking guile."

"Good girl. Now off to bed and pray God to improve your attentiveness."

"Yes, Father."

Alone in her room, Elsbeth pondered this new piece of information. A minister's wife. She tested the words out loud, trying to get used to the sound of them. *A minister's wife.* She pictured the unnamed groom she would meet some day—first blue-eyed and blond, then dark with a sweep of jet black hair, and all combinations in between. Not once did she question her father's choice. I'm in good hands, she thought.

As she often did at night, she turned up the lamp and slowly, almost reverently opened the lid of a large chest of burled oak at the foot of her bed. Carefully she fingered the fine linens and needlework, resorted the china cups, and dreamed of days to come: a house of her own with a cozy kitchen, picket fence and flower gardens. The gentle man who would be her husband, the laughing children who would fill her life.

When she crawled into bed, instead of fading, her waking thoughts slid easily into a dream, and a smile lingered on her face long after sleep had come.

All that changed the day Billy Brooster came to town.

II

He appeared first as a shadow.

Bent over in her mother's herb garden, Elsbeth noticed nothing at first as she dug into the earth beneath the yellow dock. She shook free clumps of dirt and lined the rootstocks precisely in a large flat-bottomed basket. When she had cleared this one portion of the garden for the coming winter, she moved over a row and began to collect the angelica and foxglove. Absorbed in her task, Elsbeth failed to see the murky, blue-black patch of shade slide between the slats of the rectory gate and ripple over the powdery soil. Not until it hovered over her stooped figure, did she turn a curious glance upward. The shadow became a man, young and blond, his face alight with a self-confident smile.

"Pardon me, miss," the apparition said.

Elsbeth straightened from her work and met his gaze.

A long moment of silence followed while she assessed the fierce intensity of the visitor's dark eyes and appealing cut of his nose and jaw. When she finally remembered she had a voice, she greeted him.

"Good afternoon, sir."

"It *was* a good afternoon, fair lady. Now it has become an exceedingly fine afternoon."

From a beltloop at the small of his back, the young man pulled a sprig of late-blooming aster.

"A beautiful blossom of the prairie," he said, looking at the pale lavender flower in his hand, shrugging. "It doesn't compare with the lovely flower of this garden."

With that he reached over the whitewashed fence and presented the bouquet to Elsbeth.

Even though she knew aster flourished in an

7

untended field across the road, the gesture—delivered with a charming bow—flattered her. She lowered her eyelids but could not hide the blush on her cheek.

Her voice was but a whisper. "Thank you, Mr...."

"Not mister. Billy. Billy Brooster."

"Are you newly arrived in town, Billy?"

"That I am. And looking for work."

Totally captivated, Elsbeth listened to his plea for employment. He'd traveled from a rather distant county. Though he'd had some schooling and enjoyed the challenge of learning new things, his father insisted he be apprenticed to a local tailor. At this point, Billy fashioned his fingers into a scissors and worked them through the air as if cutting out a sleeve.

"Snip. Snip. Snip."

Elsbeth giggled at his theatrics.

"I couldn't see doing that for the rest of my life, so I packed a bag and took to the road."

"Going where?"

Brooster thought for a long moment then answered. "Still deciding."

"But how have you managed?"

"Odd jobs here and there."

Intrigued by his willful independence, Elsbeth continued. "What sort of work do you do?" She giggled again. "Besides, of course, imaginary tailoring of invisible men's suits."

"Right now, I'll do anything." He glanced around the property until his eyes lighted on the barn out back. "I can tend to horses, chop firewood, muck out stalls. I'm not afraid of hard work." A shrug of his shoulders and a dimming of the mirth in his eyes told of a desperation Elsbeth found especially compelling. "Anything," he said. "Anything."

8

"I'll speak to my father," she promised. "I'm sure he'll say yes once he hears of your circumstances. Yes." She nodded emphatically. "After all, it's the Christian thing to do."

With that, Elsbeth unlatched the gate and invited him in.

She grabbed the basket and hurried ahead, toward the house and small office where she knew her father would be.

It didn't take long for Billy to settle into the daily routine of the parsonage. He greeted visitors and attended to their horses. He assisted Mrs. Elsworth when it came time to beat out rugs or chase deer from the vegetable garden. Although he balked at accompanying the family to church on Sundays, in other ways he proved a reliable and helpful presence.

Elsbeth became infatuated. Whether by happenstance or design, her daily chores soon rode tandem with his. She hung wash when Billy pruned the apple trees. She gathered eggs at the same time he milked the two cows. She felt his eyes track her movements, but she too was not innocent of studying him at work. She might sneak a look, but Billy never turned away like a schoolboy but rather flashed a crooked grin. When that happened, a warmth from within blunted the late autumn chill. Elsbeth didn't fully understand the source of this heat, but neither did she wish to extinguish it.

At night, curled snuggly under her bedcovers, aided by the glow of a single candle, she spilled onto the pages of her journal cherished dreams and youthful fantasy. The minister's son, promised by her father, no longer wavered indistinct in her mind but grew flesh and bone, gazed with brown eyes into her own of blue, and answered to a familiar name. If this unlikely blend of images made no sense, it bothered her not at all. When finished writing, she hid the diary in a niche inside her armoire, behind her good Sunday dress and kid leather shoes. She snuffed the candle with a pinch, praying softly, though if asked what for, she wouldn't be entirely sure.

Fall gave way to winter. Night came early, morning late. Outside work slacked as a blanket of snow covered the ground and an icy blast of northern air chased everyone inside.

One afternoon, not long after Christmas, the steady thunk-thunk of steel against wood penetrated the shuttered windows. Elsbeth grabbed the kindling box and headed outside in search of wood chips for the cook stove. She knew that wasn't all she would find.

Hugging a shawl tightly about her shoulders, she followed the well-trodden path toward the barn—and the sound. Her shoes scrunched on the hard-packed snow. Wisps of frosty breath led the way.

The door to the barn was partially open, just enough to let in a shaft of light, but not so wide as to allow Elsbeth to enter undetected. She remained outside and peered through the opening. Billy's back was to her, his sleeves rolled halfway to his elbows. She watched him arc the ax high over his head and land it with precision on a wedge of birch. The rhythm of his body and flex of his muscles brought to mind a great wild animal. A triangle of sweat between his shoulder blades fascinated her.

"You must be cold standing out there," he said without looking around.

Elsbeth gasped. Billy turned. Their eyes locked.

"Come in where it's warmer." He took a final swing of the ax, burying its head solidly in the chopping block.

"I...thought I might gather some kindling," said Elsbeth, out of breath despite having done nothing more rigorous than step into the barn.

"I see." He gestured toward the empty box she held. "I've saved some just for you." He reached out his hand. "C'mon, I'll help you fill that."

Timidly she relinquished the box. He guided her deeper into the barn to a small enclosure that had once been the tack room. Now it served as Billy's bunk. Though cleared of harness, the room retained the pleasant smell of oiled leather. Hay had been piled to one side and covered with a heavy woolen blanket. Propped upright in a corner was a burlap sack filled with wood shavings. A soap mug and straight-edged razor dangled from two nails driven into the wall. Despite the outside temperature, the room was warm. Billy gestured to a bale of straw, and Elsbeth sat while he scooped kindling into her wooden container. When the task was accomplished, he sat beside her.

"I like the fair weather better," he said.

"I too," she answered, glancing at him through her lashes. "The spring especially. It's a time of hope and new awakenings. Like the buds—"

He interrupted. "I meant I don't get to see you out and about as much now."

Elsbeth lowered her head and blushed.

"M...Mr. Brooster," she stammered. "I didn't realize you'd been so observant of my whereabouts."

"And you of mine?"

Her flush deepened.

Harsh winter light, streaming through a square of glass, dimmed under her half-closed eyes. Elsbeth felt him scoot closer. A finger traced along her jawline and down her neck. She drew in a breath and waited, but not for long. His lips found hers. She didn't resist. The shawl dropped at her feet. Her heartbeat filled the tiny room.

11

* * * * *

The sun had long since dipped behind the lacy fretwork of barren orchard when Elsbeth tiptoed toward the rear entrance of the house. Her dress was rumpled, bits of straw clung to the fabric. Her hair, usually neatly groomed and pinned into a knot at the back of her neck, hung loose and tangled. An inner battle of emotions raged: some soared to unexpected heights while others were blunted by a profound sense of embarrassment and guilt. Her shawl was missing. The kindling box forgotten. The closer she came to the house, the more confusing became the moral implications of what had just transpired.

If only she could make it to the sanctuary of her room, she thought, all would be well. In the quiet solitude she would sort things out. Through the kitchen, across the hall, up the steps. If only…

She sucked in her breath and opened the door.

A swirl of sweet, spicy air rushed to greet her. Two mincemeat pies waited in the bustle oven, and a new loaf of bread cooled on the kitchen table. No one was about and for that godsend Elsbeth humbly thanked the Lord. She leaped forward—from threshold to rag rug—and was calculating how best to muffle her footsteps on the bare wooden floor when her father entered the room. Immediately she stopped and choked back a startled scream.

"Daughter!" His eyes assessed her disheveled appearance. "What is the meaning of this?"

Without intending to do so, she turned her head ever so slightly toward the back door. The reverend did not miss the subtle movement nor its unvoiced implication. He brushed past her and stood at the door, peering out its small

12

window, across the snowy path to the barn door which hung open.

Elsbeth dared not move. All too apparent was the dawn of her father's understanding. The solemn black of his coat and trousers seeped into his eyes, and when his fist slammed the door jamb, rattling every dish in the cupboard, Elsbeth cowered in fear. She hardly recognized her father in this man's distorted face.

"Slut!" he roared. "Whore! You dare sully the good name of Edward Elsworth."

He slapped her—hard.

"A blight on my reputation, you are. The devil's own. Oh, that God deliver you into the flames of hell."

He raised his hand again, but Elsbeth shied away.

"Out of my sight," he bellowed.

Elsbeth saw the opportunity to flee and rushed toward the stairwell. In the dim light of the hallway stood her mother, apron twisted into a knot and pressed against her lips. Their eyes met—Elsbeth's frantic with pleading, her mother's saucer wide but unreadable. Mrs. Elsworth's head twitched back and forth between husband and daughter, but she said nothing, did nothing.

Weak with regret, Elsbeth knew at once no defense would be forthcoming from her mother. Whether fear of her husband or tacit agreement kept her at bay, Elsbeth could not guess. For the first time in her life, she felt all alone. She slipped by, dashed up the steps and into her room.

The scene below, however, was not so easily denied. The sound carried up the stairs, played out with a barrage of threats against the scoundrel Brooster, a tromp of feet, the slam of a door and march toward the barn.

The ruckus continued, volume abated only by the distance between the house and outbuilding. With shaking

13

fingers she pushed aside the heavy drape that covered her bedroom window. Frost drew fanciful shapes on the glass, perhaps Nature's attempt to obscure the scene outside. The afterglow of sunset sharpened into stark relief the profile of her father, one hand on his hip, the other balancing the rifle he used to rid the gardens of varmints. Elsbeth's heart sank further as she watched her one last hope hurry up the road, a satchel slung over his shoulder.

Billy never looked back, not even once.

III

In the weeks to follow, a cloud of acrimony settled over the household. Elsbeth barely left her room, and then only to fill a plate for a meal which she ate alone from a perch on the corner of her bed. When it became all too evident she carried inside her one more embarrassment, any chance of reconciliation was shattered.

Elsworth was beside himself. His sermons became short, in stride with his temper. He forbade his daughter's appearance outside the house and concocted excuses for her absence at church. Evenings he composed letters, searching among his network of ministers for a resolution without fully divulging his reason for such inquiries. He wrote that Elsbeth was of marrying age and desired a husband, not the promised boy from Columbus, but one whose vocation provoked an even greater calling, the will to carry the word of God to souls on the western frontier.

His search was rewarded. A recent widower, who had traveled west the previous spring and had not as yet learned of his revised marital status, would surely require a wife. With this as Elsworth's goal, hushed and hurried arrangements were made. A missive was penned in the reverend's best penmanship. It offered condolences for the man's loss and relied strongly on his compassion. Elsbeth would make an acceptable wife—despite her circumstances.

When the year's first robins appeared and melting snow made roads more passable, a final order was given. One day not long after, a wagon pulled up to the parsonage. Two small, leather-bound trunks and a shabby carpetbag, crammed with the barest of necessities—a pittance of a dowry—stood ready in the front hall. The treasures of Elsbeth's oak chest remained upstairs at the foot of her bed. Her mother pecked her lightly and quickly on the cheek while her father towered behind them in stoic silence. Traveling accommodations were discussed with the Buehlers and money for passage was handed over. Without further ado, Elsbeth was unceremoniously shipped off.

* * * * *

The plop-hiss of rain on dying campfire coals pulled her thoughts from her childhood home in the fertile river valley of Ohio to the sobering reality of the road to Oregon. The scratchy wad of bedding chafed her skin.

When Elsbeth reflected on the journey thus far, depression bore down. It suffocated like the choking dust of the prairie trail. She hated the dust. More than that she hated the unrelieved monotony, the day-after-day agony of crossing rivers, winching up steep inclines or down deep declines, the endless search for fuel to light one's cook fire.

Once an Indian with cruel black eyes and a streak of red, muddy paste zigzagging down his cheek leaped into the wagon and demanded a slab of bacon and her only tin pitcher. That had scared her. But what terrified her more was what lay beyond—beyond the monotonous prairie, beyond the great Platte River, beyond the mountains so far away...beyond the end of the trail.

A husband awaited. She knew nothing more. The great Northwest remained a mystery, no familiar face awaited, no place to conjure in her mind, no friend.

Trade goods, she thought. That's all I am. Chattel in a common business deal.

Her surroundings offered no comfort. Her traveling companions even less. The only thing she knew for certain was another day had slipped into history and found her 24 hours and an equal number of miles closer to Mr. Amos T. Warner. Her past was gone. That single name was all the future held.

CHAPTER 2

Awakenings

I

Coming to terms with her parents' harsh treatment had proven near impossible. The memories gnawed at Elsbeth's soul like a pack of vicious dogs. Even now, after a month underway, resentment was strong. It was so unfair: the cold and heartless good-bye followed by thirty days with the Buehlers. Although her parents could have cast her from their sight—alone and penniless—to find her own way, she nonetheless found it impossible to be grateful for their providing passage to the new frontier.

Her progressing pregnancy rendered sleeping in the Buehlers' wagon more and more difficult until she could barely doze more than two hours at a time. Through the many restless nights, her mind often returned to that fateful day of parting.

April should have been a time to celebrate the dawn of a new season. One expected the swollen buds on trees and shrubs to burst their seams at any moment. Elsbeth had always looked forward to spring. She enjoyed working in the gardens, preparing the soil, laying seed in furrowed rows, and attending to the perennials. That this year would be so different felt like a grave personal loss.

The Buehlers had not greeted her that day. There had been no welcome. The man merely heaved her meager luggage into the wagon bed and left her to languish in her own silence.

As the wagon rattled down the roadway, Elsbeth sat on one of her trunks and looked out the rear semi-circle of canvas stretched taut across wooden bows. The parsonage, her only home for over fifteen years, receded slowly in the distance. Soon all she could see was the crown of an old oak tree which anchored the front lawn. Its branches were still leafless. The tree appeared dead and forlorn. Elsbeth sighed, for she felt much the same.

Deep inside, she harbored the insane hope her father would relent and she'd see him in desperate pursuit, waving his arms and shouting this was all a mistake. That hope was shattered when the wagon swung onto a side lane and her old home vanished from sight. With a heavy heart Elsbeth turned and surveyed her new home. It was cramped, laden as it was with stores of goods and possessions meant to be carried across a continent. The Buehlers rode up front. She studied their backs for a clue to their natures. They sat side by side, though not so close any part of one touched the other. Mr. Buehler was stout and dressed for weather warmer than what the day offered: sleeves rolled to the elbows and a lightweight vest. His wife wore clothes more suitable for early March than April. They did not speak to one another. Occasionally Buehler flicked a long, slender osier switch to keep the team of draft horses at a consistent pace.

Inside, their son—Elsbeth guessed him to be several years younger than she—slept on a gunny sack filled with rice. His head rocked back and forth with the sway of the

18

wagon, his mouth hung open.

They had not traveled far when another wagon fell in line close behind them. The action seemed prearranged, for Buehler paid it no heed and the driver of the other conveyance made no attempt to explain his presence. From his garb—black frock coat, black hat, clerical collar—Elsbeth reckoned he was a preacher answering a godly call to travel west, there to minister to a far flung congregation. So eager was she for a small measure of compassion from another living soul that the presence of a man of God at first offered relief. She waved. He ignored her. She reasoned the afront away, convincing herself he could not possibly see her beyond his four-horse team.

A deep rut in the road shook the wagon and roused the Buehlers' sleeping son.

"Who are you?" he demanded.

Despite the boy's ill-mannered attitude, Elsbeth smiled. "My name is Elsbeth. I'm to be traveling with you to Oregon."

"That your stuff?" He pointed with his elbow at her two cases and one tapestry bag.

"Yes. That's all I—"

"Takes up a lot of room."

"I..." She hesitated, not knowing quite how to explain what a pittance this was compared to the delicate china, linens and her favorite hat which remained behind in a hope chest at the foot of her bed. Instead, she changed the subject.

"What's your name?"

"Alfred."

"Well, Alfred, there's a long journey ahead of us. We can be friends, can't we?"

For an answer, he shrugged and pretended to go back

to sleep.

By mid-afternoon the road widened into the main street of another small town. They did not stop, though Elsbeth noticed two more wagons waiting in the shadow of a white-steepled church. With a slap of leather, jingle of harness and clomp of hooves, Buehler's column of two became four.

"Alfred," she called out. "I know you're not really asleep. What's going on? There are now three wagons trailing us."

"Don't you know? Father's leading a group of churchmen. He says it's a holy mission. There'll be more in St. Louis."

"So many preachers on their way to the Oregon Territory?"

"Not all. Some'll be farmers. Others? Who knows?"

"And we're going to St. Louis?" Elsbeth, of course, had heard of St. Louis but always in terms of how very far away it was.

The boy expelled an exasperated burst of air that whistled through his front teeth. "Where else are we supposed to cross the Mississippi? Don't you know nothin'?"

Elsbeth *didn't* know. No one had told her how this journey was to begin, who she'd be traveling with, or even how long it would take. St. Louis, she thought, with wonder. She had so much to learn.

A first lesson came at eventide when the troupe arrived at a humble inn with the dubious name *The Grand River Hotel*. Although she couldn't see a river, one must have been very near, for steamboat whistles sounded at regular intervals.

Once the horses were bedded at a stable, the Buehlers, their son and Elsbeth entered the inn's dining room and ordered a meal. The fare was a disappointment. It was barely warm, and the oily stew brought on a wave of nausea. The three Buehlers were not so afflicted and ate with gusto. While Elsbeth picked among the soggy vegetables, Buehler waved over the innkeeper.

"We'll be requirin' a room for the night."

Elsbeth started at his announcement. Had she heard correctly? *A* room? One room? Buehler must have noticed her alarm, for as soon as the innkeeper left the table, he addressed her directly.

"That's for the family. Someone needs to look to the wagon. You'll do nicely. Give you a chance to get used to what it's goin' be like from here on."

He stood. "I'll go settle up. Don't be dawdlin'."

Shocked at this unexpected turn of events, Elsbeth still had the presence of mind to notice Buehler pull from his pocket a money purse. It was distinctly familiar—the one and same her father had handed over that very morning.

The greasy dinner threatened to make a return appearance. Elsbeth rushed outside and vomited in the relative privacy of a bush. Resigned to her night's accommodations, she headed for the wagon. As she passed by the other three wagons that were now part of their group, she heard the low murmur of voices. However, the cadence of the muffled words suggested prayer. For months she'd been denied attendance at church services and with it the congenial company of friends and neighbors. Here, so many miles from home, the thought of joining strangers and giving oneself over to a higher power was less appetizing than the inn's horrible dinner.

She walked on and climbed aboard Buehler's wagon where she shoved items around to make room. A chill had settled in the air with the approach of nightfall, so before all light disappeared, she opened a box of her belongings. This was one her mother had packed. Elsbeth hoped to find a warm blanket inside.

The wished-for blanket lay right on top, though it was not the one from her bedroom rather a spare they kept in an old trunk in the attic. When Elsbeth unfolded it, something clunked to the floor. It was a Bible. She regarded it scornfully. When she picked it up, a piece of paper fluttered from between the pages. Immediately she recognized her father's handwriting. All it said was 1 Thessalonians 4:3. She didn't need to search the Bible to know the meaning of this particular verse. "For this is the will of God, your sanctification: that you abstain from fornication."

Never before had Elsbeth felt so utterly alone and unwanted, and when that realization hit home, she began to weep.

II

The following morning presented itself as dull and lifeless as an old pewter jug. The neighing of horses had awakened Elsbeth. She crawled to the rear of the wagon and looked out. The missionaries were busy. Some guided their animals into position at the wagon tongues while others adjusted harnesses. The Buehlers were exiting the inn. They appeared well rested and, judging from the biscuit in Alfred's hand, well fed.

Elsbeth stepped into his path.

"Shall I go inside and order a breakfast?"

"Morning meals came with the room," he informed her. "The missus will find something for you to eat."

The something turned out to be a thin slice of yesterday's bread. It was a paltry excuse for breakfast, but her stomach still churned from the remnants of the evening meal, so it didn't really matter what she was given. She nibbled at the crust and pocketed the rest.

Buehler and his son hitched the horses, then called out to the preachers. "Movin' out in five minutes. No later."

They didn't have far to go, a few blocks at most to a dockside landing. Once again money exchanged hands. This time Elsbeth watched Buehler closely, confirming her previous suspicion that it was her father's money which placed them in the queue for boarding the ferry. She wondered if this was part of the deal. Had her father been so keen to rid himself of a fallen daughter that he had to bribe Buehler to take her along?

There wasn't time to waste on the implications, for she was ordered out of the wagon and into the service of leading the team up the gangplank. Once the horses had been unhitched and settled into an on-board corral, the ferryman began spewing instructions.

"All right. Listen up. Two abreast, midship, and get those wheels off. I won't have these contraptions rolling all over my deck."

To Elsbeth's amazement, the men began to do just that: jack up the wagon beds, remove the wheels, secure them with ropes to the side of the wagons, then lower the wagons until they rested firmly on the deck. To her it seemed like a lot of unnecessary precaution until they were finally underway. Mid-river, the current caught the riverboat and set up a rocking motion that would have played havoc with anything on wheels.

The properly-secured wagons moved not an inch, though the rolling movement brought on a wave of the

23

morning sickness which had plagued her for several weeks. She sought out a place to sit down to quiet her stomach and observe the activity on *The Ohio Belle*, the name emblazoned in red paint outside the pilot house.

The boat was large and there were plenty of travelers. The ladies wore fashionable dresses and, to Elsbeth's mind, gaudy hats. The men were a mixture of classy types and simple country folk. Their apparel reflected their stations in life. The missionaries huddled together. Elsbeth thought they looked like members of a secret society, averse to letting anyone join their tightly-closed circle. The Buehlers lounged at the deck rail.

When she looked past them toward the shoreline, she was astounded at how swiftly the boat was moving. Not even when her brother had driven the family buggy at a frenzied clip, and she had squealed in delight, had she felt they were moving this fast.

"Why, at this rate, I should think we'll be at our destination by sundown."

She had meant to speak only to herself, but another passenger overheard and replied.

"More like three days. There are ports where we'll stop and, of course, once on the Mississippi we'll be fighting the current. The weather, too, you know?"

The helpful passenger moved along, leaving Elsbeth to consider how much she was destined to experience.

On-board activity quickly took on a routine. Occasionally they pulled up alongside a dock to allow more passengers and their baggage onto the boat. So many people in so limited space was noisy, as was the almost constant call of lookouts marking the river's depth or warning of floating debris and snags. The steam engines which powered the huge arms that engaged the rear paddlewheel added to the cacophony. Elsbeth suffered a non-ending headache, and so, after four days, when she heard a cry of "St. Louis!" she murmured "At last."

Once the riverboat was secured to the shore, it was as if a whirlwind descended over *The Ohio Belle*. Passengers disembarked in a great jostle of bodies. Stewards unloaded crates of goods onto waiting drays. The four wagons were reassembled, the horses hitched. Elsbeth's assessment of the vaunted city of St. Louis was placed on hold, for her assistance was again required to see wagon and horses safely ashore. When Buehler's entourage clomped onto soil west of the Mississippi and headed toward the center of town, Elsbeth's amazement soared.

"Why, Alfred," she said, trying to make conversation. "There must be thousands of people here. And look, there's a cathedral right in the heart of it all!"

To her surprise, he appeared equally astounded at the size and bustle of the city. His eyes widened and he jerked his head from one side to the other to take it all in.

"Hope we don't get lost," he said.

"I thought you'd been here before."

"Nah. I only know there are more wagons ajoinin' us here."

"How many?"

"Four or five at least. And we have to load up the wagons with supplies and swap out the horses for oxen."

"Your father's selling the team?"

"Yeah. I heard him say horses'll be no good for the long haul, so we have to go with oxen."

Elsbeth sat back and contemplated the "long haul."

"Just how long will we take?"

"Father says four or five months if we're lucky."

No words could describe Elsbeth's dismay. Five

impossibly long months! And luck would play a leading role. She steeled her mind to the prospect, but her heart sank.

How easy it would be to blame Billy Brooster for the current state of her life. In fact, she'd tried often to pile the responsibility squarely on his shoulders, but that had never worked. Hadn't she flirted? Hadn't she followed him around like a newborn colt? She had been complicit and more— willing. In the end she had only herself to blame.

Trying to wish away the consequences of one afternoon in the barn was the devil's work. She looked for Alfred, but he had moved toward the front of the wagon and was munching on an apple. Had she wanted someone to commiserate with? She couldn't decide, but at that very moment she felt a faint tickle in the depths of her belly. It wasn't the return of morning sickness. This was different. It was a joyful feeling. A warm smile spread across her face, accompanied by a resolve that was both fierce and protective.

The tiny flutter said to her, "I'm here. You're not alone."

III

The sojourn in St. Louis stretched out to a week. They camped where they could find room, for the city was filled with what seemed like multitudes of pioneers eager to head west. Buehler took on the task of meeting with local ranchers to bargain a trade: horses for oxen. He had made several attempts before he returned from one such foray to announce a deal had been brokered and teams of oxen would arrive on the following morn. A ripple of excitement spread among the travelers.

As Alfred had forecast, Buehler's company had swelled. Ten wagons, a dozen goats, a small herd of milk cows and saddle horses, a buckskin-clad trail guide now awaited the onset of the journey. Those not of the religious persuasion were a mix of farmers lured by the unseen promise of fertile land, adventurers out for a lark, or families not wanting to travel alone.

Elsbeth wondered how much more of her father's money had been emptied from his purse in the frenzied preparations for departure. She was too intimidated to speak up but couldn't fail to notice that Mrs. Buehler's straw hat was now tied under her chin with a long strand of green silk ribbon and Alfred's pockets always bulged with a square of cornbread or piece of fruit.

One day an elderly woman pushing a small cart rolled it into their campsite.

"Sunbonnets for the ladies," she called out. "Neckerchiefs for the gents."

Elsbeth approached and examined one of the bonnets. It was expertly constructed of muslin and dyed a vibrant yellow. When she ran her fingers along the brim, it guaranteed a crisp and sturdy shade.

"Buckram inside?" she inquired.

"Indeed. The finest there is. There'll be no drooping with this bonnet. And you'll be needing it. Once out on the prairie, I hear tell, the sun is unforgiving and you with such pretty skin."

"How much?"

"One dollar."

It was a bit expensive, but Elsbeth knew the woman was right. She would need a substantial sunbonnet. The problem was, she had no money of her own. The only thing of value she possessed was a locket her Grandma Emilie had given her the year before she died. Elsbeth refused to part with it. Her only other option was to ask Buehler for the money. She asked the woman not to leave while she sought out her so-called benefactor.

"Mr. Buehler?" She found him on the other side of the wagon mounting a spare wheel to a metal hook. "I need a dollar to buy a proper bonnet for the trip. There's a woman who's just come by who has them for sale."

The man didn't answer until he had wrestled the wheel into place. He wiped his forehead with a cotton rag, then looked her up and down as if mulling his response. Elsbeth hung her head, humiliated that he might judge such a reasonable request out of the question.

In the end he stepped around the wagon to where the old woman waited. Elsbeth picked up the bonnet, but Buehler snatched it away and tossed it back onto the cart. He selected another, one not nearly as desirable, and handed the woman a smaller coin.

Speechless, motionless, and on the verge of tears as Buehler stalked off, Elsbeth barely noticed the woman step to her side until a consoling arm encircled her shoulders.

"Your father?"

Elsbeth shook her head.

"With child?"

A sigh was Elsbeth's only answer, though she did wonder if her pregnancy showed in more ways than one.

"No husband, I take it?"

"No…no husband."

Gently the woman took back the cheaper bonnet and pressed the choice one into Elsbeth's hands. "Here," she said.

"Oh, I mustn't. I have no way to pay—"

"You take this and no argument."

With that the woman lifted the cart's handles and

28

pushed it further on down the street, leaving Elsbeth to run her fingers lovingly along the fine stitching of the sunbonnet and to marvel at the kindness of strangers.

* * * * *

Jumping off day. That's what they called it. A leap of faith. Like diving into a pond without knowing what lies beneath the surface.

As they moved out of the St. Louis environs, Buehler's ten wagons were joined by others who departed at the same time. The trappings of civilization fell off by degrees. The well-worn road deteriorated, towns dwindled in size, outlying settlements became sparse, hay pastures disappeared. Finally, what spread across the horizon was open prairie. One could call it beautiful with its tall, slender stalks swaying rhythmically in the breeze and the sound it made like a soothing lullaby. Elsbeth chose not to. The prairie harbored the unknown, and she couldn't shake the unsettling presentiment that what was unknown would also be unfriendly.

CHAPTER 3

The Far Side of the Dream

I

The butt of the drover's whip banged against the side of the wagon bed and startled Elsbeth out of yet another night of fitful sleep. Dreams, both good and bad, fled before the predawn light.

"Just as well," she murmured.

She rubbed her eyes as if to wipe away all traces of the past. To face another day on the endless trek toward the Oregon Territory required all the strength she could muster. It did little good to dwell on Billy Brooster, her father's unremitting rage, or her mother's passive acquiescence. As for the other—the marriage bed into which she had been sentenced—she shuddered to think about it.

Her lips moved with the words of a humble prayer, the same one she uttered every morning. "Please, God, let him be kind."

For now, she forced her weary body into the pale gray morning. Her bulging belly strained at the dress meant for a teenaged figure. Immediately a wave of nausea washed over her, brought on only in part by the all-pervading smell of manure, unwashed bodies, and bacon fat frying over a half dozen nearby cookfires. Elsbeth clutched at her stomach and stumbled outside the circle of wagons, seeking the relative privacy afforded by distance and the tall prairie grasses. There she could be sick without the cruel teasing of the children and the self-righteous stares of the group of westward-bound missionary wives and their Bible-thumping husbands. Tears of self-pity wet the ground as well.

A rustling behind her abruptly silenced her sobs.

"Wh-who's there?" she stammered, instantly alert and aware of the dangers of being alone on the land, away from the protection of the wagon train and its armed patrol.

Who's...?" The question hung unfinished, interrupted by the deafening report of a rifle and the explosion of sod at her feet.

A scream froze in her throat. She threw up her arms against the shower of dirt. The tall grass parted and "Wild Willie" stepped forward.

Elsbeth's eyes widened in horror. Wild Willie was the son of the train's mountain man scout and his Lakota Sioux wife. Willie's straight blond hair hung past his shoulders. Bronze-colored skin and jet black eyes revealed his Indian side. Although a loner who never spoke, Elsbeth encountered his stare wherever she turned. It's as if I'm a bug on a pin, she thought. He frightened her.

The barrel of his rifle moved toward the hem of her dress, caught on a scaly coil, and with a smooth, easy motion flung the now lifeless rattlesnake out of sight. Willie raised a finger to his forehead in salute, then disappeared into the prairie. The faint swish of the buckskin fringe of his shirt was the only sound he made.

Elsbeth gathered her wits and her skirts and raced back to the campsite where she sought out Mrs. Buehler.

31

"Why is he called Wild Willie?" she asked, nodding her head in the direction of the shadowy figure who had also returned to the encampment and squatted near the tethered horses.

Mrs. Buehler's face hardened at the question.

"Half breed," she spat as if ridding her mouth of a piece of spoiled meat. She walked away, leaving a single pair of words to explain it all.

Elsbeth recalled conversations among the women, comments which conjured a long list of perversions embodied in the offspring of that most unnatural, "ungodly" union of man and Indian.

Elsbeth knew she too was the object of ridicule. It wasn't difficult to miss. How often had she seen the women gather their aprons to their lips in an effort to disguise the whispered conversations. At a different time and under different circumstances, she too might have been guilty of the same gossip. It was easy to prejudge a young and pregnant girl traveling without benefit of spouse or kin. She hoped she would be more forgiving. Youthful passion, after all, was not a character flaw transmitted like a deadly disease.

But Willie—an outcast of equal proportions—had rescued her, and that was something to think about.

In the weeks that followed, the prairie proved an ever-changing landscape. At times, it was flat and featureless, but could quickly become a challenge when wagons had to be winched down steeply-graded hills. Dusty and dirty one hour, lush and inviting the next. One such place was called Alcove Springs where a copse of trees sheltered a stream that burbled gaily over a rocky ledge. Elsbeth discovered someone named Reed had inscribed his name in the stone. She wrote her own name with a stick on the muddy bank, though she knew perfectly well the first rainfall would wash it away.

Further along the trail, great formations of sandstone suggested familiar shapes. One resembled a giant chimney. The pioneers could see it for miles. It might as well have been the needle point of a compass, for they used it to guide their way.

Great fields of wildflowers lifted one's spirits while barren expanses anticipated hardships yet to come.

The endless westward trudge continued. Each day became a monotonous copy of the one before, marked by long hours of hard work and dwindling supplies. Reprieve from the routine came in the form of violent thunderstorms, the arrival of a tiny new pioneer, or a hurried memorial to commend to God the soul of one unfortunate enough to find a promised land other than the Willamette Valley.

Despite her growing discomfort and awkward gait, Elsbeth performed her share of the daily chores. Only one thing had changed. More and more she felt the watchful eyes of Willie upon her. When the road sloped sharply uphill and Elsbeth took her turn at the ropes to help lighten the load for the overburdened oxen, Willie appeared out of nowhere to put his shoulder to the wagon. He scoured the barren countryside for firewood, replenishing her supply of that precious commodity. If the air thickened with censure of her advancing condition, Willie painted his horse and his face with streaks of colored clay and rode, unbidden, among the wagons. His ominous presence silenced the tongue of even the most condescending shrew.

None of this escaped Elsbeth's attention. Of all the holier-than-thous who surrounded her and gave unending lip service to religious perfection, it was Willie she could depend on. He didn't frighten her anymore.

At night she found comfort in private tears, not for herself or her precarious situation, but in gratitude that someone found her worthy to befriend—even if that someone was Wild Willie.

As the miles slowly passed beneath the wheels, the two quietly developed a special kinship, a silent acknowledgment of the pain each felt at being alone in the midst of many. As a result, Elsbeth stood straighter, walked prouder, questioned the tenets of her upbringing more. She began to feel much older than her fifteen years.

"We'll be coming up on Fort Bridger within the week," announced Mrs. Buehler one day.

"Is that why there is to be a general meeting tonight?"

"Things need…deciding."

"What things?" Elsbeth asked, but the fiery look of contempt which Mrs. Buehler aimed in Willie's direction was answer enough.

That evening the men gathered around the central campfire. A few women sat among them, those who had lost husbands along the way and now spoke for their family units. Drovers and hirelings were not included, for this was an owners' meeting. Elsbeth stood just outside the bobbling circle of light—silent, unseen, but privy to the agenda of complaints being aired. Chief among them was Wild Willie.

"He's nothin' but trouble."

"Never trust an Indian."

"He's crazy, I tell ya."

The list of accusations mounted as one voice fed on the prejudice and fear of the next.

"Scout reported the military's camped at Fort Bridger. They'll know what to do with him."

Elsbeth could stand the lies no longer. She breathed deeply, once then twice, to steady her trembling limbs, before stepping forward.

"Willie wouldn't harm anyone and you know it," she

said, more loudly than even she anticipated.

"What's that? Who's speaking?"

Elsbeth advanced another step, letting the yellow glow from the flames illuminate her face.

"Willie…he's not like what you say."

"This ain't your concern, girl," shouted one of the overlanders. "Get yourself back to your wagon."

When the man started to rise to emphasize his point, Elsbeth almost faltered, but she couldn't leave Willie undefended.

"My father paid full price for my passage. I have a vote, and I vote Willie stays."

Elsbeth felt almost faint at the strength of her conviction, but in the end her one vote made no difference.

Later, after lookouts had been assigned for the night, individuals drifted to their respective wagons. The summer nights had been remarkably warm. Buehler had been sleeping outside on the ground, but on this occasion he poked his head into the rear of his wagon and confronted Elsbeth.

"Let's make one thing perfectly clear. I'm the captain of this here wagon." At some point during the trek, he had anointed himself with a captain's rank and insisted his wife and son address him as such. "I won't have you taking up a stance against me."

Although unnerved by the severity of the man's tone, Elsbeth worked up the courage to answer.

"The vote was unfair."

"No backtalk. I won't stand for it." He aimed a menacing fist. "'Specially coming from the likes of you."

Contradicting this man was a fight not to be won, so she merely closed her ears to the rest of his rant.

Buehler fumed for days until the scout reported an Army fort was within another day's march.

The line of wagons arrived at Fort Bridger on schedule. Supplies were bought and bartered, oxen exchanged, rolling stock repaired. They rested three days.

This was a difficult time for Elsbeth. The months on the road had matured her, perhaps hardened her. She had come to realize her future, and that of her baby's, lay in her hands alone. But knowing was only half the battle. Hundreds of miles separated her from her father's wrath, but a decision to disobey his orders weighed heavily on her mind.

On the morning of departure, after the break of dawn and the yoking of the teams, Elsbeth laid a piece of foolscap in her lap. The paper crinkled as she shifted it here and there while she searched for the proper wording.

"Whatya doin'?" demanded the Buehler's son. He rushed to her side and grabbed at the sheet.

Elsbeth's frown warned him away, and the boy scrambled over the back of the wagon and was gone.

Alone now, Elsbeth picked up a pencil. She rubbed the side of the lead back and forth against the smooth lid of a cask until the pencil had a fine, sharp point. That's how she wanted her words to be—clear and sharp. Impeccable penmanship. No fuzzy lines. No smudges. No mistakes.

"Father," she wrote. "During the course of this journey, I have given great thought to your arrangement with Mr. Amos Warner and have come to the decision that I will not honor your pledge of matrimony to him. Elsbeth."

There. Done.

She reread the message carefully, checking for any sign her trembling fingers had betrayed the doubts and fears she was feeling. When satisfied they had not, she neatly folded the sheet and wrote his name and parish on the outside. For a moment she rested it in her lap, waiting for second thoughts. What thoughts that did come were of an

36

unforgiving father and those others who wore the cloak of God and spoke His words by rote but failed to exhibit a single note of compassion—for Willie and for herself. Second thoughts? None came.

With a gentle touch she traced the curve of her belly. She had not planned this. It certainly wasn't part of the dreams of her youth, but she would never reject this innocent little spark of life. Never.

She would also not rip the letter up. As she rose from her task, her gaze fell upon one of the trunks which held her belongings. She lifted the lid, removed the Bible, and, with a piece of string, she bound it to the letter.

A commotion outside drew her attention, for it meant their imminent departure. Captain Buehler called for the wagons to fall into line. Elsbeth had no time for her resolve to waver. Cries of gee and haw filled the air as drivers maneuvered for a favorable placement in the line of march. The clamor reminded her of the need for haste. The future would work itself out. She had to act now.

She climbed to the ground, skirted around the fort to the orderly arrangement of tents that was the Army encampment and sought out the commander. He had promised to post letters back to the states with the next detachment of soldiers.

Deep in thought, she hurried along, so distracted she almost passed by the figure clad in buckskin. After skidding to a halt, Elsbeth stood looking at Willie. She had so much to thank him for, but as yet they had never exchanged so much as a hello, and even now the words would not come. She could only hope he read her heart.

Willie raised a finger to his forehead in salute and rewarded her with the one smile she had ever seen grace his lips. Then he turned, mounted his pony, and headed, not west, but east into Sioux country.

Elsbeth regarded the Indian's retreating back a final
time. "Thank you, Willie," she whispered.

Then she stalked into the commander's tent and
dropped the bundle on the low camp table in front of the
startled officer.

"I do hope your soldiers will be heading east soon,"
she said. "This letter...*my* letter must be carried to Ohio as
quickly as possible."

Outside, the shouts and snorts of impatient men and
beasts carried through the canvas tent. Without waiting for a
reply, Elsbeth fled toward the departing train.

II

Angry voices filtered through the heavy wagon cover.
Elsbeth strained her ears to make out the words but gave up
when the pain in her side surged again. It had been two days
since the accident, two days that she had been obliged to ride
lest she slow the westward progress for everyone. The wagon
lurched mercilessly over the rough terrain, each jolt a stabbing
reminder of her injury. Elsbeth endured as best she could,
even though she silently viewed the agony as punishment
meted out by the Buehlers for what they surely believed was
her part in their recent rash of misfortune.

"It wasn't my fault," she protested, loud enough for
the sound of her voice to bolster faith in her own innocence
but not so loud as to waken the Buehler's young son, curled
up in the far corner of the wagon floor. "How was I to know
the Ramsey's mule would bolt and kick loose the water barrel.
It was only my job to fill it."

Elsbeth recoiled at the memory of the heavy wooden cask crashing against her. Even worse was the sight of thirty gallons of precious water soaking into the ground right before their eyes. The barrel shattered, rendered useless, reducing the Buehlers to dependence on one small water pouch and the charity of others.

However, this night's argument was different. Neither lost water nor injured girls provoked the harsh words being flung around the campfire. Suddenly the shrill soprano of Mrs. Buehler rose clearly out of the unintelligible mumble of male voices.

"Fifteen oxen gone. And the milk cow dead. Barbarians! That's what they are. Those red-skinned heathens will see us all in our graves if we don't do something…and fast."

"More trouble," moaned Elsbeth.

The days since departure from Fort Bridger had seen nothing but trouble. No sooner had the fort disappeared into the folds of the terrain than the two German emigrants challenged Captain Buehler's authority, sparking heated resentment—and worse. The train split, fully half the wagons and the guide retreated to take up a southern route to California. Now fewer able bodies shared the workload. Protection against the unpredictable, sometimes hostile Indians diminished as watchful eyes and ready weapons thinned to frightening proportions. Tempers flared. The pioneers squabbled about everything, from deciding when to call a halt to the day's march to whether or not the hunters should also be required to cut and clear brush along impassable sections of the route. Family groups pulled tighter together which left wanting the organization of the train as a whole.

Elsbeth knew she was considered bad luck and now,

when every extra hand was so desperately needed, dead weight as well.

She struggled to her feet just as the Captain stalked by. He glared up at her, his scowl as dark as prairie storm clouds, but he said nothing. Only his eyes accused.

Indian lover. Indian lover. Indian lover.

The stinging rebuke, although unspoken, rang in her head and seemed to echo as if shouted to the mountains.

Soon Mrs. Buehler appeared and climbed into the wagon. Cold and distant, she waded across the crowded quarters and counted out the meager strips of beef hanging from a hook to dry into jerky. Satisfied none were missing, she flopped next to her sleeping son, pulled a blanket over her head and went to sleep.

The dying campfire cast eerie shadows across the canvas walls. Elsbeth reached out to trace one with her finger, but it shifted away, lost to her touch as surely as the once-dreamlike promise of her youth was gone, in its place bitter reality, sadness and despair—the dark side of her life, the far side of her dreams.

Just as her whole body sagged from the enormity of her dreary situation, a gentle stirring came from within. Was it possible that tiny soul sensed she was about to lose heart? She patted the contours of her advancing pregnancy.

"If you had any horse sense at all," she sighed, "you'd stay in there and never come out."

The night deepened. Thoughts came while sleep would not. She redefined her future to include the little stranger she now called Charlie, a name selected for its conspicuous absence from the Elsworth family tree.

"Don't you worry, Charlie," she assured him as the first light of dawn appeared in the east. "We'll get along just fine…you and me."

The morning brought a new complication. The dust trail of a slow-moving wagon train was sighted on the road ahead. By midday it became evident the two groups would encamp together.

The Captain stewed and fretted, threatened by the second train. Even though a commingling of the two parties would provide relief to his own sorely overworked travelers and their sparse cache of weaponry, it also meant possible loss of his leadership role. He was, therefore, in a foul mood when a member of the other party approached him at dusk.

"You folks have a doctor among you?"

"Reckon not."

"We have a right sick woman. Widow lady. Lost her husband in a fall near the Devil's Gate. She—"

"Said we got no doctor."

"Perhaps if I asked around?"

As Buehler's hand dropped to the pistol resting in a holster strapped to his thigh and he took a menacing step forward, Elsbeth appeared at the back of the wagon.

"I can help," she interrupted. "Let me first collect my store of herbal remedies." After retrieving a small pouch in which she kept dried leaves and powders ground from special plants, she climbed awkwardly to the ground and stepped into the space between the two men.

Visibly shaken by Buehler's animosity, the man nodded and departed in haste with Elsbeth leaning heavily on his arm. He deposited her at a well-provisioned Conestoga and with a look of helplessness handed her a lantern and gestured her inside.

The woman was much more than sick. Elsbeth's knowledge of curatives had been learned at the elbow of her mother, but even to her untrained eye, it was evident the poor woman was beyond herbs and poultices. She wouldn't last the night. Elsbeth held a dampened cloth to the woman's fevered forehead and spoke words of encouragement, hoping only that the soothing tones would offer some small measure of comfort to one dying alone among strangers in an alien land.

Only when the raspy breathing slowed, then stopped altogether, and the oppressive silence of death surrounded her did Elsbeth notice a dark-eyed child huddled in the corner shadows. Like a frightened animal, he watched her but refused to be coaxed into the light. This was no doubt the dead woman's son. She doubted he was yet two years old. She shared his sorrow, but two sleepless nights had taken their toll. She could no longer fight the tug at her eyelids and almost immediately slipped into an exhausted sleep.

The sound of a piercing scream woke her, and a few moments passed before she realized the scream had been her own. When a second surge of pain wracked her body, she knew her time had come.

"Too soon," she moaned. "It's too soon."

Her cries alerted others who removed the dead woman and lay Elsbeth in her place. What had so recently been a deathbed now served to await the arrival of new life.

The child was in no hurry to be born. He resisted even the most torturous contractions. Throughout the endless hours of pain, however, Elsbeth experienced an undercurrent of joy and expectation until finally the attending woman laid an almost weightless bundle on her chest. A whispered voice pronounced "a boy." The new mother reached out and stroked a patch of the baby's wispy hair, then closed her eyes in contentment. Drained by the strenuous labor and lack of sleep, she drifted into welcomed oblivion.

Elsbeth dreamed of angels and cherry blossoms, kittens and softly falling snow. Billy too made a brief appearance, but not as a young man, rather as an engaging child. Of course, nothing in the dream made sense, but it didn't need to. The miracle of bringing into the world another human being made all things seem possible.

"'Scuse me, ma'am. We're gonna be moving soon. We'd be pleased to have you continue on with us."

Momentarily disoriented by the sudden awakening and by the unfamiliar voice, Elsbeth sat up, confused, and blinked away the sleep.

"What do you mean?" she asked. "I can't travel with you. I must get back to my own group."

The man shuffled nervously. "Uh…they left already."

"What do you mean they left? Without me?"

"Uh…yes'm…we found some small traveling cases near our wagons…and this." He held up a tattered carpetbag—hers. "Reckon they wanted to keep up the pace seein' as how we'll be delayed with the…uh…buryings and all."

Elsbeth forced her mind to focus on the word *buryings* and frantically rifled through the sweat- and blood-stained bedclothes.

"My baby!" she screamed. "Where's my baby?"

Only then did the thwack of a hammer's blow invade her senses. She stumbled on wobbly legs to the parted canvas in time to see a lid being nailed to a miniature wooden box.

She collapsed to the bed, too drained to cry, too empty to feel, a fragile shell with nothing left to lose. How long she lay there she did not know. It was a gentle pressure against her wrist which roused her. A small, incredibly dirty hand had found her own. Above it hovered two sad but trusting eyes. Elsbeth had forgotten about the little boy, now orphaned, who called this wagon home.

A rush of feeling poured into her and filled her up. She squeezed his fingers and managed a smile.

43

"Hello there, little soldier. What's your name?"

His upper lip quivered. "Charlie," he said.

Charlie. Elsbeth caught her breath and clutched at her chest, the beat of her heart pounding in her ears. Charlie. At last, the future was clear.

"Well, don't you worry, Charlie," she said. "We'll be all right...you and me."

III

Dust billowed around Elsbeth as one by one the wagon teams fell out of their circle formation and plodded slowly along in the wheel tracks of the ones before them. With leaden arms she lifted the whip and urged the oxen forward.

"Goodbye, little one," she cried, and her tears spilled down her cheeks and dampened the bodice of her dress. Farewell was brief. She could not bear to watch the steady column of hooves and iron-clad wheels roll over the soft mound of dirt that marked not only the birthplace but the final resting place of her son. She thought it sacrilege to trample his grave, but she also knew it must be done. Not to would invite the wolves to prowl. It was bad enough to mourn his loss and abandon him in the wilderness without fearing his tiny bones would be dug up and picked clean by snarling, howling predators.

She dried her tears, pulled Charlie close and set her eyes westward, in the direction that would yield her destiny—down the Emigrants' Road.

Over the next few days Elsbeth regained strength. She explored the confines of her new home. Charlie's parents had packed wisely and well. Bacon and beans, flour and salt were still in good supply. There were no heirloom bedsteads or weighty furniture the likes of which littered the trail as other pioneers sought to lighten their loads. A compact kitchen chest contained worn but durable tin plates and mugs, utensils and a large stew pot. A dented wash basin lay in a corner along with some essential tools. The dead woman owned a spare dress. Elsbeth measured its generous skirt and calculated how many outfits in various sizes it would yield to clothe a growing boy. A small sewing kit made such repurposing possible. To Elsbeth's delight she found a stash of small coins. If she spent them sparingly, they would last until...

Until when? She didn't want to think that far in advance, glad only that she would not have to beg for necessities. At the bottom of the chest, wrapped in crinkled paper was a stunningly beautiful quilt in shades of blue and green. She recognized the pattern as one called the Double Wedding Ring. It hardly seemed used, and Elsbeth imagined it as a treasured gift, given perhaps on the couple's wedding day. She spread it over the pallet which served as a bed, thinking this little taste of his former life would comfort Charlie.

She slept with the child cuddled close beside her. During the first night together, he woke from a troubled slumber and called out in the dark.

"Mama! Mama!"

Elsbeth hugged him tight. "I'm here, little one. I'm here, and I won't let you go...ever."

He quieted and was soon fast asleep. It eased the ache of her own loss to know she was able to, in some small way, fill the void which Charlie must certainly feel. A bond was beginning to form, and she hugged the child even tighter.

The next morning, as the company set out for the day, she settled Charlie on the spring seat next to her. For awhile she mulled the problem that had vexed her in the night. Charlie must have his own family somewhere back East. She didn't know where. She didn't know what circumstances had caused his parents to take this path. She didn't even know the couple's surname. Although that could easily be learned by inquiring among the homesteaders, thus far she'd failed to ask. What to do? There was no way she could return East by herself, and to ask the entire party to turn around was equally impossible. Each one had their own dreams which caused them to leave home and embark on this journey.

Besides, no one had yet offered this piece of information. Perhaps they too did not want to be faced with the difficult moral decision of turning around or not. It seemed to be taken for granted she would simply step into the now-empty shoes of the boy's deceased parents.

"Yo! Yay! Yo!" Charlie waved his arms above his head as if to coax the oxen into a faster pace. Elsbeth marveled at his spirit, his resilience, and decided the only plausible solution was to adopt him. It would be unofficial, of course, but this new territory out west offered many the chance to take on new identities and turn their lives around.

"Charlie?" she asked tentatively. "Do you remember what your *whole* name is?"

He scrunched up his face, deep in thought, before sucking in a lungful of air.

"Chaaarlie." He graced Elsbeth with a broad smile.

She returned it measure for measure. "You're a good boy," she said.

This required more thought. For them to have two different last names would seem odd, suspicious even, yet she refused to burden him with the name Elsworth. For now, she focused on driving the team. The question of names would have to work itself out. Charlie would just be Charlie.

Before long the unmistakable clop-clop of nearby hoofbeats broke her concentration, and she looked up into the face of a young rider. He tipped his hat.

"Sure glad to see you're taking care of Charlie there," he said, nodding and smiling at the toddler. "And he's a darn sight cleaner than I've ever seen him."

Elsbeth cherished the warm flush of pride she felt in Charlie's appearance. Indeed, a vigorous scrubbing of the trail grime had been necessary to reveal his true complexion.

The rider again touched the brim of his hat. "By the way, my name's Tom."

"I'm Els…."

"I know…and I'm sorry about…you know."

Elsbeth dropped her head, a new wave of sadness constricting her throat. When she thought she could speak without faltering and looked up, the young man was nowhere in sight.

A faint cloud of dust on the distant horizon was a telltale sign of the progress being made by Captain Buehler and her former entourage of sour-faced missionaries. She had no desire to be with them. The easy camaraderie among these travelers more than compensated for the slower pace.

When evening chores were done, the families migrated toward a communal fire. No matter how difficult the day had been, here one could find a sympathetic ear or, for a short time, forget the rigors of the trail. On the nights when a fiddle or squeeze box appeared out of someone's treasured possessions and a familiar melody filled the air, Elsbeth readily joined in, for it reminded her of home. The music and homey conversation blunted the sharp edges of

47

her father's wrath. For a while the pain of his bitter renunciation vanished in the wake of more joyous memories—of festive nights with her brothers and their families, of quilting bees with her mother and the ladies of the Altar Society.

She sat with Charlie in her lap, tapping a foot and guiding the child's waving hands to the rhythm of *Oh! Susanna*. At first, she didn't notice Tom's presence near the ring of fire until he reached out and squeezed her shoulder.

"There's bound to be dancing tonight," he said in her ear. "The Fowler's daughter has been sparkin' it with a fellow out from Indiana. Talk is they've announced their engagement."

"I'm happy for Mrs. Fowler. She's a lovely woman. Very generous in her affection toward Charlie and me. Taken us under her wing as it is."

Elsbeth hugged the child. Tom nodded.

"There they go," he said and clapped with the rest of the crowd as Mr. Fowler pulled the Missus to her feet and whirled her around and around in time to a lively tune. Others lent their voices to the gaiety by singing along with the music, humming where they didn't remember the words or making up new versions to the amusement of all.

Tom added his own slightly off-key rendition. What he lacked in quality he made up for in volume. Even old Mr. Clarke slapped his knee and roared with laughter.

Before Elsbeth realized what was happening, Tom grabbed Charlie and swung him high in the air until squeals of delight rippled through the campground and total adoration radiated from the face of the child.

When the music ended and Tom dropped to the ground, out of breath, it was at Elsbeth's side. He returned Charlie to her arms and winked at her. Embarrassed, she hid her face and answering smile behind the stiff brim of her bonnet.

At length the crowd thinned. Tom asked, "May I escort you to your wagon?"

"I'd like that, but it's not *my* wagon," she answered. "It's Charlie's now."

"True, however, he has no one else but you, so the wagon is as much yours as anybody's."

"I suppose you're right, though I never thought of it quite that way."

As they walked, Tom told a funny story about pulling one of the cows in his charge out of a mudhole.

"The darned critter nearly sucked me in with her. You should have seen me covered in that gooey, smelly mess."

Elsbeth smiled shyly, while Tom laughed at the memory. As if to slow down their passage, he lazily scuffed the toe of his boot in the hard-packed soil. He commented on the multitude of stars and sliver of moon. He noted the nights were cooling and wondered aloud if the Fowlers' daughter and her beau would consider themselves hitched without benefit of a preacher's blessing. Elsbeth was thankful he didn't inquire about the circumstances that brought her to this night and was grateful when the conversation instead turned to details about Tom.

"Last spring," he began, "Pa sold the farm and came out west to make a new life for Ma and me. He heard the soil in Oregon was so rich that even the fence posts sprout a crop. Ma and I went to live at the church rectory, helping out for our board, you know, until he could send for us." Here he paused for a moment, composing himself before continuing. "Only Ma died. The fever took her. So, I hired on with the Fowlers as a stockman to earn passage to Oregon City. I'll join Pa there."

Despite the recent loss of his mother, Elsbeth envied him for the welcome he would find when his journey came to an end.

In the days to follow, Tom seemed ever-present.

"Let me grease your wagon's axle," he offered. "Let me soak this wheel for you." "Let me mend those harnesses." To Elsbeth he became Mr. Let-Me, and she often called him that.

At the end of long, exhausting days, Tom always managed to spend a few moments with Charlie, if only to say good-night.

To repay his favors, Elsbeth told a lie.

She knew Tom ate his meals with the Fowlers. Each night she approached the other woman, wearing a sheepish grin and carrying a plate of food.

"I've gone and done it again, Mrs. Fowler. I just don't have the knack for getting the portions right. Perhaps you could share my surplus with your hireling."

Mrs. Fowler always accepted the offering with a knowing smile. Elsbeth hoped the artifice remained between the two of them and that no one else suspected the real reason she took such care to assure just enough extra to make her story believable. Nor did she mind the time spent picking vermin out of the flour so her biscuits would come up white and puffy. The look of appreciation on Tom's handsome face was her reward.

Without putting a name to it, Elsbeth fell in love.

Weeks went by. Supplies became scarce. While Elsbeth had eyes only for Tom, others scanned the skies with mounting anxiety.

"Don't like the looks of them clouds," one would grumble. Another noted a change in the prevailing winds.

"Let's push on...faster, longer, harder!" Whether

spoken or evident in the strained faces and single-minded purpose with which the pioneers drove both themselves and their animals, those words became the universal battle cry.

From more than one source, Elsbeth heard whispered the account of another party of emigrants who had been caught by the weather. That group had suffered great losses, were reduced to unspeakable behavior. She tried to assure herself her own case was entirely different. This group was not behind schedule, theirs was not an uncharted shortcut to California. But the doomsayers would not let up, and Elsbeth too began to worry about the changing weather.

By the time they arrived at the small Army post along the Columbia River, a regular part of the morning routine had become breaking the crust of ice that had formed overnight on their stores of water. The oxen huddled under clouds of vaporized breath. Men hugged themselves for warmth, their hands tucked deep under their armpits. The women spoke through mufflers wrapped tightly about their faces.

The final leg of the journey began at the river's edge. All rejoiced, for they believed this was their final obstacle. The last hundred miles, however, would not be without peril.

Some emigrants were determined to send their animals over an untested route along a ridge overlooking the deep river gorge. The Fowlers directed Tom, as their stockman, to take a different route. They had received word of a newly-opened toll road that wended south then west through the rugged terrain of the Cascade Mountains. They would precede him, for Tom had asked permission to remain behind just long enough to ready a raft for Elsbeth's treacherous river trip.

Officers at the nearby fort warned the travelers against attempting an overland crossing with their wagons.

"I hear it's a wheel-buster," said one of the soldiers.

Another piped up. "That road's so steep a body's wagon has to be lowered by ropes. And no guarantee that rope don't give way. If so, splinters is all what's left." He slapped the other fellow on the back as if enduring two thousand cross-country miles only to lose one's possessions on the outskirts of Oregon City was something to be laughed at.

"And for that, that Barlow fellow charges a toll."

This worried Elsbeth. "How much?" she asked.

"Five dollars."

"Five whole dollars for a team of oxen?"

"Nah. The five's for a wagon. Ten cents an animal."

Elsbeth pulled open the drawstrings of the small purse where she kept the coins she'd found in Charlie's wagon and counted out passage for her two oxen into Tom's hand. He hesitated a moment, but she insisted.

"I won't be beholden."

The overland groups set off immediately while the rest prepared to become river rats. Entrepreneurs from the Army post had made a business out of conveying the exhausted travelers down the Columbia, past Fort Vancouver, to another river which would take them to Oregon City. There were enterprising Indians too, but the price was steep.

Men and women alike stripped the wagons. Some dismantled them completely and lashed them onto waiting rafts while others tested fate and merely rolled them across a rickety gangplank and locked the wheels. These wagons looked precariously top heavy. The rocking motion set up by the current made them sway back and forth so their canvas covers resembled the sails of a ship.

After two days, all was ready. Elsbeth and Tom made mutual promises to exercise caution. They tasted their first kiss and parted not with goodbyes but with the words, "Till then."

The river challenged the pioneers' trespass. Its swirling, black waters tugged ominously at the moorings, daring the travelers to venture into its realm. As if to underscore the river's warning, the first raft from shore capsized immediately, paralyzing all with fear and the despair of watching precious supplies bob and dip in the angry current then sink from sight.

The second raft had better luck and, with that meager reassurance, the rest were launched. Elsbeth's was last in the queue. To save her precious pennies, she had opted to roll her wagon on rather than hire the work out to remove the wheels. As a precaution, though, she emptied the wagon bed of their belongings and secured them separately on the raft. She then steeled herself for the ride.

The space between herself and the shoreline widened. Within minutes icy water swept over the raft, drenching everyone and everything. Midstream boulders jolted the sorry lot of human flotsam or tipped the rafts to precarious angles. Screams of panic escaped the lips of even the most hardened pioneer. Elsbeth removed a shawl from her shoulders and knotted it around her waist. She grabbed Charlie, whose face was frozen in terror, pulled him to her side, and secured his trembling body against her own.

The ordeal lasted eighteen days. A final count of the river's toll amounted to two lives, four wagons, hers among them, and scores of treasured mementos from home. Elsbeth considered herself lucky to have survived the dreadful river and still be in possession of her goods. Without a wagon, though, she was stranded.

More bad luck lurked in the paradise that had lured so many. Oregon City was a disheartening sight. A tent armada in an ocean of mud surrounded a small core of wood-framed houses. To compare it to the thriving metropolis of St. Louis was outlandish. A bone-chilling drizzle welcomed her to the end of the trail. No sooner had she set a shaky foot on shore than she was greeted by news of disaster: a devastating storm in the higher elevations had blocked the mountain passes and frustrated even the most heroic efforts of relief parties. Any late-departing drovers and their livestock were given up as lost.

"Tom? Not, Tom."

Seeking others from her wagon train proved fruitless. Those who had had the foresight to immediately dispatch their stockmen, thus avoiding the storm, had hurriedly claimed their animals and scattered to outlying areas. Even the Fowlers were nowhere to be found.

Of all the losses over the previous six months, the loss of Tom crushed her heart. However, she kept the grief to herself, refusing to cry so as not to upset Charlie. The child had been through quite enough. More immediate problems demanded her attention. She turned her back on the mountain that had dealt her this most recent blow and set about finding shelter.

A dreadful number of her coins migrated from her purse into the eager hands of the owner of a local stable in exchange for a dry place to stow her belongings and rest her head at night.

For the next three days she wandered among the newly-arrived settlers and the more established community of Oregon City. She asked around. Where could she find work? Who was looking to employ? As each successive day brought disappointment, the name of Amos Warner loomed ever larger in her mind. The prospect of the measure of security the name offered was at the same time tantalizing and repulsive. As a source of pride, Elsbeth held fast to her refusal to buckle under to her father's will. She wondered how long that resolve could last?

Just as her prospects became increasingly grim, a stroke of luck stumbled out the door of one of the numerous saloons in town. The man barely avoided colliding with Elsbeth who clutched Charlie and backed away. The fellow wavered. He reached out his arm and propped himself up against the wall. He appeared to be in his thirties. A moment later he was joined by another who could easily have been his twin.

A scowling old farmer met them on the packed dirt street out front.

"Drunk again?" he shouted. "You two ain't worth a hill of beans since the old lady died."

"Pa," one snickered, "if you'd learn to cook, we wouldn't have to come here for a decent meal."

"Cook! I got the farm to attend to. Cooking's women's work."

"Well, whaddaya know. There's a woman right there." His finger pointed straight at Elsbeth. "You cook?"

Stunned and generally revolted by the trio, Elsbeth saw opportunity for what it was.

"Of course, I can cook. It's the easiest thing in the world. For a small wage and a roof to keep us dry, I'll be the best cook you can find."

The old man looked her up and down. "Kid part of the bargain?"

Shocked that the man would even ask such a question, she nevertheless kept her voice on an even keel. "Yes. Both of us or nothing."

"Hmm." The farmer scratched his head. "Let's give it a go." He pointed at a rig harnessed to a pair of worn out looking horses. "Hop on."

"My things are at the stable."

Not until they all arrived at the stable did the old man introduce himself as Gresh Tobias and his sons as "two of the most worthless human beings on the planet."

They were brothers, not twins. The family had been in the territory for two years, but the wife had a weak constitution and the dampness of the region did her in.

While Elsbeth expressed condolences over Tobias's recent loss, secretly she rejoiced that one man's unfortunate luck had netted her the position of cook.

Before he had the chance to change his mind, Elsbeth hurriedly gathered all she had packed and watched as the boys tossed them onto the back of the flatbed wagon.

"Be careful, Charlie. Hang on tight!" The two clung to each other as the wagon pulled out of town and bounced along a stretch of rocks and washouts the farmer insisted on calling a road. Charlie clung to her, terrified he might fall off. Elsbeth gripped him in return but more out of dread for what new nightmares this opening chapter of her life would bring.

Charlie's dark eyes searched her face. "Where are we going?"

Elsbeth didn't answer right away. She looked around instead, surveying the purple-blue mountains heavy with snow, the towering pine trees, the black soil that held so much promise for so many. Her arm relaxed around the shoulders of the little boy she now called her own.

"Home, my little soldier," she said. "We're going home." And she prayed to God it was true.

IV

Home.

Elsbeth couldn't imagine what she expected. Her mother had always been a stickler for neatness. *Cleanliness is next to godliness* was her favorite saying, especially when it came to the boys dragging mud in from the barn. The Tobias place needed more than a cook. Three men living on their own saw housekeeping as more of that "women's work" and, as such, ignored it entirely.

She dared not complain that cleaning up after the men was not part of the bargain, merely resigned herself to the extra work. She was relieved, though, when Mr. Tobias lugged her cases into a room separated from the rest of the house. The room was small and crowded but private. At her insistence one of the younger men installed a latch on the inside of the door which she could lock, although on nights when drunkenness reigned, she also dragged the heaviest of her trunks in front of it.

At first meals were simple affairs until she dispatched one or another of the boys into town with a list of much-needed supplies. If they found the improvement to their liking, it was their secret. No compliments came Elsbeth's way, but she felt she had done a good job.

For the first few months, the Tobias's were occupied with outside chores. Then the weather deteriorated dramatically. Winter arrived as a cruel master, bent on doling out as much misery as possible. Dampness generated by wet, heavy snow, often mixed with rain, penetrated the stoutest of walls and dared the fireplace to keep it at bay.

"Mama, I'm cold!" complained Charlie one night deep into January.

Indeed, the child looked pathetic with his runny nose and crusted eyes. To distract him, Elsbeth said, "Did you know tomorrow's your birthday? I'm going to make you a special cake."

Charlie brightened. "It's my birthday?"

"Yes, sweetie. You're going to be two years old."

Of course, she had no idea on which day or in which month he had actually been born, but he looked about two. He needed a little celebration to cheer him up, and everyone needed a birthday.

Knowing the Tobias sons would wolf down such an extravagance as cake, she divided the batter and baked a smaller portion just for Charlie. Alone in their room, she sang a little song that she remembered from her own birthdays. She didn't sing it loud, almost under her breath, so no one outside the room heard and questioned her purloining a small piece of what they might consider theirs. When they had eaten, she rocked him to sleep.

In the middle of the night, a noise awakened her. One of the men was coughing. It was a terrible sound, phlegmy and painful. Each expulsion was followed by a wretched groan. She ventured beyond her door to investigate and discovered the elder Tobias in a chair, bent in agony.

"Mr. Tobias, when did this come over you?"

"Been buildin' for days, but this is the worst."

"Are you chilled?"

"Strangest damn thing. Hot and cold at the same time."

She threw a blanket over his shoulders and filled a kettle with water. From her own store of medicinals, she mixed and measured and brewed and finally fed it by spoonfuls to the poor, sick man. She sat up all night to watch over him.

The wracking cough with bouts of fever lasted for weeks. The patient would improve, then worsen, then improve again. Eventually he steered a steady course toward renewed health.

Cook. Housekeeper. Nurse. The added duties were exhausting. Charlie grew cranky for being neglected so much of the day, and Tobias returned to his grumpy old self.

The only thing that sustained her was the fact her money pouch gained weight with each passing week.

V

"Miserable old coot!" muttered Elsbeth, and she didn't care who heard. With Charlie balanced on her hip, she struggled to push and pull at the several cartons of her possessions that had been left in a heap outside the general store by the Tobias clan.

"Imagine! Dumped here like a sack of potatoes!" The escalating vehemence in her voice kept pace with its loudness, and Charlie began to whimper.

"Don't worry, Charlie." She now whispered, hoping to calm him. "We don't need those shiftless louts anyway," she continued as quietly as her anger allowed. "Oh, they needed us all right. 'Specially in the dead of winter to cook and mend, not to mention nurse the old man through a sick spell. Yes, they needed us then. Were glad to have us. But let the gold fever strike and we're out on the street—literally."

Elsbeth looked around. Over the winter months a building boom had transformed Oregon City. A well-constructed livery and blacksmith shop dominated the central street while a church awaited only a cross to call itself complete. Although some establishments were still nothing more than tents, the many others had been fortified or enlarged to accommodate the growing population. Raised planks formed a boardwalk to save one from the worst of the mire in the streets. A general store boasted substantial log walls and a real roof.

She tried to assess their situation and visualize a solution, but all she saw were her failures—to her father, to Willie, to her own baby, and now to Charlie. She sagged under a weight much heavier than the child in her arms.

Then she heard it. As if through a muffling fog, out from a dark, distant corner of her soul, she heard the name she had long sought to forget. It was, however, several moments before Elsbeth realized the voice had not come from within but through the open door of the general store. A scrambling of feet across the wooden planking behind her echoed with the dreaded name.

"Amos, Amos…been awhile since you've been to town. Joey, quick. Get Mr. Warner's order ready."

She listened as the conversation drifted out onto the street and wondered what sadistic power had orchestrated this chance encounter. Was this to be her final punishment…or, by some cruel twist of fate, her redemption?

Within minutes the man called Amos Warner exited the store and walked across to the blacksmith shop. Elsbeth's heart sank. Warner was not the dashing young man of her childhood dreams. He was old with leathery skin wrinkled and burnt by long hours in the sun. His hands were gnarled and his back slightly stooped. With aching heart she made her decision, squared her shoulders, and crossed the street.

"Mr. Warner…?"

"Yes?" He turned from his inspection of the smithy's work and regarded the young girl before him.

"I'm Elsbeth Elsworth."

"Elsworth, you say?" His eyes narrowed. "The reverend's daughter?"

She nodded.

"A mite overdue, aren't you?"

The unexpected sarcasm of his words stung like the flick of a bullwhacker's whip, but the toddler who clung to her neck with innocent trust soothed the wound and gave her strength. She straightened her spine, looked Warner square in the eye, and launched into an abbreviated explanation of her journey, ending with the simple statement that she was now prepared to abide by her father's wishes.

"If you'll have me. Us, that is. It must be Charlie and me. The two of us."

Warner took his time before speaking.

"Elsbeth, you say?" He scratched the week-old whiskers on his chin. "Elsbeth, huh?"

He again lapsed into silence, a silence stretched so thin and tight Elsbeth feared she was being rejected.

"Come out to the homestead with me," he said at last. "The decision isn't mine alone. You know how to cook?"

"Yes, sir."

"Well, you throw together somethin' for dinner. We'll talk after that."

They loaded up Warner's supplies along with Elsbeth's trunks and rode into a countryside greening up with the promise of spring, but their silence was as bleak and barren as a cold winter wind. Elsbeth forced her eyes to focus on the parallel wagon ruts in front of her although every now and then she could feel Warner's eyes rake over her body. Her skin crawled. What *had* she agreed to? She hugged Charlie tightly for no other reason than to convince herself there had really been no choice.

The farmhouse was larger than she expected and boasted a wide porch out front. Inside, a hallway led to individual rooms. Overall, the place was surprisingly neat and clean. Elsbeth sized up the cooking arrangements, took off her bonnet, rolled up her sleeves and went to work. Warner disappeared into a small room off to the side. When he returned, it was with a fresh shirt and a clean-shaven face.

"I hear Junior coming now. Dinner ready?"

Whether or not she answered the question Elsbeth never knew, for just then the door opened and framed the familiar, sorely-missed figure of Tom...her Tom.

His appearance so rattled her that she almost missed the introduction.

"Elsbeth, this here's my namesake," said Mr. Warner. "He thinks he's too modern for the name Amos so he goes by Tom." He clapped his son good-naturedly on the back, his face aglow with a conspiratorial smile. "Something tells me you two already know each other."

Tom stared, open-mouthed. Elsbeth was speechless. Only Charlie knew what to do.

"Tom! Tom!" he screamed and wrapped his arms around the young man's legs. "I missed you. Where were you?"

The father chuckled. "Lost in the woods, Charlie, my boy. Thought he was a goner, but he made it out in one piece. Praise the Lord. C'mon, young fella. Let's you and me go feed us some chickens. I think these two have some getting reacquainted to do."

When the old man and the boy were out of sight, Elsbeth reached across a deep chasm of despair and embraced the man she loved.

Tom found his voice. "I heard stories about the river voyage claiming wagons and lives. Nobody in town had any

62

notion where you might have gone or even if you'd survived. I thought I'd never see you again. This is like a dream come true."

"Yes," Elsbeth agreed. "A dream."

CHAPTER 4

Running West

I

Billy Brooster hunched his shoulders against the chill night air and wondered if the three years in a Missouri jail would have been preferable to the misery of a one-year sentence as a defender of Fort Kearny.

"What'll it be?" the judge had said, emphasizing the question with the crack of his gavel. "The hoosgow or the frontier?"

In the relative comfort of a St. Louis courtroom, Billy had weighed his options.

The road to this perdition had begun the moment he heard the slam of a door and a red-faced Reverend Elsworth barge into the tack room where he'd been staying. He was in the process of carefully folding the shawl which had fallen from Elsbeth's shoulders.

The man was livid, incoherent, and waving a long gun carelessly in the air. The preacher seized the shawl. He grabbed Billy's shaving mug from its nail on the wall and threw it to the floor. The impact launched its handle into a far corner. One by one Billy's possessions were flung into a pile amid a torrent of language Billy thought beyond the scope of a clergyman's vocabulary. Quickly he bundled his belongings and hightailed it outside.

He knew he'd done wrong by Elsbeth, but it had seemed so natural, even preordained. As he made his way up the road, he was afraid to turn around. Despite the cold, a sweat of mortal fear coated his body. He remembered the parson's gun. Would a man of God throw away the tenets of his faith in a fit of madness? Bill had serious doubts, so he put his head down and hurried as fast as he could without actually running. When he crested a small hill and was on the other side without a bullet finding his back, he breathed a sigh of relief.

His immediate concern was vacating the town where the Elsworths were well-known and liked. If word spread of his banishment—and the reason for it—he might find himself the target of someone else's gun. The setting sun created an arc of paling light in the western sky. Billy marked it as his compass point and set off in that direction.

His basic needs were food and shelter. Small towns and villages dotted the state. In many he was able to secure odd jobs or short-term employment. He moved often, afraid to linger too long in any one place lest the breadth of Elsworth's influence stretched beyond the borders of his home parish.

If a job presented itself, Billy never turned it down whether it be below decks in a steamboat or on roof tops as a chimney sweep. With the little money he accumulated over the winter and into spring, he bought himself a good rifle and a sturdy pair of boots.

As the weather improved, jobs were easier to come by. This time of year farmers always needed a strong back and an extra pair of hands. Billy had both. Over the months and as the distance from Elsworth increased, he had developed a sense of confidence when seeking employment, so as he neared the city of St. Louis and spotted a farmer standing in his field, he approached the man.

"If you're looking to hire for the spring planting, I'm available," he said.

"Got three strappin' sons. Don't need no help with planting."

"What about—"

"What I *do* need," interrupted the farmer, "is someone to clear out stumps over yonder. Demand is going up, and I want to expand my fields."

"I'm not afraid of hard work."

"That being the case, you're hired, but you'll have to sleep in the barn." He shrugged. "The missus don't want no more men in her house."

"Perfectly acceptable," said Billy.

In hindsight, he reckoned he should not have been so eager. When shown the acres of felled trees and the density of stumps left behind, it would be a monumental task and, in the end, his downfall.

For two full months he toiled, first clearing the brush and digging out the smaller roots before moving on to the more substantial stumps. Besides stumps, the soil yielded stone which had to be removed. The summer's heat arrived early and sapped his strength even more than the backbreaking labor.

He worked seven days out of seven, even on Sundays when the community as a whole paraded off to the local church. That was when one particularly stubborn stump stymied all of Billy's efforts to pry it free. At other times, he would fasten a rope to one of the farmer's draft animals, but on Sundays they were hitched to the family wagon for the religious outing.

There was a mule grazing in a neighboring pasture. Without giving it much of a second thought, Billy looped a rope around its neck and led it to the obstinate stump. If he hurried, the mule would be safely back in its own field before church services were over.

That was one thing he was sure of. However, there were two other things he didn't know. While the two farmers were neighbors, they didn't much like one another. In fact, there had been an ongoing feud between the families for several years. Too, the second farmer's wife was feeling under the weather that day and had opted to stay at home. She sat by a window in the drawing room of her house and witnessed the "theft."

Sickly or not, she had the energy to confront Billy with a shotgun.

"Stealing my molly, are you?"

"No ma'am," said Billy, shocked to see two barrels pointed at his head. "Just borrowing." He indicated the recalcitrant stump.

"Not the way I seen it. And caught you red-handed at it too."

No amount of reasoning would change her mind, and soon Billy found himself facing the presiding judge and listening to his words: "The hoosgow or the frontier?"

Billy fingered the brass buttons on the government-issued shirt. It hadn't been much of a choice.

The trek from St. Louis had been punishment enough for his small sin of borrowing a farmer's mule. As one of several who were serving out sentences in government uniforms instead of cells, he was forced to walk while the regular infantry sat astride horses. The march went on for many miles. Food was third rate, and shelter amounted to a row of tents staked to hard, unforgiving ground.

Duty at the fort was at times boring with nothing more to do than menial labor at the behest of soldiers who found it entertaining to order him around. Newly-established, Fort Kearny was there for protection of the westbound wagon trains, but the natives in this area were not generally aggressive. The travelers mostly needed assistance with wagon wheel repair, reshoeing horses and oxen, and information about the road ahead. Billy found this work rewarding, the lending of a helpful hand to strangers whom he would never see again. Once the emigrants' supplies had been replenished and its people refreshed, they moved on and the fort relapsed into boredom.

This cycle was repeated time and again throughout the summer. By late fall activity at the fort was at a standstill, for the last of the trains had surely departed. There was not much to do other than wait out a prairie winter.

Billy stood in front of his assigned quarters and stretched his legs. He shivered, for the season was well along and the nights were turning. Coarse laughter and the smell of whiskey alerted him to the approach of fellow soldiers. The group's leader, Clayton Pierce, moved closer and held up a deck of playing cards. He ran a dirty thumbnail across the upper edge causing the cards to separate then snap back sharply, the sound echoing out into the night.

"C'mon, boy," he snickered. "How's about a little game?"

At first Billy hesitated. He tried to read the soldier's eyes, but they were shadowed by the darkness, and the words, though friendly sounding, were delivered amid a cloud of foul breath.

"Whaddaya say, kid?"

"Sure," answered Billy, still doubtful.

Someone shook out a horse blanket and spread it on the ground. "Jacks or better," he announced.

Three others joined in. They sat in a circle warmed by a campfire and their bellies heated with the help of stale coffee, laced generously with the contents of a bottle that passed among players and onlookers alike.

"Lady be good!"

"Kiss me pretty!"

The men hooted and whistled and talked to the cards. Only Billy played in silence, listening instead to the mournful howl of a coyote calling in the night. Despite the press of a dozen jostling bodies, he felt alone, once again the outsider.

Late into the night the game continued. In fits and starts Billy's money moved inexorably from his side of the blanket to the other. The string of bad luck concerned him little until the slightest of movements caught his eye. A finger out of place. A barely perceptible stroke along the bottom of the deck. His eyes narrowed into focus on Pierce's dealing hand while he drew in his breath and waited. It happened again.

"Dealer's cards s'posed to come off the top too," he challenged and jumped to his feet.

"You calling me a cheat, boy?" The words throttled the raucous crowd into silence, and the smile disappeared from Pierce's face as he also stood and glared. Billy quickly weighed the bulk of the towering figure against the principle of the thing.

"That's right, a cheat!"

The accusation hung suspended between them. Billy saw Pierce nod. An instant later the blur of a swinging rifle butt entered his sideline vision. Before he could react, a searing pain exploded at the back of his head. His knees buckled, and an onslaught of fists rained upon him, the most

69

vicious of all with a heavy silver ring. A fiery pinwheel of pain spun out of control. Only loss of consciousness brought relief.

When Billy awoke, he noticed first the sweet taste of blood in his mouth, the bitter cold, and finally the dead silence. His face scraped against the hard-packed earth. He didn't need the moonlight to recognize where he lay as the rutted expanse of the overland road. Week after week of patrol along this route, affording protection for the emigrants who passed on their way to the Oregon Territory, had incised it in his brain. The fort would be two hundred yards away, the row of soldiers' tents just to the east. He staggered painfully to his feet and headed back, marking his pace to the singsong cadence of...

"Son of a bitch. Son of a bitch. Son of a bitch."

The dying campfire served as a beacon. Soon a chorus of noisy snores led him to the tangle of soldiers collapsed in fitful slumber. Clayton Pierce grinned as he slept.

"This'll wipe that smile off your ugly face," swore Billy as he slowly freed his Army-issued Colt from its leather holster. He stood over his target, forcing the pain to the back of his mind and willing his shaking arm into readiness. The muscles of his right hand contracted. He squinted to assure his aim. But a loud grunt sounded from a far corner as someone rolled over in his sleep. The moment passed and so did Billy's anger. He put up the gun and backed away, a new plan of vengeance forming in his brain.

Turning toward the small dried-brick and wood structure of the fort, he approached the officers' quarters. A guard leaned against the stockade, rifle at his feet, but the soldier's inattention allowed Billy to slip quietly past. No sound greeted him as he inched open the door and blindly ran his fingers over the surface of a nearby table. As soon as

70

his hand brushed something, he grabbed it and retreated.

The item turned out to be a logbook jammed with handwritten notes and personal correspondence and inscribed with the name of Lieutenant Carlson. Billy smiled. Finally, some luck, he thought.

"Commander won't take lightly to finding *this* missing."

He slid the book under Pierce's bedroll—out of sight yet not so well hidden it wouldn't be easily discovered during the inevitable search of the encampment. He took one last look at his tormentor.

"You underestimated me, you did," he whispered, satisfied his revenge would soon be administered in a fitting military way. "Sorry I won't be around to enjoy it."

He left the Colt with its holster and took only his own rifle, then hurried to the horse corral. Here he patted the rump of Pierce's mount. Justice for the loss of his money and the beating would be to deprive the hated man of his favorite horse. Billy, however, passed it by and selected the worst of the lot, a sorry-looking nag that had been used only to carry supplies.

With a two-fingered salute, he saddled up and chased the lingering darkness. A short ride brought him to a thicket of cottonwoods. Moments later, the fort was out of sight. Behind him dwindled the past. Ahead lay a clean slate on which to write his future.

"Never did much like this soldiering," he said.

II

As he had done time and time before, Billy set his

sights on the western skies. His sorry excuse for a mount was slow-moving, but Billy figured by the time the morning bugle call rousted the soldiers from a drunken sleep and they realized he was gone, he would be far away. Yes, they would search, but perhaps only half-heartedly. It was wide open country. It would be anyone's guess if he'd traveled west instead of east...or north or south, for that matter. And if he read the lieutenant correctly, Carlson would be consumed with the disappearance of his journal.

Billy kept the Overland Trail to his right. He made good time despite the horse's inadequacies and outdistanced some of the late-departing trains. Caution, however, dictated he stay far enough away to avoid detection. To refill his canteen with water, he waited until nightfall, making sure no emigrant parties were camped nearby before riding to the bank of the river.

Returning from one such excursion, his horse stumbled. Billy didn't pay the misstep much attention. It was, after all, dark with only a slice of moon to light the way. A few moments later, though, the unfortunate horse caught a hoof in the rock-strewn terrain and down it went.

The animal thrashed on the ground, screaming in pain until Billy could stand its suffering no longer. The report from his rifle filled the emptiness around him. Once done, there was nothing but total silence. He left the saddle—what good would it do him?—took only what he could carry, moved a short distance away, and bedded down for the night.

For the next ten days, he followed his original course: the rising sun behind him, the sunset in his eyes, the river to his right. The going was tough. Despite it being late in the season, the sun defied the calendar. Billy was hot by day, cold at night, dirty and hungry. And tired. So very tired.

"Damned horse. What did it go and break a leg for

anyway?"

Brooster took out his frustration with a sharp kick to the stump of a water birch and scowled at the unrelenting sun. He dropped his bedroll to the ground and tugged off a boot, emptying it of stones for the second time that morning. He grumbled at that too, but kept his eyes riveted beyond a row of cottonwoods to the sparkling blue of the Sweetwater River.

If the Army had tracked him successfully, they would have by now discovered the dead horse and be hot on his trail. That he had seen or heard nothing since he rid himself of Fort Kearny was a good sign, so good that youthful optimism took hold. His canteen was empty, but it was more than his thirst that drew him toward the river. With hands calloused by the rigors of survival, he tore aside the thick underbrush and tramped ahead until, at last, he could clearly see the canvas-draped wagons of an emigrant train and relish the sound of human voices.

The river's bank teemed with oxen and cattle, cursing men, screaming children, women scrubbing a month's worth of grime out of clothes and linens. Apart from the group, a sunk-shouldered man scraped a depression in the reluctant soil. Beside him waited a corpse. Now and then the man dabbed at his brow with a square of red cloth. The time since his departure from Fort Kearny had hardened Billy's soul as well as his hands, and he hardly broke stride as he passed by the grim scene and hurried toward the commotion below.

What *did* arrest his attention was the gray-brown fur of a jackrabbit caught in a crude snare trap. Billy stooped, undid the cord around its neck, and hung the animal from his belt.

"Hey, mister. That's *my* rabbit. Give it back."

Billy whirled, swinging his rifle into readiness with

73

lightning speed, but found no target save a small boy with a large stick standing in the grass behind him.

"Give it back, I said." The voice seemed much too big for the size of the youngster.

"Now, Chet," another voice broke in. "I'm sure he didn't realize it was yours, and he looks as hungry as the rest of us."

The two men locked eyes, and a moment passed while each came to a conclusion about the other. Billy relaxed his trigger finger. The older man glanced back up the incline to the lonely grave site.

"You'll have to excuse the boy," he said, sadly, wiping his face with a red bandana from his pocket. "My wife. His mother. Chet here is already seein' himself in bigger boots."

Nodding, Billy handed over the rabbit.

"Name's Chester Holt." The man tipped back his hat and swiped a sleeve over his sweating forehead. "We could use an extra hand now. Ain't got much to offer 'ceptin' some food…provided you're willing to work for it."

Before Billy could answer, Holt's name rang out and the overlander hastened to the call to maneuver his wagon to the crossing. When the man stripped to the waist and plunged into the river to coax the frightened animals across, Billy did the same. Together they swam alongside the oxen while the fierce current pried at their feet and clawed at their arms. The struggle molded the two into a team. They emerged together, wet but satisfied the wagon had not mired in the mud and none of the stock had been swept away.

"How far's this here Oregon?" asked Billy.

Holt thought for a moment, then looked westward as if he could actually see a place called Oregon. "I guess it's about as far as you can get." The man continued, rambling on about the weather, the soil, the virgin land, but Billy had ceased to listen. The last year of his life played over in his mind, and the concept of "as far away as you can get" suited him. He extended his hand.

"Take you up on your offer, Mr. Holt."

While the decision to join up with Holt had been easy, the trail proved long and arduous. Wagons broke down, the stock wandered and needed finding, the road disappeared into rutted gullies made passable only after hours of backbreaking labor. What Billy at first viewed as a partnership, deteriorated as the miles ran long and the provisions dangerously short.

"Aw, hell, here he comes again." Brooster spat into the fire at Chester Holt's approach. "That man never wants for finding things for me to do."

From the clutch of single men and hired hands could be heard the biting taunts of "Billy, do this. Billy, do that. Sounds like you've got yourself a wife, Billy."

A tense silence fell over the group as Holt neared and dropped a grease bucket at Billy's feet. "Axle needs attendin'," he said. Next to the pail he placed a dish of watery stew and a small loaf of bread, broken apart to conceal the fact that even from this meager portion some had been held back. The meal failed to quell the gnawing pangs in Billy's midsection and served only to heighten his resentment at having to return to the circled train and crawl beneath Holt's wagon.

"This is the last time I let that old goat..."

One of the outriders heard his ultimatum. "If'n I was you," he warned, "I wouldn't be too loose with my tongue. If the old man cuts you out..." Here the fellow swept his arm wide and let his words die in the vastness of the open land and the forbidding mountains visible ahead.

Billy's heated determination cooled. He had learned

this train was the rearguard of the annual migration. To leave would place him alone and afoot. It was a picture which made him think twice and, in the end, pick up the grimy bucket and stomp toward the encampment.

He slapped at the axles with a brush thick with goo as black as his mood. In his carelessness he knocked loose an oddly-placed board on the underside of the wagon bed. Curiosity and the tip of a skinning knife uncovered a sight which curled Billy's mouth into a secret smile. He groped inside the cache, letting his fingers slowly sift through a mound of gold and silver coins, a heavy pendant, jewel-encrusted rings and brilliant earbobs. Here was wealth beyond his imagination. He selected a coin, brought it to his lips and kissed it lightly before reseating the board with a rap of his fist.

From then on, whenever possible, Billy visited the wagon when no one was around and added a coin, never more than one, to the jingle already in his pocket. He no longer groused about the hard work. He was helping himself to better wages.

III

"Says so right here!" The man stabbed a dirty fingernail at a page in the slender book he held. "Got it written in all them capital letters too so's you don't miss it."

The circle of emigrants, Chester Holt included, leaned in closer as if proximity to the words lent more weight to their dire warning.

"Mine says the same." A second man waved a small pamphlet in the air. "Says those Indians are 'hostile savages'

76

and we'd better keep a sharp eye."

The owner of the book looked over his shoulder as if expecting a war party to ride over the hill behind them.

Billy was unsure. He'd heard about these trail guides before. Back East they were commonly hawked by street vendors to those contemplating the trek to Oregon. While each purported to contain the most accurate information when it came to preparing for the trip, in reality most fell far short. They underestimated the cash one needed for tolls and supplies in far-flung locales and overestimated the foodstuffs and equipment required for a favorable journey. Folks had already jettisoned plows, barrels of molasses, heavy cookstoves and more to lighten their loads. They chafed at the waste, mollified only that the litter they encountered along the trail meant others had also fallen prey to uninformed hucksters.

This business about Indians was different. It had everyone worried.

Wide open spaces made them fear for lack of cover, and closed-in defiles put them on alert for ambush. As the Rockies strung the train out in snake-like fashion through its narrow passes, old fears surfaced anew. Every unfamiliar sound that echoed across the valleys brought with it rumors of attack until even the children fell silent under the strain of constant vigilance. In their frustration, the pioneers lashed the oxen forward, but the sting of their whips did not and could not persuade the jaded animals into a pace beyond a dismal plod.

Into this scene of desperation ran Holt's son, Chet, shouting, "Soldiers comin'! Soldiers comin'!"

The men lifted their eyes and cheered at the unexpected windfall. The women loosened the canvas flaps at the back of the wagons and peered expectantly at the rapidly approaching cloud of dust.

"Pull up! Stop the wagons!" the leaders commanded. They quickly assembled into a welcoming committee and received the soldiers with as much pomp as they could muster. Women and children, too, climbed down from their perches and swarmed around the group.

Billy hadn't forgotten his experience at Fort Kearny. With the arrival of the Army patrol, he slid behind Holt's wagon, and, with his back pressed against the rough planking and his heart pounding in his chest, he furtively edged to within listening distance.

"Sir," announced the lieutenant with a crisp salute that seemed out of place given the surroundings. "We've been ordered to accompany you as far as the Columbia River."

The emigrants plied the officer with questions.

"Why the escort?"

"This Injun country?"

"Government expecting trouble?"

To each inquiry the lieutenant calmly answered, "Just following orders, sir."

The men broke into small groups and murmured among themselves about the true meaning of the armed patrol. Into this void rushed the women who hounded the soldiers for news from the states.

Billy remained hidden—still undecided, a gut feeling directing him to linger out of sight. He closely inspected his shirt. Long ago he had ripped from his sleeves the Army insignia. Dirt and sweat had further obscured any resemblance to military garb. He began to relax.

Maybe I can pull this off, he thought.

Just then one of the soldiers laughed and Billy froze. The voice was unmistakable.

It can't be, he thought, trying to convince himself, but it took only one quick glance to confirm that the voice belonged to Clayton Pierce.

"Damn!" he swore. There could be no escaping recognition. He had to run—and now.

Quickly Brooster hauled himself into Holt's empty wagon and groped in the semi-darkness until he found the store of supplies.

"You've been holding out on me, old man," he whispered as he pocketed a small ration of salt pork and a fistful of dried beans. One more thing begged his attention. Quietly he slipped out and down between the wheels to the secret cache. Here he awarded himself a "bonus" of the last of the coins. Then he slithered along the side of the road into the cover of trees still aflame with the colors of autumn.

Once he felt the leaves close around him, blanketing him from sight, he glanced over his shoulder. Had his departure been noticed? Women calmly mounted the wagon boxes. The men picked up their whips and urged the oxen forward. The soldiers fell into an orderly line of march. The eyes of the emigrants once again narrowed in singular concentration on the dusty track that pulled them slowly toward their destiny.

All eyes save two.

In the shadows between the wagons walked Chet. He alone peered out toward the trees as if something of great interest held his gaze.

A chill enveloped Billy. He tried to shake it off. Telling himself it was merely the dankness of the forest, he shivered, turned and fled.

IV

Unburdened by the cumbersome pace of the emigrants' wagons, Billy struck out cross country. When fatigue threatened his forward progress, he thought of Clayton Pierce, conjuring up his face in every rocky outcrop and hearing his laughter in the wind. That and the biting chill of the air which lingered even after the sun had reached its zenith, renewed his determination to press on.

As the miles separating him from the troops increased, fear of their presence gave way to fear of their absence. Billy knew he was vulnerable. He enlisted caution as his companion.

It failed him only once.

It had been going on dusk and he was clearing away brush and stones on top of a ridge, a space to bed down for the night. He was tired, and hungry, and inattentive until too late. The bear emerged out of nowhere and rushed him. Billy grabbed his rifle but had no time to fire a shot. He scrambled backwards, to the very precipice of the high ground, then one step beyond. He lost his bearings and tumbled down the steep slope. His sudden disappearance satisfied the bear. It lumbered off, but Billy's desperate fall ended alongside a scrabble of brush. When he took stock of his situation, he knew it wasn't good. His hands were raw and bleeding, but the real alarm sounded when he examined his leg. A stout piece of tree branch had ripped his pantleg and pierced his thigh. When he attempted to stand, he cried out in agonizing pain and crumpled to the ground. Dragging himself to the base of a tree, he propped himself upright and waited. For what, he chose not to imagine.

Time passed. The utter blackness of the night brought

no peace, no sleep. By dawn he shivered with cold while his face flushed with an inner heat.

A feral snarl and the snap of a brittle twig raised his flesh.

"Get away. Get away, you hear?" Billy labored to his feet, aimed his rifle, and fired high and wide at the menacing sound. "Leave me alone."

He held his breath until the echo of his shot died away. When no other sound came to his ear, Billy slowly exhaled. The threat of attack over, he should have been relieved, but the incredible quiet now surrounding him served only to magnify his fear. Once more he leaned against the tree and painfully lowered himself down its rough bark to his former position, the gun now cradled on his lap. The struggle had sapped his strength and reopened the wound on his leg. Blood flowed toward his knee and drew a swarm of night-flying insects.

Another day worked its way through. Billy dreaded its exit into a second night.

As light began to fade, a coyote emerged from the bushes. For a long minute, they stared at one another. The animal took two steps forward, its teeth bared, hackles erect. Billy aimed and fired. The shot missed, or so he thought, for the coyote seemed to disappear into thin air. Had it really been there or was the fever distorting his mind?

"One, two, three, four." He counted out his remaining bullets. Then what'll I do? he thought.

He counted again—this time the hours he had lain alone at the mercy of creatures he could not see and fears he dare not name. He relived the charge of the bear, his fall, the broken snag of a birch embedding itself deep into his thigh. He contemplated how he might use the final bullet.

Billy closed his eyes and imagined himself once again

81

on his journey, whole and well-fed, but a crunch of dry leaves nearby heaved him back to reality. Instinctively he cocked his gun.

"*Qu'est-ce que ç'est?*"

Billy weakly aimed his weapon in the direction of the strange sounds. When he opened his eyes, he feared he was suffering the hallucinations that herald death, for above him hovered a most fantastic apparition: a giant, legs bound tightly in deerskin, a coarse, shaggy robe of buffalo hide encasing shoulders and torso, narrow slits for eyes, a bulbous nose, a gap-toothed mouth, all haloed by a frazzled mane of hair and whiskers.

"*Êtes-vous ça va, Monsieur?*"

The vision reached out and touched him.

"Are you all right, *Monsieur*? I heard the firing of a gun."

Only then did Billy recognize the English words as deliverance. He dropped his weapon.

"What has happened? An injury?"

"Chased by a bear. Up there." Brooster pointed up a steep incline. Evidence of his fall showed clearly from the path of crushed and broken branches and mini avalanche of stone. "Been lying here since yesterday. Thought I'd just died and you were…" Billy hesitated. He wasn't quite sure who he thought the stranger was.

"*Mon dieu!*" The Frenchman threw back his head and laughed. "Perhaps I should not ask to where you think your soul had flown. Allow me to introduce. I am Pierre Lajeunesse. And this is Genevieve." The grizzled old trapper stepped aside. A swayed-back mule greeted Billy with an ear-splitting bray.

Lajeunesse shouldered the injured boy and carried him up the slope to where Billy's bedroll and pack lay untouched by the bear. The trapper peeled back the bloodied pantleg.

"Hmmm."

"It's bad?"

"*Tres.*"

"What does that mean? I'm not gonna die, am I?"

"I do not have an answer for that question, *mon ami*. I do know we must remove the offending article and clean the wound."

Without knowing what he was agreeing to, Billy nodded permission. He stared, mesmerized, as the Frenchman built a fire and held a knife over the flames until its tip glowed red then blackened with a film of carbon.

The sun dipped below the evening clouds, bathing the earth in brilliant hues of pink and violet. Genevieve grazed contentedly nearby and paused only briefly when Billy's screams filled the air.

The following day he lay exhausted and still in great pain. Lajeunesse used the time to oil his own rifle, rearrange the mule's pack, repair traps, and cook a passable meal. Come nightfall he staked Genevieve within a few feet of their blankets.

Jarred from a half-sleep by Genevieve's probing muzzle, Billy batted the animal away. "You always sleep with your stinking mule?"

"Ah. Ill humor suggests improved health. As for Genevieve, she can smell an Indian long before the Indian can smell her." The trapper shrugged. "For that, I tolerate her...shall we say, shortcomings."

Billy tensed. "You think...Indians? Right here?"

"We shall see."

The test of Genevieve's nose came early the next morning. The mule grew edgy, snorting and tugging at her rope lead. Lajeunesse picked up his rifle and slipped out of sight. Billy lurched to his feet in an effort to follow but collapsed on the first step.

When the Frenchman returned, Brooster whispered, "My gun. It's over there."

"No need, my friend. We are in luck."

As if on cue, shadows darkened the ground at Billy's side, and he looked up into the faces of three Shoshone warriors. No dime novel had fully prepared him for the fearsome trio. The leader was bare to the waist, though his legs were wrapped in a soft animal skin. A breastplate of porcupine quills hung from a leather strip around his neck. A scar ran from his ear to his chin.

What sprang to Billy's mind were the awful trail guides. He choked back a cry and watched, unbelieving, as the trapper stepped forward, embraced the man, and kissed him soundly on both cheeks.

"Rising Storm, my good friend," he bellowed. "We meet again."

Rising Storm returned the greeting with equal sincerity although considerably less flair, and the two moved off to talk in private, the conversation a garble of English, French and sign language. Billy had no choice but to squirm under the black, unblinking eyes of the two remaining braves.

"*Je regrette*, my young friend," said Lajeunesse when he and Rising Storm returned. "You are too sick to travel much, and I have a long way to go. Snow will close the mountain passes soon, and I do not wish to be caught on the wrong side. Rising Storm is my friend. He will care for you in his village."

"You can't leave me with these…"

"There is no other way."

"I can pay you. I have money."

84

"What would poor Genevieve do with your money?"

"Well, what *do* you want?"

"You have nothing to fear, *mon ami.*"

Billy realized he also had nothing to say in the matter. He looked about for his gun but found it now in the possession of Rising Storm's companions. Protest died on his lips, checked by the greater call of reason, but even as he held his tongue, his hands curled into tight fists, draining his knuckles of color.

Immediately there was a flurry of activity. The Indians stripped saplings and lashed them together to form a travois. Lajeunesse loaded his belongings onto Genevieve's back then lifted Billy and his belongings onto the litter and covered him with a blanket.

"*Au revoir*, my friend," he said and turned, offering Billy what little satisfaction could be found in cursing his retreating back.

V

He was still alive. The Indians hadn't murdered him yet, though at times he wished otherwise. The constant bumping of the travois as it dragged over the ground enveloped him in a blur of pain. When finally the movement stopped and Billy opened his eyes, he found himself in a village of a dozen or more tepees. He could smell smoke from a campfire and the aroma of roasting meat that made his mouth water. Children and women surrounded him as if he were a sideshow curiosity. The youngsters seemed bent on touching his face which, though rimed with dirt, was much lighter in color than their own.

Eventually the kids were shooed away, and he was lifted by the shoulders and legs and deposited in one of the tepees. It was warm inside. He relaxed in spite of the gruesome warning touted in those travel guides. His eyelids drooped with the weight of sleep. He had almost achieved that blissful state when a sound returned him to high alert.

A toothless old woman entered. She was wrapped in a shawl of animal pelts. The wrinkles around her eyes were deep ravines cut into sun-ravished skin.

"What do you want?" he demanded of her but, of course, the woman didn't understand. He shut his eyes again, resigned to whatever fate had in store, only to be surprised when she began to minister to his wound, first by washing it with warm water and then applying what felt like a layer of soggy leaves. Just as quietly as she'd come, the old woman departed. Immediately a young girl appeared in her place, put a bowl to his lips and urged him to drink. The brew smelled the same as what had met his nose on arrival at the camp, and he swallowed it hungrily.

Over the course of days, this process was repeated until Billy could feel his strength slowly returning and his fears fading into the background. He looked forward to the routine, especially the arrival of the girl. She appeared to be about his age. Her name was Kiasu.

On the fifth day, Rising Storm made an appearance, his first since the day he had brought Billy into the camp. A bubble of fear rose to the surface, for Rising Storm was carrying a stick that was approximately four feet long and as thick as a man's wrist. However, he merely handed it to Billy who, with a good deal of support from the walking stick, struggled to his feet and limped out into the crisp morning. Although a dusting of snow whitened the ground, it didn't deter the activity going on around him. Women were scraping hides, men tying arrowheads to shafts, children playing with hoops made from willow switches.

Rising Storm nudged Billy and, with two fingers scissoring back and forth, indicated he wanted him to walk. Together they made a slow circuit of the village until Billy could go no further. The next day they walked the outside perimeter. The day after that, two times.

From then on, as soon as light showed through the smoke flaps and he heard the chatter of women, Billy rose and went outside. He always looked around for something to do. The women giggled when he gathered firewood, for that was children's work. They laughed outright when he used his knife to slice up roots for the communal stewpot, for that was women's work.

The native men instructed him in the art of flint knapping and soon he could complete an arrowhead in under fifteen minutes unless, of course, he struck the stone improperly and the whole thing was ruined. The men also allowed him to compete in their contests of horseback riding and hatchet throwing.

Kiasu taught him the meaning of *behne* and *aishen* in her language. *Hello* and *thank you* didn't get him far in a conversation, but his effort signaled a welcome into the community.

He especially enjoyed the evening storytelling sessions when everyone crammed into a tepee and listened to one of the elders speak. The words meant nothing to Billy. It was the resonance of the teller's voice and the rapt attention given him by the children that mesmerized him.

As winter fully established itself in the region, Billy settled into the rhythm of village life. While the days passed pleasantly enough, the nights were reserved for torment. Specters with familiar faces engaged in endless pursuit. No matter how fast he ran, they clawed at his heels, threatening to overtaken him at any moment. Not knowing what fate awaited if he lost the chase, he awoke shaking.

After one particularly upsetting dream, a scream startled him out of sleep. It wasn't his own. It came from outside. Snow, heavy with moisture, had fallen overnight and created an icy slick throughout the compound. One of the more rambunctious boys lay on the ground, convulsed in pain. His pony was still struggling to its feet. It was clear what happened. The boy, Matu, Rising Storm's nephew and grandson to the old medicine woman, had ridden too fast, the horse had lost its footing, disaster had struck.

Billy rushed to the circle of onlookers and saw to his horror the condition of the boy's arm. Blood colored the snow a flaming red. The fractured bone shone white where it penetrated his skin. A woman yelled some commands, and others picked up the injured lad and carried him into a tepee. The medicine woman was summoned, but Billy knew more had to be done.

"Sticks!" he called out. "Three. Four. Straight ones. And leather strips. Hurry!" He gestured wildly, pantomiming what he needed, hoping someone would understand.

He followed the others and knelt alongside the boy's mother, helpless until Kiasu entered and deposited the necessary items at his side. He took her hands and placed them on the boy's shoulders.

"Here. Hold him like this." He squeezed her hands with force to indicate what he meant. "Tight. Don't let go."

At that he grabbed the boy's wrist and pulled. The shriek of pain was awful to hear, but the bone retracted and nested with its other half. The boy quieted as Billy placed the splints and secured them with leather thongs. The grandmother appeared, nodded approvingly at Billy, and began to apply a mysterious concoction to the wound.

That night when he returned to his own tepee, lying on the blanket which served as his bed was his rifle, the first time he'd seen it since Lajeunesse had abandoned him to the Indians. If this was a sign of acceptance, so was the storytelling. Now the elders became more animated as they attempted with hand gestures and facial expressions to relate the stories in a manner Billy might better understand.

The days grew warmer, the nights not so cold. Snow melted. Over the remainder of the winter, the injured boy had healed. He bore the brunt of teasing from his peers with remarkable good humor. Billy too regained a state of robust health, though nightmares still haunted him. The village vibrated with talk of the first spring hunt.

Billy wondered if Lajeunesse would return or if the Indians would decamp to another location. The bigger question remained: What would he do?

VI

"Listen, old man. Nobody does that to me and gets away with it." Billy leaped to his feet and grappled Lajeunesse to the ground.

"I gotta get to Oregon." His fingers tightened around the old man's throat.

"You have to help me." He felt the muscles of the trapper's neck slacken under the pressure of his hands.

"Do you hear?" he shouted. "Do you hear me?"

Not a whisper came from the Frenchman's lips, but all around the woods reverberated with sound. Genevieve wailed. Soon her harsh cry melded with the maniacal laughter of Clayton Pierce. Chester Holt was everywhere, demanding "Fetch the water…harness the team…cut the wood…haul the barrels…tend the wheels…" A judge's gavel banged incessantly. Aunt Prissy yelled, "Billy Brooster, you little good-for-nothing. Get out of my sight!"

Into the confusion of noise and images insinuated the plaintive call of a distant coyote, bringing with it a silence so total it too became unbearable.

"Stop! Stop!" Billy's eyes snapped open.

Despite the chill of the tepee, beads of sweat dotted his forehead. Billy knew what had happened. The delirium of fever had long since passed with the healing of his wound, but the dreams would not go away.

He covered his face with trembling hands and tried to calm his labored breathing. When he looked up, he was startled to see Rising Storm, for he had not heard the Indian enter. His imposing presence unnerved Billy, no less now after months in the village than at the beginning when he lay helpless, frightened and in need.

"You dream." It was a statement not a question, but the Indian waited patiently as if expecting a response.

Billy never knew how to fill these unsettling gaps.

"I'm fine," he finally blurted out and stumbled to his feet. "Leg's as good as new." He stomped twice and slapped at his thigh—proof of his point as well as a distraction from Rising Storm's unwavering eye.

Still nothing.

"I'm coming with you, no matter what you say."

At this the Indian nodded and backed out the opening of the tepee, letting its deerskin covering drop quietly into place. Billy growled under his breath, angry with himself for allowing an Indian to trip him into a blundering defense with barely a handful of words. Besides, the dream was his business.

Outside, the camp bustled with activity, both practical and spiritual preparations in full swing. Women darted here and there, carrying provisions to the waiting pack horses and riding ponies. As they worked, they chanted. What little Billy knew of the language failed him. He assumed the incantations to be prayers to the spirit world, pleas for success of the first hunting party of the season.

To one side stood gangling boys, their sullen expressions open masks of displeasure at being judged too young to join the group. Elsewhere, excited children squealed in delight. Dogs barked. Tribesmen painted their ponies and bid farewell to families who clustered around departing husbands, sons and grandsons.

The sight of Kiasu standing nearby soothed Billy's wounded ego. During the long winter she had been his nurse, then his companion, learning his English words with high intelligence and teaching him her language as best she could. If their hands occasionally brushed, it was by accident, though these mishaps happened more and more frequently of late. Billy acknowledged her stunning beauty—burnished skin, deep brown eyes, flowing hair. She smiled often and had a playful nature. Billy found himself wanting to do well on the hunt to please her.

She stood by his horse, a gift from Rising Storm for his earnest outlay of work around the village and in no little measure what he had done for Matu. Kiasu had striped the roan's face with ochre and braided feathers into its mane. At Billy's approach she lowered her eyelids and gently blew on one of the feathers so it fluttered as if about to take flight.

"To give your pony great speed," she whispered. "For the hunt."

A quick glance to either side assured Billy that Rising

Storm was out of view. Only then did he step close to the Indian girl and gently tuck a strand of jet black hair behind her ear.

"Speed. Yes, I'll need that."

The touch brought a glow of color to Kiasu's bronze cheeks. From a fold in her dress, she plucked a piece of finely crafted leather. This she thrust into Billy's hand, and before he could say anything, she stole away among the women.

Billy examined the talisman. It was exquisitely beaded and of a similar design to the amulets possessed and coveted by many of the single young men. At one end it was secured to a narrow leather strip. He slipped it over his head and tucked it inside his shirt just as a chorus of whoops signaled the moment of departure.

Once mounted, Billy scanned the throng of villagers for Kiasu's familiar face. There was no mistaking her raven's hair and antelope eyes. He grinned and patted the small lump at the front of his shirt. As he did, the morning sun broke over the smoke holes of the tepees and brought tears to his eyes. He clamped them shut. On the back side of his eyelids appeared a startling diorama—a fair-skinned girl with golden hair and eyes the color of blue cornflower petals.

Surprised, he thought, *What trick is this?*

He blinked hard, but the image persisted. The words, "a beautiful flower blossoming on the endless prairie," came to mind. Why, he could not say, for *that* girl, though not forgotten, was forbidden. Nevertheless, he experienced a hollow ache where thoughts of Kiasu should have been.

The hunters kicked their horses into a trot, working their way through the cheering crowd. Although Billy stared in Kiasu's direction, it was no longer *her* earthy beauty which made him smile.

The smile did not last long, for the elk herds

remained well hidden, and many days passed while the party ranged far from the village and well into the wooded mountains beyond. At last, a trail was sighted, and the spirit gods rewarded them with a plentiful kill.

While the Indians butchered meat and loaded the last of the pack animals, Billy climbed a hillock overlooking the countryside.

The valleys around him had responded to the season's increasing warmth. The receding veil of snow lay bare a distinctive set of parallel lines which meandered over and around the contours of the land, heading invariably west.

"Oregon," he said, barely above a whisper. That single word, dredged from another time and place, bubbled to the surface. He couldn't fathom why an utterly unimagined part of the continent roused conflicting emotions. This Oregon held nothing for him other than it had at one time been his goal. It would be filled with strangers, yet those strangers offered something the Indian village did not. A sameness. To him.

"The white man's road."

Billy recognized the voice but not fast enough to check his body's reflexes. His hand flew to his rifle in readiness.

Rising Storm didn't move. He stood at Billy's elbow, appearing to study the serpentine trail of wheel ruts.

"It leads to Oregon." Billy waited to see if the Indian would respond even though he didn't expect it.

"S'posed to be pretty nice there."

The moment dragged on.

"Fresh start 'n' all."

Rising Storm reached out and hooked a finger under the leather thong at Billy's neck and slowly pulled until the beaded amulet had been resurrected from its hiding place.

93

Anger flashed across Billy's eyes, but only for a moment. He was fully aware of the question—although unasked—that needed answering.

The sun moved their shadows as they stood in thoughtful silence.

At last Billy removed Kiasu's gift from around his neck and hesitantly placed it in Rising Storm's hand. That resolved, the two descended to the waiting hunters. The riders repacked their remaining supplies and mounted as one. The Indians turned northward and home. Billy, too, wheeled away, only not along the same course.

Once again, he was on the move—running west.

CHAPTER 5

Yearnings

I

Billy hadn't ridden more than a few minutes before he noticed the steady thrum of the Indian ponies' hooves had died completely away. For the first time in months, he was on his own. It was a strange feeling, as if being caught in limbo between two worlds. Oregon was still a good distance away, and the Shoshone village now a place where he might no longer find welcome. Even his clothes were a mish-mash of cultures—buckskin leggings over his own woolen breeches, a soft leather tunic on top of a calico shirt, boots instead of moccasins, a wide brimmed hat. He sat atop an unshod horse.

After a few moments' pause to consider the confusion of his feelings, he struck out in the direction of the stronger pull.

The set of parallel ruts was not far ahead. He felt no sense of intimidation, for it was much too early in the season for travelers to be this far along the route.

At the first stream he came to, he washed what remained of the dried yellow markings off the horse's face and brushed the feathers from its mane. He thought about discarding the clothing which the Indian women had made for him, but they added a layer of warmth he didn't want to give up.

He was not entirely right in his thinking about the emigrants' route. Following the same tracks made the going easier one day but harder the next. While he knew if he stuck to the road, it would inevitably lead him to this place called Oregon. The wagon trains, however, reached this far west in the late summer or autumn when streams and rivers were at a low point. Creeks they must have simply splashed across were now overwhelmed by the spring melt and turned into deep, fast-moving torrents. Often he had to scour upstream for a suitable crossing before doubling back to the trail.

Grumbling over getting his boots wet a second time that morning, Billy heard the unmistakable click of a rifle being cocked. He extended his arms away from his body to show he carried no weapon. Slowly he turned.

"Howdy, stranger." The greeting seemed out of place considering the barrel of a long gun was aimed in a direct line with his heart.

"Howdy, yourself."

"Whatcha doin' here?"

"Just passing through. Mean no harm."

"Why're you dressed like a danged Indian?"

What did this fellow want? thought Billy. Clearly the man had no love for the natives. Should he lie? Tell him he'd killed one of those "danged Indians" and stripped him of his clothes? He took a deep breath.

"Happened upon a friendly village back a ways and swapped out a spare blanket."

"How far back?"

"A five-day ride."

"Ah! Well then, welcome to the neighborhood." He

swung the gun down to his side. "The name's Zeke. That's short for Hezekiah. The mum had to dig through the Bible to come up with that one."

He laughed and Billy relaxed.

"Surprised to find you—or anyone—out here. You a trapper?"

"That I am, though it's getting harder all the time. Beaver're petering out something fierce."

"I met a trapper last fall by the name of Lajeunesse. Ever heard of him?"

"Who hasn't. He's practically a legend."

"If you happen to stumble across him, tell him Billy Brooster relays his thanks."

"What does that mean?"

"He'll know."

The two men parted company on better terms than upon meeting. Billy wished him good luck with his beaver traps, and Zeke left Billy with advice on avoiding the "danged Indians."

"Keep a clear head and a sharp eye. Good idea to keep your gun loaded too. I got mighty close to you without so much as a *Who's there?*"

Billy picked up the trail, much pleased the chance encounter with Zeke had allowed him to mend fences with Lajeunesse for the way he'd cursed him, that is, if the message were ever delivered. He didn't dwell on the odds of that happening, but it relieved his troubled conscience that he'd tried.

Others had left messages too. Not by word of mouth, but actual letters impaled on sticks planted in the ground. Most were illegible. The punishing storms of summer, the snow and ice of winter proved more-than-adequate adversaries to the scraps of paper. Billy wondered how many of these messages had connected with the neighbors or family who followed on the west-bound trek.

Eagerness for this new territory grew with each passing day. It meant, of course, a new life among his own, but he was also struck by the awesome beauty of the country. It was nothing like what he'd grown up with in Ohio. Everything here seemed bigger, more dramatic. At certain times of the day, the mountains took on a deep shade of blue. There were virgin forests, high desert wasteland, a spectacular river gorge. When he came to a gate and a man demanded a toll, he willingly doled out the required coins. He was on the last leg of his journey, full of anticipation. Surely paradise lay ahead.

II

Oregon City smelled as bad as any hardscrabble town Billy had had the bad luck to drift through. An oozing channel of mud and manure sliced through its makeshift business district, relieved only by a plank walk on either side. An insistent rain had soaked his clothes, so he sought refuge in a tent structure that boasted a hand-lettered sign misspelling the proprietorship of "Vernon's Salloon."

"What's your pleasure, boy?"

Billy really just wanted a place to dry off, but looking around at the crowd of drinkers, he thought it better to order something.

"A shot of your best." Billy leaned against a wooden bar and slapped a coin down in front of the bartender. The glint of gold drew two shadows out of a far corner.

"New in town?" asked one.

"Maybe," answered Billy cautiously.

"You'll be needin' a business partner, perhaps?"

Billy chuckled. He had once used that same line in Missouri when he needed some cash to make it through the night, though he'd managed to pay it back after a few weeks of hard labor in a farmer's field. From the looks of these two characters, he reckoned a loan would quickly turn into a gift. He shrugged off the anticipated loss, as long as it wasn't too much, in return for what information they could give him about the lay of the land. Oregon City wasn't much of a "city" and certainly not the paradise he'd imagined. He nodded again to the barkeep, this time including his newfound "friends" in the gesture.

Once the drinks were poured, he asked, "How many folk call this place home?"

He hadn't directed the question to anyone in particular, but it was the bartender who answered.

"Numbers depend on the time of year. In high summer and early fall, wagon trains will bring in plenty, though they don't tend to hang around long."

"No?"

"Nah. They restock what they can then settle on land up and down the valley. We count about eight hundred as permanent."

Billy nodded and gestured out the door. "So just a stopping off place?"

"Don't get me wrong. It's here they come for supplies. Most are regulars but didn't think you were asking about that."

"Not quite sure what I was asking. Only curious." Billy upped his glass and drank it in. "Thanks, though."

Despite the dreary weather and questionable companions, the whiskey tasted of civilization. For a second

99

time he regarded the slice of Oregon City he could see out the door. Not only did the town offer the security of familiarity but an anonymity in proportion to the number of miles, mountain ranges and rivers that separated him from other times.

He only half-listened to the two jabbering moochers at his side. Instead, he watched the trousered pedestrians and a few skirted residents parade past the saloon on the street outside. The rain had stopped, and a weak hint of sunshine offered promise of a better day. The comforting warmth of the liquor lulled him into inattention until a flash of color caught his eye. Brooster straightened, on the alert. The movement, however slight, did not go unnoticed. The man to his left sighted along Billy's line of vision and snickered.

"Hey, Jake." He elbowed his friend. "Man here is lookin' for a little piece of pantaloon."

Jake peered out on the boardwalk too. "Sure picked the right one." He snorted at his own joke. When Billy didn't answer, the man anxiously fingered his empty glass and continued. "Word around town is, that one done got herself in the family way back East."

Jake's companion, seeing that another free drink might be on the line, jumped on the band wagon. "Heard her paw sent her way out here. Tryin' to save her virtue or somethin'." He laughed openly.

"Got a kid an' all."

Dry throats loosened their tongues even more.

"Hear she's a reverend's daughter. Guess there's fire in thems you'd least expect."

"How do you know that?" demanded Billy.

"Bunch of preachers passed through last fall. They brought letters and such from back East."

"And talk of the crossing," added the second man.

"Where are these preachers now?" Billy wanted to know.

"Oh, scattered to the wind. Seems they was eager to get out and spread the word."

Billy had heard enough. He ignored the intruding voices and watched the young woman with a child in her arms cross the street. As she disappeared into the general store, he willed himself back in time to Rising Storm's camp and allowed the strange vision to once again flicker before his eyes. Blonde hair. Blue eyes. A fragile beauty.

Billy had always left belief in destiny to the dreamers of the world, but how could he explain the circumstances that brought two people over so many miles to the same street in a distant country?

"Elsbeth," he whispered and stepped out into the light.

CHAPTER 6

Sunlight and Storm

I

Three new chicks had hatched the morning before to Charlie's utter fascination. Since then, except for meals and bedtime, he had been riveted to Amos's porch, his legs dangling over the edge, enthralled with watching the mother hen and her brood.

The scene plucked at Elsbeth's heart, for it reminded her of years past when she and her beloved grandmother would sit on just such a porch on quiet Sunday afternoons. Grandma would rock while Elsbeth sat at her knee on a low stool. It was where she learned to embroider and braid colorful rag rugs. Grandma knew how to sing too. Her lovely voice took the place of conversation. The songs were mostly hymns and sometimes Elsbeth would sing along. Her grandmother would have loved Charlie and likely spoiled him to no end.

She called to the boy to join them, but he refused to vacate his post. At other times, his stubbornness might have been upsetting, but secretly Elsbeth treasured moments alone with Tom. Like this morning when they walked hand in hand along the southern border of Amos Warner's land claim. The field was cleared and ready for the spring planting.

"Tom, your father has done a remarkable job in two short years," she exclaimed.

"Yeah. He's a real work horse, but he had little choice. You've got to clear the land, get a crop in and build shelter to secure your claim. Several of his neighbors joined together to form a collective of sorts. You know, helping one another. With your two oxen, they were able to double up on the work."

"I'm glad the animals could be put to good use."

"It was presumptuous to keep them, but we thought you...I mean, we didn't know if..."

As Tom struggled to put into polite words what they assumed might have happened to her on the final leg of her journey, Elsbeth took pity on him and patted his arm.

"It's all right, Tom. It really is."

"Anyway, it helped that our old plow made it across," he hurried on. "Too many others were forced to ditch the heavy stuff for the sake of the draft animals. And the hens. Pa did without in order to salvage the two best layers, and now he sells eggs in town sometimes."

"You come from good stock. Amos's house is the best I've seen."

"Ma insisted. She swore she wouldn't live in a shack. That little room where you and Charlie sleep was going to be her sewing room."

"It's very cozy. I'm sure your mother would have loved it."

They walked on in silence, Elsbeth reluctant to say anything further about Tom's poor, dead mother.

Finally, they came to the end of Amos's property. The neatly-plowed earth abruptly changed and patches of coarse, knee-high grass took over. Tom stopped. He laid an arm on her shoulder and pointed to a large pine tree several hundred yards away.

"Pa put in a claim for me too, knowing I'd be coming along. You can see he's cleared some of it out already. The bigger trees and such. My land would be from here to that pine yonder."

Our land, Elsbeth corrected without saying it out loud.

"What a generous government," she said instead, gazing at the tract.

"The law's not exactly final yet, but those that know such things say it will be soon. So Pa and the other folks here are just getting a head start."

"Is that allowed?"

"When the time comes, who's going to argue with an up and running operation? It's good for everyone all around."

"Then we shall be ready. C'mon, Tom."

She slid an arm around his waist and pulled him over the invisible line that defined the beginning of their future homestead. The soil caressed her feet. The sun peeked from behind a brooding cloud as if to acknowledge their right of ownership. Even a honey bee in search of nectar seemed to be welcoming her home in its own insect language. Elsbeth almost burst with pride at the promise inherent in this property.

The heat of Tom's body so close to hers was reassuring. The unkempt state of the field was not. They would have to begin work soon to prepare the ground for its first crop.

"I'll put in my own fair share of a day's work," she said. "With the two of us together, and maybe with help from that cooperative you mentioned, this field will be shipshape in no time."

A wistful look came over Tom's face as his gaze drifted to points beyond the tract of land. Elsbeth felt sure he was visualizing future fields and harvest-ready crops. When she closed her eyes, she too had visions of the largess this virgin soil could produce. She forgave him for not responding, for at that moment the clouds gathered to cover the sun and a light rain began to fall. They joined hands and ran to the house.

II

"Drat!" Elsbeth inspected the piece of handiwork in her lap and wrinkled her nose. With the help of the needle and tip of her fingernail, she undid the last two uneven stitches.

"That's what I get for daydreaming."

Charlie looked up from the corner of their little room where he played with a pair of pinecones he'd found.

"What, Mama?"

"Oh, it's nothing, sweetheart."

She held up the sleeve of a green shirt meant to fit the boy. He'd grown out of his other shirt and the only fabric she had was what she'd salvaged from his mother's dress. After measuring and cutting a pattern the night before, she'd set about sewing the pieces together, but on this day the sun streamed through the window and the view outside was of Amos's plowed field and the one beside it which would be hers and Tom's.

She abandoned the project and thought about what those fields meant. Her future surely, although the role of a farmer's wife had not been part of the dream she'd always imagined.

The parsonage back in Ohio had maintained a vegetable garden and she helped her mother tend to a good-sized flower and herb garden as well. But acres and acres! Running an entire farm would be vastly different from the social and spiritual responsibilities of a minister's wife, but she was determined to make it happen. She'd be the best farmer's wife she could be. And there was a ready-made family here in Oregon. Charlie was a delightful child. Amos had welcomed her without reservation. And Tom? On the trail he'd been so caring and funny and helpful and... She closed her eyes. Yes, Tom would make the perfect husband.

She stood and walked to the window. Of immediate concern was the state of the unbroken soil in the field next to Amos's. It had been two days since she and Tom had walked along its perimeter and still it lay untouched. They would have to do something about it soon. Start small the first year, of course, then expand.

As she was working out how to broach the subject with Tom, there was a light tap on the door. Charlie jumped to his feet and ran to open it.

"Good morning, everyone," said Tom cheerfully.

Charlie pulsed with excitement when Tom stooped to eye level and laid his hands on the child's narrow shoulders. "You up for a day of work, little man? Lots to do around here."

The answer to his question was an enthusiastic head bobbing. Elsbeth felt encouraged by his words, for hadn't she just been thinking about the same thing?

Tom rose and invited Elsbeth into an embrace.

"I can help too," she said.

"Oh, no. This is man's work." He winked at Charlie.

106

"Out to the barn, my boy."

In a flash the two were gone, but Elsbeth was overcome with curiosity as to what inroads one man and a very small boy could possibly make against a large untamed field. She pulled a shawl over her shoulders and quietly exited the room. Amos was nowhere in sight, so she let herself out the door and approached the barn. Peeking inside she witnessed what "man's work" amounted to. Tom was instructing Charlie in the proper way to spread straw for the four oxen and one buggy horse. Tom raked. Charlie collected an armful of the straw and scattered it on the dirt floor. It wasn't exactly play, although she could hear laughter—Tom's deep and throaty, Charlie's high-pitched and full of glee.

She smiled at the picture they made together. Father and son was how she thought of them these days. It wouldn't be too many years before they became a real team, working to make the land produce. She thought of a time in the future when a little sister or brother would round out the crew of helpers.

Beset with these pleasant musings, Elsbeth wandered away. Without intending to revisit their land claim, she found her footsteps leading her in that direction. On the verge of the tract, she bent over and grabbed onto a handful of the grasses growing there. And tugged. And tugged. Finally, the fast-holding roots relented and she wrested the clump free. Clearing this field was going to harder than she expected.

III

A small bell jangled cheerfully as Elsbeth opened the door to Parker's Mercantile. The sound woke Charlie. He had been dozing with his head against her shoulder, but now he was alert, transfixed by the marvelous variety of shapes and colors burdening the shelves and the smells that emanated from barrels crowding the back wall.

Elsbeth smiled at his curiosity and indulged him by walking slowly among the displays until a bolt of yellow gingham caught her eye. She ran her hand along the fabric. It would be an extravagance, she thought, but already she could picture it stitched into curtains, brightening the rooms of a cozy little farmhouse.

"You like yellow, Charlie?" she asked.

The boy paid no attention. A glass jar filled with candy held his gaze. Elsbeth laughed out loud.

Her good mood vanished as muffled voices filtered through the open door. A dozen men gathered on the boardwalk outside. Their lively conversation quickly escalated to a feverish pitch.

"Gold!" Elsbeth ground out the word in disgust. "Don't they have anything else to talk about?"

The news from California had ignited a frenzied excitement among the townsfolk for over a month. Glowing · reports of walnut-sized nuggets just waiting to be scooped up blinded the most level-headed and made fools of the rest. To Elsbeth it was as if a deadly contagion, far worse than cholera, had settled over the town, extracting a costly toll from the community. Each new day saw a steady stream of men fall victim to the toxic lure of riches. It seemed nothing could hold them back.

Elsbeth had only contempt for such talk and the irresponsible men who answered its call. How many more, she wondered, would forsake the obligations of family and farm to offer up their souls at a temple called Sutter's Mill?

"We're two of the lucky ones," she whispered to

108

Charlie, giving him a gentle squeeze that served more to reassure herself of Tom's steadfastness than to comfort her son.

"What'll it be for you today, Miz Elsbeth?"

The question startled her, for she had not noticed Mr. Parker step from behind the counter and stand at her side.

"I think we'll just have one of those candies today."

"A red one, Mama, please," added a delighted Charlie.

"Shall I load up the supplies Tom ordered?"

"Supplies?" She looked at Parker, bewildered, then along the line of his outstretched arm, past a pointing finger, to a wooden crate on the floor. The box held an assortment of equipment—heavy canvas pack sacks, a pick ax, shallow pan, and shovel.

"There must be some mistake," she said, though her throat filled with the taste of dust. Her tortured heart clearly transmitted a message to Charlie who dropped his candy and flung his arms around her neck.

"Miz Elsbeth? Shall I...?"

"No!" She cut Parker short.

An awkward silence followed. The merchant inspected his pockets, fiddled with a bit of frazzled twine he found there, while Elsbeth labored under the weight of what Tom was clearly determined to do.

"I mean no thank you, Mr. Parker. If Mr. Warner wishes these things, he'll have to come get them himself."

With that she turned and hurried out the door, oblivious to the shadowy figure which lurked so near that the hem of her skirts brushed the mud-splattered leather of his boots.

Elsbeth sought refuge in the street, away from the hated box with its cargo of doubt and the implements of her despair.

109

"It's a mistake. I know it is. He wouldn't leave us." She thought of Tom, tried to imagine him teasing her over this silly misunderstanding. Yet in the core of her heart a seed of doubt was growing.

How long she stood in the mud amid passing carts and wagons she did not know, but gradually she realized it was the very same spot on which the Tobias men had so recently dumped her before heading for the goldfields. The parallel, once drawn, could not be denied. She shivered.

Charlie, until now wide-eyed but wordless, sprang to life and whimpered, "Find Papa."

"Papa? Charlie, you've never called..." The words died on her lips, for in his eyes she saw a fierce look of urgency amid a reservoir of unshed tears. His short life had been filled with pain and loss. How could she even think of trampling this fragile sprout of trust under the heel of her own uncertainties?

In this moment of hesitation, she looked within herself, cringing at an unwelcomed yet familiar sight. The contours of nose and chin mirrored her own. A clerical collar shone stark and white against a backdrop of shame. The vision wavered ghostlike before her eyes, reminding her of shattered dreams and the dark side of love.

Elsbeth sighed. "Don't worry, little soldier," she said. "We'll find him. We'll make him stay. You...we...won't be hurt again. I promise."

Resolutely she shifted Charlie's weight to her other hip, whirled around, and stepped headlong into the arms of the man who quietly stood outside the general store.

"Oh! Excuse me, sir," she began, smiling apologetically. "I didn't see..."

Although the young man politely released his grip and tipped his hat, recognition slowly dissolved her smile. He was unshaven and disheveled, rougher around the edges, but his face swept Elsbeth back just the same to a bright autumn day and the charming stranger at the rectory gate.

Her hand flew to her mouth.

"Billy?"

IV

"That's right, it's me...Billy."

"What are you doing here?"

"I *was* trying to put the past behind me...at least the disagreeable parts, but I see the agreeable parts have managed to travel the same route. So, I ask you the same question: What are you doing here?"

"I...I..."

"Your family make the move out west?"

She shook her head.

Billy smiled. "You know, you haven't changed a wit."

The two stared at one another. Elsbeth's lips formed around a response, but it remained trapped inside. Anger bubbled up, then a curious, fleeting feeling which she could not put a name to. She remembered the first time she laid eyes on him, his boyish appeal, the offering of flowers and flattering words. In the meantime, Charlie rubbernecked his head between the two. His expression asked a thousand questions, but Elsbeth barely noticed. Had his tiny voice whispered them in her ear, they too would have gone unanswered.

Elsbeth felt an eerie darkness descend, as if a heavy gray curtain had been draped across her eyes, or perhaps it only seemed that way, for at that moment a menacing cloud

111

passed in front of the sun and rain began to fall, not as the usual drizzle but in great swollen drops. Even as passersby headed for shelter and horses hitched to posts up and down the street eased their backsides into the storm, Elsbeth remained rooted to the ground, studying the man who stood before her.

The sound of wheels swooshing through the mud, interrupted her train of thought. An ox snorted loudly nearby, and she heard Tom call her name. The past once again became the past.

"Elsbeth! What are you doing standing out in the rain?"

Tom reached out for the boy then offered his hand to Elsbeth, pulling her into the wagon box. He spread a waterproof tarp to protect her head and skirts and settled Charlie at his side, under a flap of his jacket. Then he shook the reins, urging the team into motion. They had almost quit Main Street when he asked, "Who was that?"

Elsbeth paused, considered both Tom's recent secrets and Charlie's straining ears. "Just a man," she said. "New in town."

She looked back toward Parker's store and with a certain amount of relief saw that Billy Brooster was nowhere in sight.

The homeward-bound oxen trudged laboriously along the road. The sound of their rhythmic breathing competed with the rain. Charlie chattered away about a cat he'd seen and what he would name it if it happened to follow them home. The two adults rode in unnerving silence.

When they neared the familiar lane which led to the Warner farm, Tom lifted Charlie over the side of the wagon and sent him running toward the house. Meanwhile Elsbeth raced to the barn. She unlatched the double doors and swung them wide to allow Tom to pull inside. Two milk cows, a pair of oxen and Amos's riding horse greeted them. Together they unyoked the team, each performing certain tasks routinely and without a glance toward the other. This and the steaming bodies of the animals, mingled with the stifling humidity and leaking roof, created an unbearable atmosphere in the crowded enclosure.

Elsbeth swallowed hard and spoke first. "Jeremy Parker has the supplies you ordered."

She prayed for him to say he had no idea what she was talking about and was disappointed at the spark of eager anticipation that crossed his face.

"You should have…uh, I mean…no mind, I can pick them up tomorrow."

"I saw the equipment, Tom. Didn't appear to have much usefulness for the spring planting."

"I…I was gonna tell you about that."

"When, Tom? Before or after you loaded up your bags?" Tears moistened the corners of her eyes, but she stood her ground. "How could you?"

"It's for us, our future."

She took his arm, led him to the open barn doors, and pointed to the unbroken field that was theirs.

"That's our future. Those acres out there that you claimed. For us…when we're married."

"You don't understand, Elsbeth."

"I understand that chasing after gold is like trying to harvest the morning fog. It's so thick you're sure you could bale it up right along with the hay. So, you grab at it only to come up empty. Then the sun climbs above the treetops and burns the fog away. It's gone, just as if it had never been there at all. Only the land is real, Tom…the land is our future."

"What you don't understand is…" He took a deep breath. "I've sold my claim."

Elsbeth staggered backwards as if she had been struck. She groped along the wall to support her failing knees.

"Tell me it's not true."

"I got a good price, money I needed for a stake, equipment and mules and such, passage to California." He hurried on defensively. "It's not what you think. There's plenty of gold. I've heard stories."

"Fairy tales, you mean."

"There's a meeting tomorrow in town. Come and listen. It'll change your mind, you'll see."

"More fairy tales. I've seen and heard it all."

"I'll be back in six months. We'll be rich. We can get married then, make another claim or buy all the land we want."

"Aren't you forgetting something?"

"What?"

"Charlie."

Tom threw his arms up in the air then let them flop limply to his side. "I'm going," he said, pronouncing each word emphatically. He stomped out, slamming his hand against the door so hard the hinges rattled.

Alone, Elsbeth was left to struggle not only to comprehend Tom's stubborn decision but to secure the barn for the night. As she tugged the doors shut, a movement in the dim light startled her. It was Charlie.

The rain had drenched his clothes, and rivulets of water trickled from his sopping hair, along the curves of his cheeks, to meet at and drip relentlessly from his chin. His shoulders jerked up and down in concert with a chorus of anguished sobs. His eyes accused her of a most unforgivable sin.

"You promised," he cried.

V

Elsbeth reached up and pulled the sides of her bonnet close over her ears, hoping to shut out the boisterous, back-slapping revelry of the farmer-boys-turned-would-be-goldminers.

She had not wanted to come to this meeting, but Charlie's accusation of the day before weighed heavily and she changed her mind. If she knew what the men were jabbering about, she reasoned, perhaps she could apply good old common sense and talk Tom out of going after all. She assured Charlie she would only be gone a few hours, then ran to the barn just as Tom swung onto the saddle. His equally dark mood lifted when she yelled, "I'm coming. I'm coming with you." He quickly dismounted and readied the wagon instead.

The ride into town had even been tolerable. Lingering tension between the two staved off any serious conversation. They spoke instead about the improving weather and the early-morning arrival of twin calves. Elsbeth still harbored confidence in her ability to convince him of the foolishness of this gold-seeking nonsense. However, as the meeting got under way, it took but a few minutes to prove her expectations overly optimistic at best.

Tom forced an opening in the crowd and jostled them to the front where, amid talk of the advantages of pack mules over wagons, he promptly forgot she existed.

Elsbeth startled when he leaped from her side to an upended box and began shouting words of encouragement to

115

the remaining undecided few who watched.

"Ran into Rowdy Pinkham from down the valley," he said. "'Cordin' to him, prospecting is as easy as walking across a stream. When you get to the other side, just empty the gold out of your boots."

Yahoos erupted from all sides.

Elsbeth had enough. She pushed free from the throng. When her absence went unnoticed, she shook her head sadly and aimed for a small circle of women.

"Pretty soon there won't be a man left in town," said one as Elsbeth approached. The others nodded and clucked knowingly.

"Both my husband and eldest up and left last week."

"Martha! That means you've only little George to tend to the planting. What will you do?"

"I've still got the girls. We'll manage."

"Aren't you angry?" asked Elsbeth tentatively.

The woman shrugged. "What good would it do?"

Elsbeth was horrified. How could these women be so resigned? Her mouth tightened into a frown as she thought that any man who treated his family this way wasn't worth...what? She was too miserable to come up with a comparison. After all, her man was now one of them.

She felt a comforting arm go around her shoulder. "They'll come back. You'll see."

Another hand patted her sleeve. "They've got a hunger in the belly that has to be satisfied, dear, but they know where home is."

"That's right. Soon enough our men will snap right back to their senses."

Elsbeth didn't answer. Anger plowed twin furrows across her forehead as she considered how heartless Tom had been to ignore the pain he was causing not only to herself but to an innocent, adoring child. An unexpected chill passed through her, a coolness that refused to be dispelled even when she pulled her shawl closer around her shoulders. In her pocket Elsbeth felt for a small lump which she had purchased and hidden there, a little piece of hard candy—a red one. What *was* she to do? The answer came as no surprise, and in her heart she knew there had never been a choice at all.

She wandered toward the wagon and the patiently waiting team. The oxen seemed always so accepting of their lot, be it a light load or a heavy one. She felt a strange kinship with them. Yes, she would wait. In the end, Tom would return and Charlie would have his family.

The warm sun on her face seemed a good omen, and she tried to smile.

"You believe in Fate, Elsbeth?"

Her hand flew to her throat as she whirled around to face the speaker. "For pitysake, Billy Brooster," she gasped. "You've scared me near half to death."

He stepped from behind her wagon and casually rested an elbow on its wheel, mere inches from where she stood while she anxiously looked about for curious bystanders.

"Fate. You believe in it?" he repeated.

"Whatever do you mean?"

"You and me...finding each other this way."

She took a small step backward. "I wasn't looking, Billy."

"That's why it's Fate," he said softly, at the same time reaching out and touching a bit of lace at the cuff of her sleeve. "You're still as beautiful as a field daisy, you know."

"Please, Billy. Mind your words. It's not mannerly."

"I think those are right smart courting words."

117

"C…c…?" Elsbeth shuddered. "Your talk is madness. I'm spoken for. Planning to be married as soon as he…well, soon."

"But not hitched yet. I've asked around about this fellow. Tom's his name. Tom Warner."

"You had no right, Billy. That's my business."

He ignored her accusation. "Oh, I know he's chasing down to California along with the rest of them fortune hunters. A foolish man to leave the best behind."

"Just leave me alone, please, Billy."

From behind his back he pulled a small bouquet of droopy-headed campion mixed with pennycress, laid them gently on the wagon seat. "Fate," he said, then turned and walked away, leaving Elsbeth alone to stare at the delicate white petals and fight the warmth that flashed to her cheeks.

For a long moment she stood there. Then with a fierceness that surprised even herself, she reached out and swept the flowers to the ground. As she watched, they caught the breeze and somersaulted away.

VI

The Warner household hummed with activity. Elsbeth had no choice but to pitch in, for there was beef to dry, foodstuffs to prepare, and woolen shirts to patch and launder. The peaceful barnyard sounds she had come to know and cherish were now shattered with the noisy protest of mules as Tom hastened to break the animals to harness and packs.

By the end of the second day, her nerves had worn so thin the need for escape was overwhelming. She hitched a single ox to a small farm cart, plunked Charlie in the back, and took off into town. Charlie's usual gentle humor had been fading at Tom's impending departure, and even the diversion of the ride failed to bring relief. Reminders were everywhere they turned. Partners in the venture called out to her.

"Tell Tom we'll be seein' him first light."

Newly-shod horses lined the street in front of the blacksmith shop. Young men and old loudly bid each other farewell, while others fortified their resolve at one of the many half-tent saloons on the street. Elsbeth's spirits slumped ever lower, and an uncomfortable feeling of being watched set her further on edge. She gave up and prepared to head for home.

At that moment a horse and rider she had failed to see approach came to a halt directly in front of the cart. Elsbeth looked up in annoyance.

"Right fine day, Miz Elsbeth." Billy Brooster touched a finger to the brim of his hat as he sat astride his Indian pony. Elsbeth frowned, for he blocked her advance.

"Let me pass, Billy."

She glared at him to emphasize her demand but saw soon enough his eyes bore down, not on her but on Charlie, as if studying his features, searching for an answer without being quite sure of the question. Instinctively she pulled the boy under the protecting curve of her arm.

"Please. Move your horse."

He made no effort to do so.

"You...uh...had a...uh..." His voice trailed off even as he continued to stare into the child's face.

Elsbeth felt the blood drain from her cheeks when she realized what it was he sought.

"This here boy's more than two years old. There's

119

nothing tying you and him or you and me together," she said.

"Nothing?"

The question made her pause. She looked over his head to the snow-covered peak of Mount Hood. Despite its bulk, she clearly saw through and beyond it to a little mound of dirt so far away. She thought of lying, but that would deny the life she'd carried and grown to love. Instead, she said, "Not anymore." Billy had a right to know. "There was but he's at rest now."

"He?" So quietly did Billy utter the word it might have been mistaken for a faint puff of air. With the barest movement of his knee, he urged the horse forward and out of her way. Elsbeth snapped the reins, sending the ox into a slow walk and leaving Billy lost in thought by the side of the road.

So all-consuming had the preparations been that when the following morning arrived, the sudden calm rankled with an ominous threat of its own, and a glorious sunrise mocked the somber mood with which Elsbeth prepared their morning meal.

Charlie refused to eat and stirred out of his seat at the table only when Tom asked him to follow him outside and hold the mules' leads while he loaded sacks of flour, sugar and coffee onto their backs. The boy showed no enthusiasm for hurrying along the leave-taking, and once Tom had finished, he wandered despondently back into the house. Elsbeth watched quietly, her heart aching for the suffering Charlie so plainly endured.

Tom muttered something about a missing piece of equipment and disappeared into a shed attached to the barn. His absence allowed Elsbeth to slip unnoticed to his waiting mount. She tugged at the thin leather strings that held closed a saddlebag. Inside she slipped a small golden heart. It was

120

one of the few personal possessions she had brought from home—a locket etched with a fancy "E," dangling from a golden pin wrought into the shape of a bow. It had been gifted to her by her grandmother who shared the same initial. The locket contained a tinted daguerreotype of herself taken two years before when she still wore her hair in braids. Her face had been cut out and into a heart shape to fit snugly inside. There had been a picture of her father too, but she had long since torn it from its place. Now a dark curl of Charlie's hair, secretly snipped from the child's head while he slept, nestled in the small enclosure.

"Don't you dare forget what you've left behind, Tom Warner," she whispered with a vengeance.

Within minutes the man Elsbeth had once dreaded to part with on the banks of the Columbia River was ready to go again. The mules, however, displayed more than the average reluctance, leaving Tom no alternative but to loop a rope around their necks, drape the ends over his shoulder, and lean heavily against their stubborn resistance. Elsbeth walked behind the comical parade, cheered by his inelegant departure while at the same time chiding herself for such unchristian thoughts.

Amos waved his son off, his face a mix of emotions. That he had chosen to accompany Tom no farther than a few paces from the farmhouse door suggested to Elsbeth a disappointment approaching her own.

Warner's rutted lane intersected the more traveled north-south road that connected Oregon City with smaller settlements up the Willamette Valley. The men assembled there were clearly impatient to be off and obviously cared little about the picture Tom presented as he took his place among them. Shouts of "Head 'em up!" and "Let's get a move on!" rang through the air, and the motley column began its slow advance.

Tom practically leaped into the saddle, but once settled he leaned down and took Elsbeth's hand in his. He squeezed it lightly and brought it to his lips.

"I'll miss you, Elsbeth. I expect to be back in time for Christmas."

At the warmth of his touch and the sincerity of his goodbye, a flush of remorse swept over Elsbeth until the meaning of what he had just said fully registered.

"Christmas? Tom, that's eight months away."

"'Bout that." He bobbed his head up and down in agreement.

"You said you'd be gone only six months."

"The boys and me figured we'd be needing a little more time."

Elsbeth's mouth dropped open, but she was speechless. Instead of words, she frantically looked toward the house. Did Charlie know? The answer was forthcoming.

"Tell Charlie for me, will you," he said, before yeehawing the mules to life.

Elsbeth stomped her foot, but Tom had already fixed his gaze southward, and the sudden motion served only to startle a nearby mule, already jittery in the general hubbub. The mule's hooves banged at the wheels of the caravan's single supply wagon. The driver cussed—the presence of a lady be damned—as he fought to calm the beast.

Elsbeth didn't care. She reflected on the four weeks that had transpired since she had first ridden down this very road in the company of Amos Warner, fully prepared to sacrifice her future to his bidding. A miracle had happened then. Despite the generally drab Oregon weather, the intervening days had been filled with the sunlight of her reunion with Tom. But now dark clouds churned into a storm and brought them to this cross in the road. She watched Tom take his place in the column. Only seconds had passed, but his figure receded rapidly. How small he became. Would there be another miracle for her? For Charlie?

Too late to fret about it now, she told herself. There's work to be done. Before the last of the glory seekers straggled by, Elsbeth turned homeward. Immediately a splash of color caught her eye. Curiosity drew her to where a partial fence defined the far western corner of Amos's property. Warped and splintered by the winter, the wood of the top rail splayed open like a giant hand. In it was wedged an offering of peace—a small nosegay of wildflowers. She plucked it free and buried her nose in the sweet fragrance.

"Oh, Tom!"

She looked up, half expecting to witness his return. A lone horseman greeted her, but it wasn't Tom. Billy Brooster pushed the hat back on his head and gestured toward the spring flowers.

"See you found my little surprise."

Elsbeth dropped the bouquet as if it had been on fire.

"What are you doing here?"

"Took a hankerin' for some of that gold they say's in California."

"You're traveling with this group?" she stammered.

He nodded and they fell into a strained silence. Both turned to watch the receding line of hopefuls and the hypnotic swish of horsetails. After what seemed an eternity, Elsbeth said, "Why?"

"I hear life's rough in the mining camps. Dangerous too they say. Some aren't cut out for it. Some don't make it back. But don't you worry none. I'll take good care of that one for you."

With that Billy kicked his pony into a trot and

seconds later was gone.

Alone. Elsbeth wrestled the demons of her emotions. As her whole being slumped and her chin sagged onto her chest, she remembered the flowers lying at her feet. Slowly, almost against her will, she stooped, selected a blossom the color of an Ohio sunrise, and carefully tucked it in the waistband of her apron. She wasn't entirely sure why she did so, only that it somehow seemed important.

Then the demons returned and chased her up the lane.

CHAPTER 7

The Glory Road

I

Everyone was out of sorts in the days following Tom's departure. Had it been a week already?

Charlie lost interest in the baby chicks and often had to be reminded to scatter their portion of grain in the yard. Amos threw himself into work. He opened more acres than the previous year, necessitating leaving the house at first light and not returning until after sunset. Elsbeth found solace in the kitchen, cooking up stews, baking breads, rolling out pie dough, until Amos begged her to stop.

"I can't possibly eat all you place in front of me!"

"But you work so hard," she protested.

"You fill my stomach just fine, Elsbeth. Work satisfies another emptiness."

"For a woman, it's not so easy. Everything I see or touch is a reminder of that same emptiness and nothing seems to fill it."

As the days grew longer, idle hours became intolerable. Amos refused her offer to help in the fields and household chores were quickly put to rest. Charlie moped about, his prized collection of pine cones forgotten in a corner. Elsbeth thought to start an herb garden, but her heart wasn't in it, and though she managed to clear a small patch of ground, not a single seed had been planted.

One particularly warm afternoon while Charlie napped, she filled a jug with spring water, spread butter on several thick slabs of bread, and walked into the field where Warner labored under the sun.

"Amos," she called, "it's dreadfully hot out here. You simply must take a few moments for refreshment."

"You chastise me like a mother, Elsbeth, but today I appreciate it. It's much too warm for this early in the season."

He mopped his brow on his sleeve then lifted the cloth covering the basket she carried. His expression conveyed an obvious pleasure at her thoughtfulness.

"You miss him, don't you?" he said.

"Very much. And Charlie misses him more than words can say. But you must feel the void too. Aren't you even a little bit angry he left just when you need him most?"

"Tom's a good lad. He's well on to becoming his own man. I can't fault him his dreams. I had my own ambitions. There're what landed me out here. But, yes, I do miss him."

Dreams, thought Elsbeth. She wanted to shout that she too had dreams, but what good would it do to question Tom's lack of responsibility when Warner seemed all too willing to justify it?

With the now-empty basket in hand, she wandered back toward the house. Her path took her very close to the promising land claim that had been so recently snatched away by Tom's impulsiveness. She dared not step onto the soil for fear the new owner might object, but she found a grassy area on the verge and sank down to the ground to take stock of her feelings.

126

The warm sun and gentle breeze couldn't coax her from her melancholy mood. She thought of the twists and turns the trajectory of her own life had taken in the past year. Hadn't she survived and, dare she say, prospered? Perhaps it was better Tom sold the land. Though she mourned the loss of its security, there were other courses one could follow to support a family. Tom was good with animals. A stable hand then. Or even owner if he struck it rich down in California. He was also well educated and loved children, if Charlie were an example, so a teaching position in a schoolhouse was not out of the question.

Bolstered by this rosier outlook, she stood, intent on waiting out the next eight months with a more positive attitude. She would pass the summer and fall at the Warner farm. Help with any work, of course. Tend to Amos's household in preparation for one of her own. She would have to help Charlie see a brighter side to Tom's absence. As it was, he suffered dreadful nightmares. He woke wailing Tom's name. During the day he sulked or cried, the pain of losing a mother and two fathers in the space of one short year plainly written on his face. She would make counting down the days a game with rewards along the way.

To rally herself when the empty days seemed too long, she recalled the parting words of Billy Brooster. Tom's safety and his health in primitive mining camps weighed heavily, and while Brooster might be a poor substitute for a guardian angel, she clung to his assurance: "I'll take good care of him."

The intervening days, however, chipped away at her ease of mind, for Billy had also suggested a darker possibility. One morning she awoke to the cold realization that Billy had also suggested Tom might not make it back at all. Brooster's comforting promise, delivered with a spray of springtime

127

blossoms and the look of a smitten schoolboy, took on a new and sinister meaning.

What had he meant? She closed her eyes and willed herself to recall every word, every inflection, every gesture. What had he *really* meant? Anxiety ballooned into panic until one evening she stood before Amos and made an announcement.

"I've heard the widow Mrs. Larkin has a farm wagon she would be willing to sell for a pittance. I can manage the cost with what little I've saved. If you would help me rig some stays and part with that old canvas cover you have in the barn, it will make a suitable covered conveyance."

"Whatever for?"

"I…we, Charlie and me…will be following Tom to California."

"Elsbeth!" exclaimed Warner. "That's madness. It's much too dangerous for a woman alone. He'll be back. I know Tom. Trust me. Trust him."

"No, Amos. This is something I must do." She left it at that. She did not wish to explain Billy Brooster, and how could she worry this man with her fears for his son's life, supported by nothing more than a handful of wildflowers and the ominous shadow of a woman's intuition.

"At least leave the boy here."

"Oh, Amos. Look how he grieves over Tom's absence. It would break his heart for me to disappear too."

"Then I'll accompany you."

"That's right Christian of you, Amos, but allowing your land to sit idle risks your claim of ownership. I can't ask that of you. And, as you say, when Tom returns…when we all return, we'll buy back his land, if possible. Or file a new claim. Or do something entirely different."

Elsbeth knew Amos's faith in his son was strong. She

also knew her resolve matched it in equal proportions. The old man relented.

With the decision made, they acquired the wagon and equipped it as best they could. Amos insisted she take the two stronger oxen. Elsbeth packed her meager belongings and accepted with gratitude provisions from Amos's larder. On a cool, spring morning, she and Charlie were off.

II

The California-bound trail was paved with Forty-Niners as they called themselves. Many of the men rode a horse or mule. It seemed one tried to outpace the other. They jostled for position at narrow fordings or sought out shortcuts through the heavy forests, while her wagon forced her to follow a pitted road. Most were provisioned with the barest of necessities, as if speed were of paramount concern and judicious planning an afterthought. Those who traveled with a wagon also drove their animals with an urgency Elsbeth considered foolish given the terrain, the uncertainty of the route, and what might or might not await them at the other end.

The Valley of the Willamette rose up into the coastal range. She found herself on rough trails with names like Applegate and Lassen. Day after day she and Charlie trudged along. Although she advanced at a much slower rate than the others, Elsbeth was rarely alone, moving first with one group, then falling behind into the company of another.

The going was difficult, though not impossible. Those determined for the goldfields carried with them a multitude of talent that had nothing to do with gold digging. Any service Elsbeth needed was eagerly exchanged for a hot meal. A blacksmith filed a burr from her ox's shoe for a pan of cornbread. A harness maker rigged a serviceable winch to hoist her wagon up the steep inclines. For that she paid with a hearty soup of wild herbs and onions. Her reputation as a willing and excellent cook fanned out before and behind her like ripples on a pond.

At long last, as weary emigrants, she and Charlie entered the heart of gold country. Each evening Elsbeth poked to life a crackling fire under the much-used Dutch oven. Her stewpot drew men like moths. As she handed each a bowl or plate, she looked beyond their bristling whiskers and into their sunken eyes, searching, always searching for a familiar face. Her questions were always the same.

"Tom Warner. Have you seen him? Are there Oregonians among you?" Reluctantly she inquired after Billy Brooster. The answer? A shrug of the shoulder, a shake of the head.

Charlie knew they were trying to catch up to Tom. This perked him up. His mood changed from one of utter depression to, if not optimism, at least normality for a child his age. He paid attention more and tried to help when Elsbeth unyoked the oxen each evening.

One day as they passed into a forest, he tugged at her sleeve.

"Mama!" he exclaimed. "Look at the trees."

"I think they're called redwoods."

"How did they get to be so big?"

"They've been growing a long, long time."

"Will they ever stop growing?"

"Eventually, but not for a while."

Charlie mulled her explanation but continued to point out one giant tree after another.

"This one too?" he'd ask.

Elsbeth looked around as if seeing for the first time more than just the trail ahead. This place called California was vast. How would she ever find Tom?

Brooster's talk of the perils inherent in such an adventure as hunting for gold now haunted her anew. While most of the men she'd encountered thus far had been friendly, it was clear the earlier congeniality on the part of the gold seekers had frayed. The cardinal sin of greed blanketed the rough and tumble encampments that sprang up seemingly overnight. There were quarrels. An occasional fistfight over who had rights to a twenty-foot stretch of streambed sometimes exploded into a free-for-all from which Elsbeth hastily fled. Baseless rumors of easier pickings emptied a camp as quickly as if the bung on an overturned water barrel had been suddenly yanked free.

In the beginning she flung heavenward a host of silent prayers: Give me direction. Give me strength. Little by little, though, she recognized the success of her mission depended solely on one person—her.

III

Midnight. The lateness of the hour brought scant relief from the noisy celebration. Business flourished in the half dozen canvas-sided saloons which huddled together to form a nameless town in the California landscape.

Gunshots split the night. No fear, Elsbeth told herself. Just someone's drunken idea of merriment. The blast, however, scared Charlie, and he trembled against her side. She tried to block out the sounds by folding closed the rear flap of the covered wagon, but all that accomplished was to cut off the thin rustle of air that would have made sleeping bearable if only quiet prevailed.

It had been over a month since she'd made her decision to leave the tidy Warner farm. Sometimes a faint shiver of regret tiptoed up her spine, especially on a night like this, but in general she held fast to her commitment to find Tom and bring him to his senses.

"Mama, where are we?"

"I don't rightly know, little soldier."

Where are we indeed? she asked herself. One camp seemed nothing more than a copy of all the others they had passed through. Hardscrabble, Dogtown, Cryin' Shame— California boom towns with names as desolate as their surroundings, inhabited by men in the throes of wanderlust and gold fever, the twin afflictions of the men who marched along this glory road.

"Is Papa here?"

"No, honey. Maybe in the next camp."

Elsbeth wrapped the little boy in her arms and sighed. Had she been wrong to follow Tom into the Sierra Nevadas to catch up to his dream? The question gnawed at her this night just as it had every other night since leaving Oregon City.

"Stay here," Amos had urged, but she would have none of it.

A fly buzzed at Elsbeth's ear. As she swatted it away, her eyes opened to the pale glow of dawn. She had fallen asleep after all. The weight of Charlie's head on her arm told her he had too. Gently she rolled the boy onto a cotton quilt and stepped outside.

On the ground near her wagon, two young men sat patiently, tin plates balanced on their laps.

"Oh, dear," said Elsbeth when she saw the small cups of flour they held up as if an offering to a pagan god. "I had planned on moving a little farther south before breakfast."

Just then a third walked up, bearing kindling for the fire. Elsbeth relented and reached for her cooking utensils. She measured water and flour into a large bowl but stopped, hopes soaring, when the newcomer said, "Some new fellas landed in camp last night. Come down from the north, they did. One of them was askin' after the same 'un you was."

"You mean Tom Warner?"

A look of confusion passed over the young man's face. "No...sorry, I must have..."

Elsbeth straightened, hesitated, then said, "Billy Brooster?"

"That's the one."

"He's here?"

"Yeah...uh, I mean, no. The one askin', not the Billy fellow." When Elsbeth didn't reply, he stammered on, "Thought you might be interested...seein' as how you were askin'...same name an' all..."

Still Elsbeth remained silent. Her mind, though, whirled with a thousand scenarios to explain this turn of events.

"That's him, over yonder."

She looked along a row of crude lean-tos that hadn't been there the evening before. The object of her scrutiny wore a soldier's shirt. Recently discharged, she thought, or maybe he was just one of the many who had abandoned their posts in the frenzied rush for gold.

The sound of hot bacon grease sizzling in the iron skillet pulled her back to the business at hand. Who is he? she quizzed herself even as she stirred and ladled, tested and flipped. What does he want with Billy? The smell of flapjacks

133

filed the air. A sleepy-eyed Charlie appeared, as did ten other hungry men. For a moment, curiosity about the soldier moved to second place.

Elsbeth cooked and served by rote until the men signaled the end of the meal by extinguishing the fire with the dregs of their coffee cups. Then one by one the prospectors approached, murmured "Thank ya, ma'am," and pressed a few flakes of shiny yellow metal into the palm of her hand. As always, their shy, awkward gratitude embarrassed her, although by now she should have been used to it. The scene was a familiar one, repeated in every mining camp she visited.

At first Elsbeth had protested with, "No need. It was my pleasure." She thought of the many wives and mothers left at home to worry about the well-being of their men. She did it for them, a small act of kindness that required no payment. Circumstances, though, finally forced her to admit their contributions were necessary. As the number of men increased, she used a portion of the gold to restock her makeshift kitchen. The men had insisted, just as they did this morning, and she accepted.

"You're too kind," she whispered to each, but under her breath she said, "Prettied up dirt, that's all this gold is. Nothing but trouble."

When the final straggler wandered away, Elsbeth did what she always did. She brushed the golden flecks into an old blue and white crock jar and tapped the corncob stopper firmly into place.

"Hear you're lookin' for Billy Brooster?"

Elsbeth whirled, stifling a scream when she realized the unexpected voice belonged to the soldier.

"Uh…yes, that's true." She fumbled to collect her wits. Up close the soldier frightened her. The smell of whiskey clung to his breath even though it was well before noon. A twist of his lips suggested he took pleasure in her obvious discomfort. Despite the efforts of the climbing sun, Elsbeth felt a chill crawl along her spine.

"Any luck?" he asked.

"None at all." It was the truth, yet instinct warned her to economize with the particulars.

"Been up to Rich Bar?"

She shrugged.

"Mormon Island then?"

Elsbeth stepped toward the wagon, assuming an air of dismissal. The soldier ignored it and moved forward.

"We could help each other, you know. I got some unfinished business with Brooster." He nodded down at Charlie who peered out from between the spokes of the wagon's wheel, eyes locked on the stranger as if under a sorcerer's spell. "Maybe you do too?"

Quickly, deliberately, Elsbeth moved alongside the wagon, her skirts now a shield between her son and the man who wore the outward trappings of law yet filled her with a fear that his interpretation of justice might clash violently with her own.

"Sir, that's truly none of your concern."

He sneered and spat on the ground near Elsbeth's feet. Despite the man's despicable manner, she stood, unflinching. If he was looking for Billy, it stood to good reason he'd have no idea of Tom's whereabouts. She glared at him, but didn't say a word. The conversation obviously over, the soldier turned and stomped away, packed his gear, and within minutes had hiked up the ravine and out of sight.

"I don't like that man, Mama."

"Neither do I."

"I wanna go someplace else."

She smiled at Charlie's simple logic. Swallowing the

135

sour-tasting bile that had risen from her stomach, she said with a nod, "Me too."

She looked around the campsite for a long, thin switch which she stripped of leaves and handed to the boy.

"First, let's go into the meadow and tickle those oxen into coming back here to the wagon."

By the time they returned, the temporary town had emptied of its miners, leaving Elsbeth to hitch her team alone. The solitude suited her, gave her time to think. She boosted Charlie into the wagon. When she had the oxen in place, the tableware rinsed, the frying pan restored to its hook, she found him sitting on a pile of bedding, staring into a small book bound in leather. The book had been a gift from Tom. It held neither poetry nor tale of great adventure but pale blue lines on which to record their farm accounts. All blank. A dream on hold. Empty, save for a dainty yellow flower, salvaged from a spring bouquet, which she had pressed between the pages.

"Why are you saving this?" Charlie asked as he pointed at the flattened petals.

Elsbeth dropped to her knees and closed the book. "I don't rightly know, Charlie dear. I really don't."

IV

From the vantage point of outlying rises, Sacramento resembled a fine cut diamond. The sun flashed along the surface of the American River, breaking into a thousand dancing points of light. A multi-faceted prism of canvas roofs reflected hot and white from the valley floor. It almost hurt the eyes to look upon the city.

Tears streamed from Elsbeth's eyes but not from the brilliance of the view. She peeled away the outer skin from yet another onion and dropped it into the stew simmering in a pot at her feet. A strand of hair slipped from the confines of her now-faded yellow bonnet and fell across her face. With a quick puff of breath, she blew it to one side. There was no time for otherwise. Six men sat at her table—a full house, the second since noon.

The table wasn't much, a plank really, secured against the wagon at one end and balanced on an empty keg at the other. It jutted at right angles just far enough to make room for three patrons on either side. Over the table Elsbeth had spread a small square of cloth with lilacs embroidered along the hem, another of her precious possessions. She dispatched Charlie to gather field daisies, and with these touches sought at least a semblance of home. A crude canopy, fashioned by detaching the canvas wagon cover from its frame and draping it over two poles anchored in the ground, offered a small rectangle of shade in the mid-afternoon heat.

For five days this patch of field on the outskirts of town had been home, the wagon doubling as living quarters by night, kitchen by day. And still no sign of Tom. Had it not been for the advice of a brown-skinned miner up from Mexico City, Elsbeth might have continued to wander haphazardly through the higher elevations.

"*Senora*," he'd said, wagging a knowing finger. "You waste your time running from one camp to the next. Go to Sacramento City. Stay there. Sooner or later he will go there too. They all do. Panners and dry diggers, peddlers and card sharks. Take my word."

Elsbeth took it.

With equal parts reluctance and relief, she staked claim to a bit of hillside and placed all her bets on a man's need to eat. She set up shop and never wanted for customers. Six of them now grew impatient for a meal.

The young woman moved among them, serving up the stew, passing thick slabs of bread from her Dutch oven, and pouring coffee into their mugs. She watched them eat, wondering where they all came from, this mass of humankind with hope burning in their eyes. Some brought her flour, dried beans or perhaps a brace of ducks. Others measured gold into her hand. The latter filled the blue and white jar, the former her cookpot.

One by one they filed away.

"Shore was good fixin's, ma'am." The voice belonged to a boy, one barely old enough to shave. "Don't get much up t'camp and what we do ain't worth nothin'."

Elsbeth acknowledged the compliment. "It must be difficult for you up there in the mountains. The work. The loneliness."

"Least I'm not on King Street." He nodded knowingly down toward the city.

Curiosity aroused, Elsbeth squinted down at the sparkling gem of order and industry that was Sacramento as if straining her eyes would reveal the secret of King Street.

"The sick ones end up there," the boy continued. "A bugger can flop for a dollar a day…out of the weather."

Elsbeth's eyebrows arched in disbelief. "A dollar. So much?"

"Yep. 'Course somethin' to eat might be thrown in— if they're lucky."

"What about the unlucky ones?"

He lifted his shoulders, unconcerned, but Elsbeth persisted. "And medical treatment? You said they were sick."

The boy laughed into a ragged shirt sleeve. "Ma'am, it tain't exactly what you'd call a hospital." He was still laughing when a moment later he disappeared over a rise, pick and shovel clanking loudly on the back of a sandy-colored burro.

Elsbeth watched him leave. She could understand neither his skewed sense of humor toward the suffering of fellow miners, nor his eagerness to return along the path that might eventually lead him to the same desperate fate.

She longed to run after him, throw her arms around the boy and shake him free of his foolish notions of gold and riches. Indeed, she had taken two full steps forward before reality caught her by the arm. She sank to the ground and wept.

The outburst lasted only a minute. Dabbing at her cheeks with the corner of her apron, she wondered if this moment of weakness was due to frustration over not being able to find Tom or perhaps because the young man reminded her so much of one of her own dear brothers.

For an instant a lifetime of memories flooded her heart and threatened a fresh overspill of tears. She ached for family, for familiar scenes, lively discussions at the dinner table, guessing games in the parlor during the long winter evenings, a book to read.

"Stop it, Elsbeth," she admonished herself. "What's past is past. There's only the future now." She squared her shoulders and rose. "Sundown will be around soon enough with another swarm of hungry mouths. Best I give Charlie some attending to while I have a moment's peace."

She expected to find him playing in the shade under the wagon, but when she looked, he wasn't there. Nor was he inside. Just to be sure, she climbed aboard and rifled among the jumble of housewares. Not a sound. No impish face. Again, she checked under the wagon bed, this time crawling on hands and knees.

"Charlie!" she screamed. "Where are you? Charlie!"

Nothing in Elsbeth's sixteen years prepared her for the soul-wrenching panic she felt when the last syllable of his name faded into utter silence.

V

Long, fingerlike shadows crept over the gentle hills, enveloping the verdant fields and coloring them with the blackness of night. No matter how hard she ran, or in which direction, darkness lurked. It mocked her. It tricked the eye. How often did she see the silhouette of a frightened little boy only to rush forward and find a bush, a stump, a pile of stones.

Two men appeared on the horizon.

They pulled up short, for despite their obvious advantage in size and number, the disheveled appearance of the lone woman must have been alarming. Elsbeth's hair swirled recklessly about her face, free of the bonnet which hung useless at her back. Her eyes glowed bright with the look of a madwoman. She called to them in a voice shrill with hysteria.

Before the two could react, Elsbeth stood before them, toe to toe, the jacket lapels of one caught firmly in her grasp.

"Charlie. Little boy. Dark hair. He's lost. Have you seen him?"

"*Mein Gott im Himmel,*" bellowed one of the German immigrants, wrestling to free himself from her grip. The man and woman grappled with each other, neither comprehending the other.

Elsbeth tried again, this time speaking slowly, loudly as if that alone was sufficient to break the language barrier.

"Little...boy. Have...you seen...a little...boy?"

"*Bitte. Ich spreche kein Englisch.*"

Wild-eyed, Elsbeth turned to his companion. He only smiled weakly and said, "You cook, please? Pay gold."

"No. No." She pounded her breast with her fists and sobbed. "My boy is lost. I must find him."

The man, now unfettered, lost no time in fleeing, his companion close behind. Helpless, Elsbeth watched them retreat then stumbled off, reaching her own wagon moments before the last faint crack of gray in the western sky slammed shut to total darkness.

She clambered aboard and fumbled around until her hand landed upon the wire handle of the lantern. Dragging it out to the ground, she tried to light the candle inside only to be thwarted by the utter pitch blackness of the night. Not a star or sliver of moon aided her attempt. She burnt her fingers twice.

On the third try, the match connected with the wick and a flame was born. Even with this small success, Elsbeth knew she could not venture far from the wagon. The yellowish aura of the candle's glow penetrated the darkness only so far. If she wandered far, she would lose her way. Sobbing with hopelessness, she crawled back into the wagon, though not before propping the lantern in a conspicuous spot on the ground—a beacon to light a little boy's way home...just in case.

The security of the wagon afforded little comfort. Visions of Charlie, alone and afraid, tortured Elsbeth. The familiar surroundings only intensified his plight. She whispered his name over and over as if repeating it a magical number of times would assure his safe return. Finally, spent by guilt, she groped around in the dark until her fingers brushed the polished marble of a small cross, one of her few

141

personal things that had survived the journey west. Dropping to her knees, she bargained with God.

"In the name of all that's holy," she prayed, "send him back to me."

By chance, she also found Charlie's red kerchief. Into its folds had been knotted a treasure trove of little-boy things. She fumbled at the corners until the knots gave way. For the remainder of the night Elsbeth rocked back and forth against the hard wall of the wagon, cradling in her hands the bundle's contents—the smooth river pebbles, the bristly pinecone, even the two dead spiders.

With the first light of dawn, she renewed her search.

The morning dew soaked her hemline but went unnoticed as she scrambled over the same territory she had scoured twice the night before. No living soul escaped her interrogations. If one were wrapped in a blanket and dozing under a tree, she woke him up and peppered him with questions. If one were trudging along with shovel and pan, she stepped into his path, forcing him to stop. What followed was the same barrage of inquiries. To a man, they shook their heads sadly. Some patted her sympathetically on the back. Most promised they would help widen the scope of the search. She thanked them all but took no consolation from their good intentions.

A rumor here, a nugget there, she thought bitterly. How important could one small child be when paydirt was all around?

A curl of smoke rose above a nearby stand of pine. Elsbeth followed it to a group of four or five men bent over a campfire. She approached repeating, "Have you seen a little boy around here? He's lost. Dark hair, brown eyes. About so tall." She held out her hand to indicate a height slightly below her hip.

Those facing her looked up blankly. Only when the one whose back was to her turned slowly did the trim of his uniform become evident.

"Well, we meet again," he said. He doffed his hat in an irreverent salute. At the same time his eyes roamed over her body, beginning at the top of her snarled hair and ending at the bottom of her rumpled dress.

"Clayton Pierce. At your service, ma'am."

Elsbeth remembered their last encounter and wished only to be gone.

"So, you've lost the kid, huh?"

"Charlie. His name is Charlie."

Pierce reached out, lifted a twisted strand of Elsbeth's hair and let it slide between his fingers. "How careless of you."

Revolted, Elsbeth backed away.

"In such a hurry to be off, are we? Too bad…considering what a help I could be."

"Mr. Pierce, if you know anything about Charlie's whereabouts, I demand you tell me."

A smirk. "Just takin' my time…judgin' the measure of your gratitude, if you know what I mean."

Elsbeth dug her fingernails into her palms to stop herself from raking them across his face. After Charlie is found, she told herself. After. She glanced toward Pierce's companions, hoping for assistance, but they only kicked dirt onto the smoldering fire and hastened away.

His rough hand massaged her elbow, unnerving Elsbeth, but only for a moment. She quickly shook free of both the crippling disgust and the unwelcome hand.

Clayton Pierce made no effort to conceal a laugh. "Always did admire a little spunk." He reclaimed her arm, this time lodging it in a viselike grip, and pulled her toward him.

143

"Allow me to escort you, ma'am. We can talk about Billy Brooster along the way. Let's see. Where's that wagon of yours?"

"Billy Br...? You said this was about finding Charlie." Elsbeth dug her heels into the soft earth and jolted to a stop. Pierce barely broke stride.

"Damn it, girl, c'mon," he growled, yanking her onward. "We're gonna negotiate a simple contract. You help me sniff out Brooster, and I show you where the kid went."

"Why's Billy so important to you?"

"We've a little score to settle's all. 'Bout what don't concern you none."

Elsbeth's stomach constricted. From the look on Pierce's face, the score was anything but little. Billy's intentions toward both Tom and herself were troublesome but, until proven otherwise, a product of her imagination. This man Pierce, however, left no doubt he meant serious harm...or worse. She feared the very devil had come to barter, and, as usual, the bargain weighed heavily in his favor.

Responsibility for Billy's fate appeared to reside in her hands, but that was something she'd deal with later. For now, the one thing that mattered was Charlie's whereabouts and, according to Clayton Pierce, he held the only clue.

VI

The morning sun made its appearance as Pierce carelessly dismantled Elsbeth's makeshift kitchen, positioned her team at the wagon's tongue, and tied his horse off the trailing end.

"Just where are you proposing we go?" she demanded

from her seat at the head of the wagon.

In answer Pierce merely climbed aboard, released the brake, and swung the animals onto a course leading toward town.

"You're going to Sacramento? Charlie would never…"

"Boys will be boys."

"What are you talking about? Charlie's a mere child. I don't believe you have any idea where he is." She grappled for the reins. "Stop this instant. I do not want to leave this area. Do you hear me?"

"I hear ya. But if you want to find the kid, you have to go where the kid went."

"You saw Charlie go into the city?"

Pierce's lip curled in an unreadable grin. "Him an' another brat," he said while glancing sideways at Elsbeth. "Climbed aboard a big ol' box wagon and off they went."

"You're lying." But was she really willing to gamble Charlie's safe return because the man repulsed her? He'd dangled a carrot of hope and she had no choice but to follow, no matter where it led her.

Pierce ignored her accusation, appearing instead to be intent on guiding the oxen. When the wagon teetered precariously over the uneven terrain, he pressed his leg firmly against Elsbeth's thigh, coarse laughter rumbling from his throat when she jerked away and huddled uncomfortably on the far outer edge of the seat.

A small brown bottle appeared from beneath Pierce's Army shirt. With his teeth, he tugged at the cork until it popped free and, amid a spray of saliva, sent it flying into the passing scenery. Whenever the wagon wheels passed over an even spot in the road, he lifted the bottle to his lips and drank. If the smooth places took too long in coming, he

145

drank anyway, the amber liquid sloshing over his chin.

Elsbeth concentrated on the approaching city. At first it appeared only a brush stroke of civilization across a canvas of green. As the miles fell away, though, streets emerged, then shops and houses. Soon painted signs were readable: saddlery, gunsmith, general store. Dozens of sloops and schooners bobbed alongside the quays, a forest of masts waving merrily to their more firmly anchored brothers on shore. Although canvas tents remained the most common means of shelter, everywhere construction progressed at a feverish pace. More substantial buildings, in various stages of completion, dotted a grid of streets. The thwack of hammers and shouts of laborers added yet another dimension to the hustle and bustle of Sacramento City.

Elsbeth drew her breath in utter amazement, for the activity and the numbers of people hurrying about their business reminded her of a colony of ants. How would she ever find Charlie among so many?

"Whoa!" shouted Pierce. They lurched to a stop at the end of a street. He tossed the reins carelessly aside and clambered down, losing his hat as he did. Even with his boots planted in a wide stance, the soldier had difficulty standing without wavering. He belched loudly.

"You wait right here, Missy," he called over his shoulder.

Elsbeth obeyed. She waited while he teetered onto the boardwalk and waited some more as he stumbled into a saloon. She even waited after he reappeared with his fingers wrapped tightly around the slender neck of a whiskey bottle. Two equally drunken companions emerged from the tavern and joined him in the street. With arms draped over shoulders, they vanished around a corner.

Elsbeth ended her vigil. "You miserable...you no

146

good…you…" What she lacked in words, she made up for in action. Putting her foot firmly to the side of Pierce's rolled-up pack of belongings, she kicked it resolutely overboard. After untying his horse and slapping it on the rump, she gathered the reins of her team in her hands and vented both anger and frustration on the backs of the oxen. They rattled away, leaving in their wake Pierce's hat, now encrusted with mud and parted neatly through the crown with a deep impression of the wagon's wheel.

Wishing only to disappear from view as quickly as possible, Elsbeth drove forward, into the heart of the city. If the streets became a maze, she didn't notice. If pedestrians pressed close, she didn't see.

"Hey there, watch out!"

An itinerant merchant interrupted his singsong litany of wares just long enough to scream and frantically leap aside. Tin pots clattered to the ground when the corner of the ox wagon clipped his handcart. Elsbeth felt as if a thousand eyes witnessed her embarrassment. However, the pulse of the city wavered not the slightest, and within seconds the hawker retrieved his merchandise, shook his fist but proceeded on his way.

"Lord have mercy," Elsbeth sighed wearily, "Lord have mercy."

Unnerved by the mishap she reined sharply into a patch of knee-high grass between an apothecary shop and a frame building under construction. There she hitched the team securely to a signpost that read, "City lot for sale— Inquire at Hotel."

Now on foot, her attention turned once again to the search for Charlie. Free to inquire of shopkeepers or passing citizens, she roamed the streets, darting here and there, trying to imagine what sorts of things would attract inquisitive little boys. The activity along the Embarcadero? The boisterousness of saloons? The stable with its horses?

Up close the city paled dramatically from her earlier assessment. There was noise. Confusion. People everywhere. Animals. Street vendors. Strangers. Dangers. The more she searched, the more she was convinced Pierce had fed her an outright lie. She pictured Charlie returning to their campsite in the hills and discovering the wagon gone. She ought to get back to her wagon, but reason prevailed. Right now, she was in Sacramento City. She would first look for the boy here.

"It's far too big a task for one person," she admitted. "But who is there in this place to help me?"

Up the street a small crowd had gathered. Elsbeth drew near, hoping someone among them would volunteer on her behalf.

"What's going on?" she asked of a young man on the edge of the throng.

"Bet's up to five hundred dollars," he answered breathlessly, "and stakes have been upped again."

"Gambling? Out here in public? On the street corner?"

"Sure thing."

A cheer erupted. The crowd surged forward, carrying Elsbeth with it until she found herself next to a small table draped in green felt. On one side stood a man dressed in an outrageous plaid suit with a bright yellow vest and a bowler set rakishly atop his head. He held up a deck of playing cards for all to see then shuffled it with carnival showmanship. Across from him a man smiled through a dusty beard. This man clutched a bulging leather pouch which he occasionally waved in the air to the delight of the bystanders.

"Double or nothin'," he called.

The dealer drew off the top four cards and laid them

in a row. He signaled the player who pushed two of the cards to the side. A jack of spades and a seven of hearts lay exposed. The dealer waited. A hush fell over the crowd.

"Lower," called out the player, pointing to the face card. He beamed at the approval he received from those around him.

Slowly the dealer drew from the deck. King of diamonds.

A universal groan united the crowd.

"Ring-a-ding damn," yelled the gambler, although he seemed to take his loss in stride and even handed over the poke of gold with hardly a second's hesitation. "Guess I'd better find me another gold mine," he joked and, amid good-natured laughter, walked away.

Elsbeth could only stare in disbelief. "He lost a thousand dollars," she whispered. "A fortune. That would buy a farm, a whole farm and then some."

She looked around, expecting to see her reaction echoed by the others but was sorely mistaken. The people began to disperse as if nothing out of the ordinary had happened. Seeing them leave reminded her of the reason she was there to begin with.

"Wait!" she called.

The dealer paused as he folded his table and glanced her way. Words formed on her lips, but before she could give them a voice, a woman passed between them. It wasn't her shocking red hair styled in outlandish ringlets, nor was it the fancy green dress with daring neckline that choked Elsbeth into silence. The woman rustled by and was almost to the corner when Elsbeth stammered, "That pin. How did you come by that...pin?"

The woman reeled around, confused, her hand protectively covering the golden heart at her breast. Elsbeth regained her manners.

"Excuse me," said Elsbeth, catching up to the woman. "I didn't mean to startle you. That piece of jewelry…?" She pointed, hardly believing what she saw.

The woman relaxed and let her hand drop. "It was a gift," she said proudly.

"I had one just like it. Mine was also inscribed. With an E…like yours."

Caution clouded the woman's face.

"It was more than a pin. It was a locket." Before the woman could react, Elsbeth stepped forward and caught the hidden clasp with the tip of her fingernail. "Opened like this."

The locket sprang open and something fell to the ground. Elsbeth knelt to retrieve it. "Who gave this to you?" she demanded, but when she looked up, the other woman had vanished. Still on her knees, she unfurled her fingers and stared aghast at what lay in the palm of her hand…a dear little circlet of dark brown hair. Slowly she rose, the questions that gnawed at her soul now twofold: Where was Charlie? How had this woman acquired the locket she'd given to Tom?

Gazing about, she realized she had come to the end of a long, winding road. Thousands had taken the same road, seeking its promise of riches and glory. For her, the only gold that mattered was shaped into a heart and held a few precious strands of hair.

People streamed nearby, coming and going about their business. Elsbeth barely noticed. She fixed her gaze on the lopsided sign at the corner, appreciating immediately the irony that her journey had come to its end at the foot of King Street.

CHAPTER 8

"Seeing The Elephant"

I

The fourteen men—Billy counted the others—were in high spirits as they filed out of Oregon City. From his position in the rear of the column, he witnessed a good deal of backslapping and raucous shouts of "California gold...we're comin' to get ya!"

The single supply wagon was piled with their belongings, heavier equipment like shovels and pickaxes on the bottom, bedrolls and gunny sacks of food and extra clothing on top. Pack mules shouldered tents, cooking equipment, and an odd assortment of useless bric-a-brac foisted on the men by well-meaning wives, mothers and sweethearts.

A warm breeze cheered them onward. A passable road led south, connecting outlying homesteads. Gentle hills conjured easy traveling and the speed to outrun those gold seekers who delayed their departure until the next day or next week.

Their numbers seemed destined to swell. At the first tilled field the group came upon, a pair of brothers, apparently having gotten word of the intentions of the Oregon City crew, fell in with the others, one horse between them and not much gear to weigh them down.

At another farmhouse, the farthest from town, a man and a boy waited by the side of the road. Next to them was a cart drawn by a dark brown donkey.

The man waved at Tom Warner, but it was Billy who reined in and said pleasantly, "Howdy. You're out and about early this morning."

"Heard tell you folks were heading down to California."

"That we are, sir," said Billy.

"This here's Cephas. I've been watching after him ever since his daddy died. He's been yammering on and on about wanting to find some of that gold, so I packed up his stuff and as much flour, bacon and beans as I could spare. We've been coming out here every day hoping to find a group willing to take him on, but they all refuse."

Billy eyed the lad. "He *is* a might young."

"Don't let his size fool you. He's all of thirteen, going on fourteen. Just small for his age."

The boy wore an old, well-worn hat and trousers a bit long in the leg, but there was an intensity in his demeanor that reminded Billy of his own younger self.

"Well, Cephas, looks like today is your lucky day. Mount up."

"He'll work hard," added the man. "No worry about that."

"I'm sure he'll do just fine."

While Cephas turned toward the patient donkey, Tom rode up.

"See here...uh, what was your name?"

"Billy. Billy Brooster."

152

"Well, Billy Brooster, I noticed you joined up at the last minute and so's not aware of the rules. We stick together. Can't have any of the party lag behind."

Billy nodded toward Cephas. "I picked us up a new recruit. He's young, but I've been informed he's a good worker. Just ask..." To his dismay, the nameless man was already disappearing into a gray barn a hundred yards away. "Anyway, his name's Cephas."

Tom studied the boy's awkward movements as he wrestled with the donkey's trappings. "At least he seems to be well-provisioned if that cart is as loaded as it appears."

"That's my understanding."

Tom hailed the boy. "Step lively, young fellow. That gold's not going to wait forever."

At the sound of his name, Cephas's face lit up with a crooked smile. He swept the hat dramatically from his head and swung it in the air in a wildly-enthusiastic arc. As he did, his foot tangled in the loose-lying reins and he promptly fell to the ground.

Tom groaned. "Hurry him along, huh?"

The men grumbled about the new addition to their numbers, for Cephas's donkey could not keep up the pace, and the miles they traveled that first day fell short of expectations.

They camped on a wooded hillside where a clear stream gurgled conveniently nearby. Without a vote or any kind of acknowledged consensus, Tom was looked upon as leader, so when he called the halt, there was no mutiny. They merely acquiesced.

"We'll need firewood and water for the animals," said Tom.

No one questioned his authority to make such demands.

Cephas's benefactor had promised the boy would be a hard worker, and he immediately proved that prediction to be true. He ran around picking up deadwood. When he'd accumulated an armload, he dumped it in the space designated for the firepit. Then he led the horses and mules by twos to the stream and let them drink their fill. He ran his hands over their flanks and inspected hooves.

The real test of the boy's worth, however, came in the dead of night. Slowly, at first, the horses began to agitate. Their anxiety steadily increased until they chuffed noisily and tugged at their tethers. Only Cephas, who had unrolled his bedding closest to the picket line, heard them and recognized a looming danger. He leaped to his feet and, as if he had the night eyes of a feral cat, made a beeline to where Warner huddled under his blanket.

"Mr. Tom!"

Warner rolled over. "Cephas, can't you see I'm trying to sleep?"

"Something's excitin' the horses. Maybe it's injuns."

"Or a field mouse."

"No, no! Horses ain't afraid of mice."

"I was only being… Never mind."

Tom pushed himself upright, grabbed his rifle and roused a fellow from Indiana named O'Brien who he knew to be a good shot. They set off in the dark.

Meanwhile, Cephas returned to the horses and began to hum, here and there throwing in a few words that meant entirely nothing. He had a sweet voice, and it calmed the animals.

Soon the crack of a rifle echoed through the trees. Others woke at the sound and lighted lanterns from the embers of the dying cook fire.

"What's going on?" they demanded.

"Injuns," said Cephas.

"Relax everyone." Tom and O'Brien emerged from the woods. "Not Indians. A mountain cat."

"A dead one now," piped in O'Brien.

"Good call, Cephas," said Tom as he ruffled the boy's hair. "That's a good ear you have."

Grinning widely, Cephas cupped his hands behind both ears. "I got two of 'em."

Over the next several days, the gang of would-be prospectors traced the curves of the Willamette River through virgin forests and grasslands lush with the spring's new growth. They now numbered twenty, including a former trapper, disillusioned by the decline in demand for beaver skins, and a fellow named Youngblood who wove his life's story with more twists and turns than the river they followed.

It didn't take long, however, for the men to develop a camaraderie among them, swapping stories of westward journeys, women and anticipated wealth. They all came to accept Cephas in spite of some original skepticism and the lad's obvious shortcomings. They pretended not to notice his blank stares when they debated the virtues of panning versus hard rock digging, or his awkwardness at simple tasks like pitching a tent.

Billy reckoned this had to do with Cephas's gentle and open nature as well as his innate skill with the horses and mules. The boy knew how to extract a stone from beneath a horseshoe without injuring the hoof. He sang to the animals when something disturbed their calm, though Billy suspected the men also found the music soothing. Visions of gold and riches were one thing, but life on the trail, any trail, was difficult. The nights were lonely, and thoughts of home and family at the end of a hard day were a sad reminder of what they'd left behind.

One evening well into their southbound excursion, the trapper-turned-49er, stood by the campfire and raised by its neck what could only be a bottle of whiskey.

"There's cause for celebration tonight, boys," he announced as he took a long swig and passed the bottle to the fellow next to him. "We've crossed what the Indians call the Siskyous. We're in California!"

A cheer went up even as the level of liquid in the trapper's bottle went down until nothing remained.

California.

The very word reignited their enthusiasm. The next day they rode with straighter backs and spirits buoyed.

California. Their dreams were about to be realized. Instead of counting up the miles—"we've traveled fifty so far," then seventy, then a hundred—they counted down. Two hundred fifty to go became two twenty-five, two hundred.

Soon after crossing the border, Tom pulled Cephas aside and led him to the edge of a small stream.

"It's time for you to master a few basics before we get to our destination."

The youngster had taken a shine to Tom, had even begun calling him boss. For that, Tom assigned him various menial jobs whenever and wherever they camped. Now he handed Cephas a shallow, black pan with ridges circling the inside surface. It was only about fifteen inches wide but looked much bigger in the small boy's hands.

The size and weight of the pan did not dampen Cephas's glee at being once again singled out. Dutifully he followed Tom's instructions and waded into the water.

"Oh, oh. My shoes is wet."

"Don't worry about that. What's important is to learn the proper technique for scooping up gold."

"Lots of gold?"

156

"You bet. Only this is how you do it the right way. First collect some of that material from the bottom of the stream."

"Like this?"

Cephas plunged his hands into the cold creek and deposited two fistfuls of mud into the pan.

"Now slowly swirl the water and little by little spill some over the sides."

The first attempt turned out to be a disaster. The pan, weighted down with water, sand and stones, tipped and all was washed over the sides. They tried again and again until Cephas got the hang of it. When not a single flake of gold made an appearance, Cephas hung his head at the shame of his failure, but Tom slapped him on the shoulder.

"To be expected, my boy. We're not in gold country yet."

This perked the lad up, and he went to sleep that night, ignoring his sodden stockings and clutching the metal pan to his chest.

Although excitement among the men reached a fevered pitch the deeper into California they went, misfortune did not abandon them. When a wheel of Cephas's donkey cart bounced over a jagged rock, the axle broke and the cart fell onto its side. The frightened donkey bolted, further damaging the cart and strewing the poor boy's worldly goods over a twenty-foot stretch.

Tom inspected the mess. "There's no repairing it," he said. The wrecked cart had to be left behind.

Billy, along with several of the men, gathered up clothing and what foodstuffs could be salvaged and stowed it all in the one supply wagon. Billy consoled Cephas for his loss while Tom grabbed the boy by the shoulders.

"Look at it this way, my man. Your stuff is now

mixed in with everyone else's. We all share. That makes you a full-fledged member. Congratulations."

Cephas beamed. Billy retreated a few steps to where an old, floppy hat lay on the ground. He picked it up.

"This yours, Ceph?"

"Yup. It belonged to my daddy. It's my lucky hat."

Billy thought about the bitter irony, considering Cephas's father was dead.

II

After ten days together on the road, the disparate band of hopefuls had evolved into a collegial company of men bent on a single-minded mission.

During the day, a pause at a stream to water the horses, presented an opportunity to seek what they had come the distance to find. Some employed a nascent skill at panning. Scoop-swirl-spill. Others simply lifted rocks from the streambed, peering underneath for elusive flecks of gold. At night, after a hard ride, each spread a blanket or rolled a length of deadwood close to the campfire and swapped stories. Billy laughed and joked with the rest of them as they spent and respent gold they had yet to see.

One evening, talk turned to a more serious topic.

"We've come a long way, but we're close, ain't we, Tom?" asked one.

"By my calculations, and without any undue delay, another week should land us in the middle of paydirt."

"I was warned to beware of no-good claim jumpers," the man continued. "You no more than leave to take a piss and when you come back, someone's sittin' on the riverbank, claimin' they have a right to your spot."

A universal nodding of heads attested to everyone's agreement. One by one eyes shifted toward Tom. Since the beginning he'd been regarded as the de facto leader. Warner, however, had no ready answer. Instead, he picked up a pair of twigs off the ground and broke them in half. Piece by piece, he threw them into the flames.

Finally, he said, "Well, boys, if those claim jumpers can't find us, they won't be presenting a problem, will they? I suggest we vote on an alternate route, one off this beaten path we've been following."

The men all glanced around, but no one seemed to have a better idea. A chorus of cheers then went up. There was no need for a formal vote. All agreed.

The plan was executed at first light the next day. The trapper, whose name was Piotrowski, though everyone called him Pete, set out on his own through the woods, scouting for the best route. He was gone a long time, so long the men were getting edgy, but he returned and announced he'd had some luck.

"Up over that rise, the ground's been trampled by the passing of deer or elk. Not only will following it keep us out of sight, but, in my experience, it will lead us straight to water."

"What about the wagon?"

Pete resurrected an ax from the wagon and raised it over his head. "We'll clear the way."

The going was slower than anticipated. If Pete had taken the time to measure the width of the wagon against the backside of a deer, he'd have known they were in for a long haul. As it was, all axes were called into service. Enthusiasm for the plan waned, but the choice had been made. The group forged on.

That first night, the men were spent. After supper most cleared a level piece of ground and dropped exhausted into their bedrolls.

A crescent moon had risen over the surrounding treetops, washing them with a silvery glow. Billy squatted next to Tom, who sat on a rock by the slowly-dying campfire. His eyes were not on the orange and golden embers rather fixed on the darkened sky above.

"There's a legend," said Tom, speaking softly as if talking to himself. "A half moon…" He nodded overhead. "…is a sign of good luck and wealth."

"Is that what you're expecting when we get to where we're going?"

"No doubt in my mind. The stories I've heard…" His voice trailed off as if there were no sense repeating what everyone knew. California gold was easy pickings.

"Luck for some."

Tom went on as if he hadn't heard. "Oughtn't take no time at all to buy a right impressive *rancheria* down here in California. Won't take long before this place is a state," he added thoughtfully.

Billy tossed the dregs of his coffee into the fire, which exploded with a robust pop and hiss in the otherwise quiet night.

"Sounds like you're fixing to stay."

"Not out of the question. I hear the winters ain't as dreary as up north." Tom chuckled. "And then there's the gold."

Billy pursed his lips. "What if the gold runs out?"

"I'll just have to cross that mudhole when I come to it."

Holding his breath, Billy asked, "Oregon City's got no hold on you then?"

Tom rubbed his chin and adjusted his hat. He stared at Billy yet seemed lost in a personal reverie. Finally, he simply stood and walked away.

Billy exhaled.

No one else appeared to share the opinion that the venture into California was anything but the first leg of a two-way road back to Oregon—a brief interruption of their lives during which they would get rich fast and beat it home even faster.

Pete's reading of the deer path had its pros and cons. They did indeed find water, but the small, natural watering hole proved a dead end, a place where animals quenched their thirst then turned and retreated the same way they'd come.

The men tired early, for chopping saplings and clearing out underbrush all day was hard work. Eventually, though, the forest thinned and gave the workers a reprieve.

Daily speculation about the goldfields turned to more pressing problems.

Mules proved a tribulation of surprising magnitude. One managed to outsmart a poorly-tied knot and wandered off during the night. They found it at dawn with eight arrows in its neck, resurrecting fears of the dreaded Digger Indians.

Another mule came up lame and stumbled headfirst over a precipice, taking with it two hundred pounds of supplies.

Jack Stoker's younger brother, Nate, carelessly walked behind a third in his haste to answer nature's call and was kicked in the ribs for his trouble. Nate's injury was serious and marked the company's first real dispute. Jack insisted they lay by for a few days.

"Gold's waited a long time in these hills," argued Billy, siding with Stoker. "A few more days can't harm none."

Others wanted no delay. Recent evidence of Indians

had spread jitters throughout the camp, and for some the goldfields beckoned with hypnotic urgency. Tom fell in with this group.

"Men," he said, "are pouring into California by the thousands. We came for the gold. Can't let them others get a jump on us, cheat us out of what's ours."

He lobbied hard the case for pressing forward at any cost and, in the end, won out.

Writhing in pain, Nate was lifted onto his saddle and, to prevent him from falling, strapped into place...legs to the stirrups, wrists to the pommel.

For two days the men endured the consequences of their decision, for Nate never let up his dreadful moaning. On the morning of the third day, he obliged them by dying, and they buried his body beneath a pile of rock. The group gathered around the crude gravesite. Some shook their heads sadly. The dead man's brother mumbled what appeared to be a personal farewell.

When everyone remounted, Jack broke formation and turned northward with his share of the provisions. Hardly a day had passed, however, when he reappeared.

"Ain't no help for it," he said, shrugging. "Fact is, Nate is dead, and the gold's still in Californy. Can't do nothin' about the one, so might as well do something about the other."

The company now numbered nineteen.

The days blurred. One seemed the same as the next. In fact, several in the company complained about being lost and blamed Pete.

Billy watched Tom closely. He didn't like the man much. On the one hand, Tom was quick to laugh and maintained a staunch optimism which kept the others true to their stated objective. Billy dismissed the notion that Tom

162

had somehow been responsible for Nate's death, for he had not been alone in his vote which ultimately sealed the Stoker boy's fate.

Call it a gut feeling—and Billy frequently did—but he sensed certain incongruities in Tom…the surface man and the hidden part that bothered him so.

What, he thought, does Elsbeth see in him that I don't?

"I'll take care of him." His own words dogged him across the miles. The promise to Elsbeth burned at his insides, like a rock that had sucked the day's heat to its inner core, then gave it up slowly in the dark of night.

If I turn back now, he tried to convince himself, I can tell her he died. Lots do. Nate Stoker did.

But, no. No…

Brooster rocked back in his saddle and looked around. They had covered considerable ground while he had been lost in thought. It surprised him.

When Pete's unfortunate route didn't pan out, they had forged on, relying only on the sun's position to assure them they still headed south. They'd ascended a wide mountain pass, but the downhill side deteriorated into a narrow ridge, crowding the horsemen into a tight column of pairs. While before them spread a convoluted maze of ravines and gullies, all agreed they were in the foothills and surely within striking distance of the much-touted fields of gold.

"Ho!"

"Ho!"

"Ho!"

The call passed from rider to rider until it reached Cephas who repeated it, though he and Billy held the rearguard position, behind even the pack animals.

"What's up?" Billy asked, careful not to let young

163

Cephas see him smile at the needlessly repeated call. He raised himself in the stirrups and could see Tom, far ahead, dismount and stand, with eyes shaded, peering down a steep embankment.

"Blasted mules," said Billy, assuming another mishap. He untied a rope from under his bedroll and dropped to the ground.

"C'mon, Ceph. Looks like we're going to have to haul some horseflesh up the side of this mountain." Together they hurried up the line and arrived with the others just in time to see Tom skid down the slope.

"What…?"

"Cook tent broke loose."

"At least that'll come up easier than one of these long-eared beasts."

Billy freed up the coils of his rope and tied one end to the bole of a sturdy pine. The other end he tossed in the direction Tom had disappeared. Before anyone could decide what next to do, Tom came back into view at the bottom of the ravine, dusty and rubbing an elbow, but flushed with excitement.

"Come down," he shouted. "C'mon down. I think I've found it." No one needed an explanation of what *it* was.

Jack Stoker was the first to loop his arm around the rope and scuttle out of sight. He slid and stumbled through the scrub growth, dislodging a shower of dirt and vegetation in his eagerness to reach bottom. The others quickly followed suit.

Billy took his turn.

"Lookee here, boys."

Anticipation rippled through the company. All gathered at the brink of a swiftly-moving stream. Water whirled and danced over the rocks at their feet. Midstream a giant wedge of moss-covered granite divided the course in two. On the leeside of the boulder, where the water slowed temporarily, sand had settled out and formed a wide level bar. Tom splashed across the water and scooped up a mound of sediment. He let it drain slowly through the crevasses of his cupped hands. No one missed the significance of the tiny yellow specks that clung to his fingers.

"Guess we'll be staying right here," he said.

III

"Hey, Billy. You'll never get rich that way."

"I'll say. Them shovels fer diggin' not fer leanin' on."

Billy chuckled at the good-natured ribbing. His mind had wandered, along with his gaze, out of the deep, dark-walled cut in the mountain where the Oregon City company had staked claim to a gravel bar, out and over the rimrock, down into the lush green valley far below.

"Guess I ain't possessed of the fine eye for gold as you boys are," he called with a laugh. "'Spect I'll be here washing this rock long after you've all made your pile and headed home."

No one answered. Conversation never lasted long among the workers, and this exchange had used up the afternoon's quota. The others turned back to their work.

Billy spat on the palms of his hands and rubbed them together. He tested his grip against the wooden handle of the shovel. Blisters, festering at the base of his fingers, stung like fire, but he hoisted the shovel nevertheless. Load up the gravel. Toss it into the pan. Wade into the icy stream. Fill the pan with muddy water, swirl it around and slosh it over the side. Swirl and slosh. Swirl and slosh. Endlessly monotonous. It did, however, give him time to think. Mostly he considered there must be a better use for the California landscape than to pitch it one spadeful after another into a tin pan and rinse it all downstream.

Wearing out that topic, Billy turned to wondering if his feet would ever again be warm or dry. He had developed a persistent cough...but was not alone. When the sun set and the clank and bang of the workers' tools ended for the day, the dark hours resounded with the harsh, guttural noise of men expelling phlegm from their lungs. One miner would begin the serenade; soon others filled in the chorus, the piteous sound echoing among the crude shelters and on into the night.

The one thought which brightened Billy's day was of Elsbeth. The many weeks of absence had rewritten his memory, so Billy had largely forgotten the cutting edge of her rebuff at the moment of his departure and accepted as reality a more endearing image. Unfortunately, any thought of Elsbeth set him also to puzzling over Tom Warner.

Warner was only a glance away, directing Cephas in the art of hauling up sand from the creek bed. More than once did Billy ask himself why he had ever promised to look after this man. But he knew the answer. He had wanted to please Elsbeth, to see her smile and so he had made the promise. It was the single tie which bound them. A pact. A pledge. The force which set him on the road toward this frigid stream on a lonely mountainside.

IV

Spring settled into summer.

As luck would have it, Tom discovered their claimed section of stream, while out of sight from the schemes of claim jumpers, was poised within reach of Sacramento City. The city was a hub of industry. Once gold had been unearthed in the region and would-be miners began pouring in, what was once a sleepy settlement, grew by bounds.

Warner's gang plotted a scheme of their own. When supplies ran low, they pooled their money and took turns driving the wagon into town. A new face showing up at the general mercantile—its driver sworn to secrecy or scripted with a fantasy about his purpose—had so far successfully failed to expose the location of their camp or the size of their strike. Tom volunteered more often than the others but never twice in a row.

A certain frontier order permeated the camp. The men labored within shouting distance, but kept apart, far enough isolated to allow each the solitude to gauge his own progress against an established goal—measured in ounces. No one knew, or cared, the magic number for the fellow working ten yards away, but no sooner had the gold dust filled the desired bag or bags, than he would straighten his spine a final time, pack up his gear, and head for home. A few ranted at the stubbornness of the gold to find its way into their pans faster than it was spent on supplies and the occasional night in a Sacramento bar. They too eventually gave up.

One by one their numbers dwindled. Only fifteen worked the placer diggings on a hot afternoon in July of 1849.

"How long before Mr. Tom gets back?"

Cephas had moved in closer to Billy and asked the question while his eyes shifted up and down the narrow gorge and along the ridge above, alert for any sign of Tom Warner and the supply wagon. Billy paused, his shovel wavering knee high, weighted with rock and heavy sand.

"Soon, Ceph. I'm sure it'll be soon." He dropped his load and patted the boy on the back.

"Wish he'd a-taken me along."

"We've talked about this before." Billy pulled the boy in front of him and looked him squarely in the face. "It has nothing to do with you, Cephas. We mustn't advertise the fact we're pulling gold out of this streambed. That would be a bad thing. Do you understand? We'd be swamped with diggers. The gold would play out faster than you could untie that knot in your shirt."

Cephas looked down at the sleeves of his red flannel shirt. They had been carelessly rolled and tied, beltlike, around his waist. The body of the shirt flapped over his backside. Cephas squinted down at it and bit at his lip.

"He coulda brung *me*," he protested. "I'm his friend."

Words formed on Billy's tongue, but he swallowed them and offered a patient smile instead.

"Mr. Tom's good to me," the boy continued. "Lets me work with his pan all day long."

"I know, Cephas," said Billy. He picked a piece of pyrite off the ground and considered the advantage that had been taken of this simple-minded boy. With barely concealed anger he flung the rock as far as he could. "I know."

"That danged wagon has a bad split wheel too. Hope he don't have no trouble."

"Tom is lucky to have someone like you to worry about him."

168

"Mules're jumpy too."

A moment or two passed while Billy sought to catch up to the abrupt turn in their conversation.

"Uh," he said finally, an edge to his voice. "Mule trouble again?"

He glanced up toward their campsite where the animals stood tethered to a heavy line strung between two trees. Usually content to nibble grass in the shade, they now jostled and bumped one another and tugged wildly at their rope halters. Billy dropped the shovel and picked up his rifle.

"Maybe a bear or mountain cat in the neighborhood," he said. "I'll go topside and check."

Billy took one step. Suddenly his legs wobbled. Before his eyes flashed the memory of a long-ago night in Independence and a half-drained bottle of bald-faced whiskey. His legs had refused to obey then. Now he was stone cold sober, but the feeling was the same. On step number two he fell.

"It's the ground, Cephas," he yelled. "The ground's moving!"

He struggled to his feet, only to tumble again. Cephas had fallen too though the boy managed to crawl within arm's length of Billy.

"Gosh, Mr. Billy. This here California's no better 'n a dog shakin' loose a bunch o' ol' fleas."

"And we're the fleas."

While the two of them gawked in disbelief, towering pines swayed violently against an unseen force, then released a decades-old grasp on the ground and, with roots waving nonsensically in the air, tumbled from the uplands. A wall of earth broke free and heaved in their direction. Rocks caromed down the steep slopes, cracking like gunshot as they ricocheted off each other in a mad race to the bottom. The avalanche spared neither horses nor humans. Terrified screams split the air, ungodly loud amid the racket of sliding turf and the tumble of trees.

"Run!" screamed Billy.

He picked himself up and sprinted toward the giant midstream boulder. He was almost there before he realized young Cephas hadn't budged.

"Cephas!"

Billy flew back across the creek and locked his hand on Cephas's arm, half dragging the lad to his feet, and pushed him roughly toward the shelter of the boulder. Billy once again neared the safety of the granite shield, but before he reached its protection, a rock the size of a tar bucket slammed him from behind and propelled him the rest of the way. He landed in the stream, conscious of a searing pain and the steady plunk-plunk of stones cascading into the water all around.

Beside him Cephas whimpered like a frightened child.

As quickly as it had begun, the quaking ceased. For a few brief seconds, no sound disturbed the dust-congested air. Then chaos.

Distant shouting reached Billy's ears. Boot heels skidded on loose stone. Rifle shots quelled the cries of anguished animals, creating a void in the concert of hellish suffering into which poured the wails of dying men.

Cold water slapped at Billy's face. He coughed it away, but the pain in his back knifed deeper. He winced but struggled to his feet.

Cephas still sat in the water. He rocked slowly from side to side and stared with blank, expressionless eyes. He appeared lost, though for the moment safe.

The earth shivered again and Billy dropped to his knees. The aftershock had little strength, barely dislodged a stone, but the fear...the fear was still very much alive.

"Brooster!" It was Jack Stoker calling. "What shape are you in?" His voice cracked. "George is dead. Can't even find the Landner brothers or Cal Swain and his helpers and they wasn't workin' but a spittin' distance away."

"I'll do for now," answered Billy. "Cephas is down by the water. He's all right too."

Both glanced quickly around, taking a grim, mental census. One by one Jack's stubby fingers shot skyward. "That leaves six killed or missing. Not a horse or mule in sight either, lessen' you count the dead ones."

"What about Warner?" Billy asked, his voice lowered and his eyes shifting nervously toward Cephas.

"Dunno. He was due back with the supplies. For all we know he's dead and buried right under our feet."

"I don't see any sign of the wagon."

"You're right. He's probably still underway. Danged lucky timing if you ask me. Everything up top the ridge has sheared away. He coulda landed himself right in the middle of all this."

The stunned survivors gathered in a tight knot to gape at the wreckage of their camp. Gnarled roots and stumps jutted haphazardly from the mounds of earth alongside the limbs of half-buried animals, and the bloodied remains of George Gluck.

No one issued a command, but as one the men set about the gruesome task of locating and burying their friends. They found two besides George. It seemed useless to dig among the rubble for the missing three only to bury them again, so they merely fashioned crosses out of broken tree limbs and the busted handles of shovel or pick and erected six markers in a neat row.

One more? Billy wondered.

The job was difficult, for none had come through the experience unscathed. Someone retrieved Cephas from the stream and settled him on a level piece of ground where the boy continued his rhythmic sway, eyes wide and fixed though on nothing in particular.

When the work was done, they huddled near the little graveyard.

Stoker cleared his throat. "The elephant," he said.

Heads bobbed in solemn agreement.

"Elephant?" asked Billy, hunching against the pain that stabbed his side with each labored breath. "You mean the one sitting on my chest right now?"

"No. Being scared outta yer wits. Seeing the elephant. You know?"

At first Billy wrinkled his brow. He did *not* know. Then he recalled the overlanders whispering about the great ordeals of the crossing. The tests of their fortitude. Knowledge through experience. The elephant.

"Yes, the elephant."

Soon the men drifted apart, each to rummage through what had once been their camp, collecting anything usable or edible. Billy found a length of rope and a dented coffeepot. He clawed at the ground around a piece of checkered cloth and unearthed, dirty but whole, someone's shirt with scarlet patches stitched neatly to the sleeves. He wrapped his meager hoard into a ragged square of material cut from one of the tents. After months of backbreaking work, it was a dismal reality to come away with so little.

The work progressed slowly, for each man also had choices to mull, decisions to make. Most opted to salvage what they could and begin the long trek to Oregon and home. Two announced plans to venture farther south, perhaps clear to the dry diggings on the Tuolumne.

172

"What about you, Brooster? North or south?"

Sharp edges of rock bit through the thin, worn soles of Billy's boots. Stoker's words still rang in his ears: "For all we know he's buried right under our feet."

Despite his injury, a faint smile formed on Billy's lips. "North," he said.

V

The sky lightened from pitch to opaque.

Billy's skin flushed with a warmth that had nothing to do with the still-hidden sun. Each breath he drew emerged as a ragged wheeze, a terrible reminder of his injury. It had been a mistake to wait. Billy knew that now. Too late. He had traded away valuable hours by resting the night, hoping to recoup his strength and quell his fever. There had been no relief, rather an intensifying of his injury, and the security of traveling with others had been lost.

"C'mon, boy." He reached out and nudged Cephas awake. "Time to shove on. It's just the two of us now."

Cephas sat up. "Three with Mr. Tom."

Billy pulled himself to his knees. One advantage of their delay had been a marked improvement in his companion's state of mind. The boy had gradually shaken off his stupor, enough to help scour the site a final time before darkness settled in. Their store of supplies grew by one old blanket, a battered hat, a gold watch and fob knotted into a bandana, and Billy's rifle which Cephas had fished from the creek. The rifle wouldn't be of much use until it dried out, but Billy was glad to have it. For now, it served as a crutch, and with it as leverage he managed to rise to his feet.

"What about Mr. Tom?" Cephas chewed on his lower lip.

"What about him?"

"We've got to go look for him."

"Reckon I have busted ribs or worse. We'll be slow moving. Tom can catch up."

"No!" A look of panic flashed across Cephas's face.

"We're going to have to worry about ourselves for a while," said Billy. "Tom can take care of himself."

"What if he's hurt?"

"I'm hurt!"

"I don't want to leave Mr. Tom." Cephas hung his head. The backs of his hands worked feverishly at the corners of his eyes. "What if he needs me?" he mumbled.

"I...never mind. We're heading north, back to Oregon City, and that's that."

The climb to the ridge top was long and arduous. Familiar pathways and footholds had been ironed smooth by the slide. Every step or two Billy doubled over with a spasm of pain. He cursed his misfortune. He cursed the elements. They rested often.

To make matters worse, a morning fog obscured what might be a reasonable way to go and forced the pair to retreat and try a different course. When the sun finally appeared and reduced the fog to an intermittent, hazy cloud, both Cephas and Billy turned their faces upward. At first grateful for the light which eased the search for the best possible path out of the ravine, they soon realized this same sun proved a formidable enemy and baked them with unrelenting ferocity. The climb ate up precious hours. At the end of it, Billy stood looking back down into the devastated valley. He didn't say anything. Not only was he exhausted, feverish and in unremitting pain, but lightheaded at the realization of how narrow their escape had been.

After a moment the scene around him came into focus. This area was surprisingly untouched by the earthquake and landslide. Lavender-colored flowers softened the craggy profile of the land. A light breeze stirred the treetops, and from somewhere he could hear a bird calling to its mate. It was almost pleasant.

During their ordeal, a strained silence had fallen between him and Cephas. It wasn't hard to understand why. They disagreed on what to do about Tom: make the effort to determine his whereabouts—and fate—or give him up for lost and head for home. Now he twisted around to look at the boy who sulked a few yards away. The movement set off a hacking cough. He bent at the waist and clutched his chest. Had it not been for this, he might have missed it altogether. In the dirt. At his feet. A narrow groove packed more firmly than the ground around it. Billy studied the unmistakable markings. A wagon had pulled up, stopped, then backed over its own tracks, retracing its path in the direction of the afternoon sun.

Billy kicked at the dirt. A sound rumbled around in his throat, not words, but a low, angry growl. He swiped again with his boot, this time digging away at the marks of a wagon wheel with a badly split rim.

"Lousy son of a…" The sound of his own voice startled him, and he looked up quickly to make sure Cephas had not heard. He knew now for sure why he did not like Tom Warner and just as surely he knew what he had to do.

He stared northward, aware of an ache that tore at his insides, a pain unrelated to his injuries. Then his gaze shifted slowly to the west. For the second time in less than a year, the faint lines of a wagon trail beckoned, this time leading toward Sacramento City.

175

Below in the ravine there was a movement...or had he only imagined it? Had the sun's rays given the semblance of life to a monolith of granite, or had he really seen it? A great hulking shape, gray and exotic. Had he encountered *his* elephant?

He edged closer to Cephas and draped an arm over the boy's shoulder for support.

"I think," said Billy, "we'll be making a little detour."

CHAPTER 9

Promises To Keep

I

"Get away!"

Elsbeth swung her leg, kicking dirt and stones at her four-legged tormentors. A dreadful place this King Street.

She flushed with panic at the thought Charlie might be here. Right and left, shacks charaded as inns and boarding houses. A few unsavory-looking characters idled about. Castoff goods, dead animals, garbage, waste lay about in total disorder and varying degrees of decay. Elsbeth closed her eyes and willed herself forward, concern for the boy alone spurring her on.

No sooner had she entered the street than two mangy dogs appeared and stalked her every step. Occasionally one or the other sprinted near and nipped at her skirts.

"Let me alone!" She kicked again.

No kindly gentleman was on the street to come to her rescue. No one appeared and claimed ownership of the mongrels. They alone appeared to be the guardians of King Street. Its snarling defenders. She feared she had crossed an imaginary line and trespassed the very gates of hell.

Slowly Elsbeth advanced, wary of the collection of hovels crowding in on all sides. Tar-papered siding and flimsy tin roofs flapped in a sudden gust of air as if vying for her attention or issuing a warning.

Nearby was a building larger than most. From the shadows of its doorway stepped a bearded man, his rolled-up sleeves exposing sunburned arms. He leaned against the frame and watched her approach.

"Watcha lookin' for, lady?"

"A small boy."

"Tain't none 'round here."

"Mind if I look?"

"Ain't gonna like what you see."

Elsbeth stiffened. Months on the Emigrants' Road had prepared her for almost anything. Hadn't the preceding year served her up a lifetime of hardship? She hardly felt threatened by a roadside flophouse despite its rickety appearance.

"I'll be the judge of that, thank you."

She stooped at the low-hung door and entered what had been heralded on a crudely-lettered sign as Queen Victoria's Hotel. Her stomach lurched. The queen would have ordered executions had she known what was being touted in her name.

Cots crammed the center of the narrow, airless room. Along the walls heaps of moldy straw identified additional, lower-class accommodations. Mice scurried across her path. Every available inch of space writhed with human tragedy. Some thrashed about, snoring. Others rocked back and forth, blindly staring at motes of dust which choked the air. Despair had drained their faces of expression. Many were curled into tight balls, knees drawn to chests, moaning loudly and hugging themselves against the convulsions which wracked their bodies. Elsbeth's hand flew to her mouth. The smell of men caught up in the business of dying overwhelmed her and she stumbled backward, out the door.

"Warned ya," said the proprietor. His face collapsed inward around a toothless grin.

She pitched him a disgusted look then hurried away from his house of horrors, almost welcoming the company of the four-legged devils who once again worried her hemline. The next establishment proved no different. Nor the next. Often the unfortunate overspilled the four walls and lay huddled in the narrow strip of shade that framed the building, searching for relief from the stifling interior.

Just ahead the buildings ended, and the street faded into the overgrown landscape beyond. Elsbeth paused at the last shabby cabin. Her shoulders sagged as much from relief as exhaustion.

"Thank God you're not in this awful place. But, Charlie, where *are* you?"

She began to retrace her steps, ignoring the persistent dogs but now aware of an unexpected anger which rose in her throat.

"I blame you for this, Tom," she muttered. "If you hadn't gotten it into your head to chase after gold, I wouldn't have had to come looking. Now Charlie is lost. I'm here in Satan's parlor picking my way among these living corpses. My locket is dangling from the dress of some painted Jezebel."

Even admitting she was partly to blame didn't mitigate her anger toward him. Her fingers curled into fists, and she sucked in her breath only to be sharply reminded of the stench all around. It brought her back to the present. She quickened her pace. In her haste to be away, she almost stumbled over a pair of legs protruding from beside an adobe wall. The man might have been dead so still he lay. He was half hidden in the shadows, and a wide-brimmed hat obscured his face, yet his checkered shirt scratched at her memory until an image of Tom rolling belongings into a blanket came into focus.

"It couldn't be."

She looked again. As she watched, the man threw an arm over his head and a cloud of buzzing flies lifted away. The elbow of the shirt flashed red, a pattern of broadcloth so familiar Elsbeth could feel the needle pricking her finger as she sewed the patch over the frayed fabric of the shirt.

"Tom?" she whispered.

For the briefest moment she hesitated, listening to the voice of a still-smoldering anger telling her to turn and flee.

"Tom," she repeated, this time louder.

The unfortunate man had once again lapsed into deathlike stillness. Elsbeth rushed to his side and fell to her knees, her anger now fully in check.

"Tom, is it really you? Wake up. It's me, Elsbeth. Charlie's lost. We have to find our little one."

No answer.

"Tom!" She pulled at his arm. Sickness and want had taken their toll. The man's skin was sallow, his lips cracked, hair matted.

"Dear Lord!" she gasped, realizing at once her error.

The shirt was Tom's, but the man was Billy Brooster.

Without thinking, she glanced over her shoulder, half expecting to see Clayton Pierce. Only the dogs stared back. She picked up a rock and hurled it, forcing them into watchful retreat.

"Billy?" Her voice became gentle. "Billy, what's become of you?" Hesitantly she reached out to wipe away the beads of perspiration dotting his forehead. Her fingers drew to within inches of his brow before she jerked them back.

"Billy," she said instead, "do you know there's someone looking for you? A loathsome creature. A soldier. He's here in town." Once again she looked around. "You can't stay here."

To herself she asked a final question, "What are you doing wearing this shirt?"

Elsbeth gathered up her skirts.

"Listen to me, Billy." Though not sure he could hear, she explained, "I'm going to get the wagon. It's left on *K* Street—not far from the river. I'll be back, though it might be a spell."

She made a move to rise, but Billy moved too. Quickly. He bolted to a sitting position and, with surprising strength, clamped a hand tightly about her wrist.

"Oh, dear God!" Startled, she lost her balance. One arm flailed wildly in an effort to prevent herself from toppling while the other desperately tried to wriggle free of Billy's grasp. She lost on both counts and, with a thump, landed in the dirt only as far away as Brooster's reach would allow.

"Let go." Her voice pitched higher. "Let go of me."

Almost immediately she realized there was nothing to fear. His eyes were open, but Billy's gaze drifted unseeing over her shoulder. Slowly she laid her free hand on his crushing fingers and one by one peeled them away. His only response was a cough accompanied by a wince of pain.

"I'll be back," she whispered. "I really will."

Elsbeth picked herself up and ran, leaving Billy sitting alone, staring blankly, as if contemplating a distant, uncertain future. She turned back once to look at him. He hadn't moved an inch.

II

"Where are they? Oh, dear God in heaven, where are they gone?"

Elsbeth was sure this was *K* Street, just as surely as she knew that's where she left her team and wagon. Pierce, she thought sourly, that evil man has found them and, out of pure spite, absconded with all I possess.

She swiveled on her heels to retrace the length of the street though she'd already done that once before. Squinting into the late afternoon sun, she embarked on a second pass.

Long, blue-black shadows propped up three of Sacramento's many saloons, along with a dentist's office and a purveyor of scarred and dented articles useful only if one were heading to the rivers and streams on the outskirts of town. More buildings, remarkable only by the size or placement of a window or door, crowded among them. Foot and wheeled activity had picked up considerably since her arrival hours before. Horses snuffled. Loose stone under their hooves scrunched. Drivers cursed. She thought to inquire of one or the other of them, but their rough appearance put her off.

Suddenly a sound of a different sort alerted her to a blessed discovery. The snort of an ox, loud and guttural, pointed her in the direction of her team. They were there all along, hidden by the depth of shadow and the traffic obscuring her line of sight.

The urge to rush forward was checked when she thought of Pierce. Was he there, lying in wait? Quietly she approached, lifting her skirt by inches so it did not rustle in the scruffy grass. She put an ear to the canvas cover. Nothing. Not a voice, not a snore, not a hint of movement.

Emboldened, she circled to the back of the wagon and peered inside. All was as she'd left it.

"Thanks be to God," she whispered.

Quickly she climbed aboard, released the brake, and steered the team toward King Street. There she found Billy stretched full on his back. The shade had moved with the advance of the afternoon, so the sun beat on him without relent. Sweat soaked his shirt—Tom's shirt she corrected herself. The barest of twitches assured her Billy was still alive.

"Billy." She put a hand on his shoulder and gave it a gentle shake. "It's me, Elsbeth. I told you I would come back. We have to get you to the wagon. It's only a couple steps away, but you are going to have to help me. I can't lift you by myself."

Although his eyes flickered open, he did not seem to recognize her. Elsbeth swallowed a bit of disappointment at that, then convinced herself it was probably just as well. She maneuvered his arm so he could raise himself to an elbow. With her fingers wrapped tightly around his belt, she tugged him to his feet. Together they wobbled the few necessary steps. Once she had him leaning against the wagon, she unlatched and dropped the rear gate. To her amazement and immense relief, he managed to crawl inside without assistance. There he crumpled to the floor. She did not consider whether his position afforded any comfort. It was imperative they leave.

She'd grappled with the decision to tend to Billy, for it meant neglecting Charlie. The little boy had never been far from her mind, and she now resumed her search with a heightened passion.

The road leading out of town, usually well-traveled given the burgeoning population of Sacramento, was strangely deserted. Perhaps it was the time of day, for evening

183

was fast approaching and a layer of gathering clouds hurried along the advent of darkness.

Elsbeth devised a simple plan. If Charlie had only wandered away and become lost, there was hope he would recognize a familiar landmark and find his way back to where they had camped before. Not for one moment did she believe Clayton Pierce had told her the truth. With all her heart, she believed Charlie was still in the hills up yonder, waiting for her to return. She must hurry, for a little boy, no matter how tough he may seem at times, would not last long on his own.

She had wanted to inquire of anyone she encountered along the way and was sorely disappointed there was no one to ask.

After some time she spied the figure of a man on the road ahead. He was walking slowly, so she climbed off the wagon seat in order to meet him head on. He was a gnarled old man, weathered by sun and hard work, a prospector, most likely. Elsbeth took a deep breath.

"Good evening, sir. Have you—"

He interrupted with his own question. "You the lady that cooks?"

"What? No! I'm—"

"Do you...?" He wriggled two wiry eyebrows in a suggestive manner. "You know, have a hankerin'...?"

"Absolutely not!"

"Then what are you doing out here?"

"I'm looking for a lost child."

"Don't know nothin' about that." He glanced over her shoulder, seemingly eager to be on his way, but Elsbeth sighed so despondently he paused and waved a hand toward a distant ridge. "Came across a tent village back a ways. The women there weren't hankerin' either, and the husbands didn't much cotton to me inquirin' about it. Maybe they can

184

help."

"Women, you say?"

"Yeah. Sprouts too, running around and yelping like wild dogs."

"Was there a little one, about two years old, with brown hair?"

"Can't say as I much noticed. I was in a hurry, you see."

He edged past her and scuttled off before she could thank him. The information was sparse, but it was something. For a long, undecided moment she weighed her options: return to the patch of ground she'd claimed for her kitchen or seek the settlers' camp. Neither one assured success, but women and children...

Elsbeth grabbed the wagon traces and guided the oxen in the direction the man had indicated.

III

"Damnation!"

The torch, sparsely pitched with tar, sputtered twice and died. "Hell and damnation!"

Elsbeth caught up her breath. Never before had she uttered such words. She was immediately contrite, and a flush of embarrassment crept along her cheeks despite there being no one within miles to hear. The acrid smell of smoldering tar burned her nostrils as she debated what next to do.

"I must move on. I must."

A smudge of yellow-orange stained the horizon, confirming the old man had steered her right. It was a beacon, a goal to pursue.

"That must be the camp," she said to herself. "It has to be. Doesn't look *too* far. Not impossible."

She slid her hand between the heavy rope halter and warm cheek of her lead animal and with a tug and soft clucking of her tongue urged the beast along. Slowly. Cautiously. One toe after another darted out from beneath the ragged hem of her dress and probed the ground for dips or ruts, rocks or vines which the darkness rendered impossible to see.

In this manner, Elsbeth advanced for the next quarter hour.

The glow in the sky promised campfires, other folks—women—perhaps even the end of her search. She thought of the children, a lad perhaps, someone whom Charlie encountered by a twist of fate, a newfound playfriend who enticed him to explore too far. Yes, that's it exactly. She thought how good it would be to hear his squeal of delight when the two lost souls were reunited. It brought a smile to her lips and, for the briefest of moments, diverted her attention.

Without warning, the heel of her foot rolled on a stone. Unbalanced, she dropped the useless torch and staggered sideways, finally pitching into a narrow, muddy ditch. Soft earth oozed between her fingers and plastered the side of her face. She grimaced at the mess, but her expression quickly turned to one of horror as she remembered the animals.

"Oh, no! The team." Her voice tightened with self-reproach. "Stupid, foolish me to risk the animals by fumbling around in the dark." Above her she could hear the chuff-puff of the oxen's breath. Clawing toward the sound, she threw her arms around their necks, a silent prayer spilling from her soul.

"Dearest Father, I pray Thee, do not punish these poor beasts for my careless haste."

Gently, she ran a hand along their limbs, sending heavenward a simple thanksgiving with each passing inspection. Hardly had the eighth "Praise Lord" passed her lips when a feeble groan emerged from the wagon.

Her shoulders slumped. Once free of Sacramento City, pursuit of her lost boy had pushed from her mind any thought save that of finding him. She had forgotten about Billy. And now the night had conspired against her, first cutting short her search, and reminding her of this added responsibility. She sighed. "What am I to do with you, Billy Brooster?"

With outstretched arms, Elsbeth slowly fingered her way from ox rump to brake handle to wheel hub. She needed neither lantern nor taper. Darkness was complete but so was her familiarity with every knot and nail and groove that shaped her "home." Still a sense of unease settled over her, and she stopped to listen.

A thousand crickets chirped midnight greetings. From somewhere in the distance the plaintive cry of a nocturnal creature rose into the night. Elsbeth shuddered. A whisper of a breeze played with her hair. It was warm and smelled of Sweet Clover but would not explain away the gooseflesh which puckered her arms. She considered the possible dangers—both of man and beast. Who knew what lurked within arm's reach, for the territory remained to her a foreign land, mysterious, unpredictable, and, despite its beauty, forbidding.

She tried to shrug free of the invisible, strangling anxiety that threatened her usual calm. Hurry, she thought. Past the rear wheel. The tailgate. The step-up. Inside. I must get inside.

One foot gained the wooden step, but in the darkness, in the muggy, midsummer California night, Elsbeth's heart froze. An unknown someone nudged against her shoulder blades the hard, cold steel of a rifle barrel.

Afraid to turn around, she reached forward, hoping to seize upon a weapon of sorts but felt only a single hinge, rusty yet firmly riveted into place. No iron skillet. No tool. Not even a loose bolt to pull from its socket.

"Ma'am." A voice, a human voice so close it gagged her.

"Yes?" she answered.

"Whadaya go and steal Mr. Billy for?"

She strained to hear. The voice sounded boyish, but she couldn't be sure.

"Steal?"

"He's in that there wagon, ain't he?"

"*Mr.* Billy?"

"I've got the rifle."

Elsbeth was painfully aware of that, but she was also becoming quite certain its owner was young and perhaps as frightened as she.

"I'm going to turn around now." She did. One tiny step after another. She allowed not the barest swish of her skirts to add to the nervous circumstances of their encounter. Face to face revealed little more than before. The shape of the intruder showed only an inky outline against an even murkier backdrop of night air and nothingness.

"This here's his rifle. I have to give it to him."

"Him?"

"Mr. Billy."

"Do you mean Billy Brooster?"

"My friend. It's his gun. I only borrowed it for a minute." Suddenly Elsbeth found the rifle thrust into her hands. "I was afraid back there. There was some real nasty dogs. And I wanted to look for Mr. Tom while Billy was asleep. But it's not my gun."

The boy's explanation raised more questions than it answered. In the silence that followed, Elsbeth made a decision.

"Would you like to give it to Billy yourself?"

She reached out blindly, hoping her reassuring pat would connect with his shoulder. It proved to be lower and bonier than she anticipated.

"Yes 'am," came the answer.

"Then you shall." She handed him back the rifle.

IV

The pale pink of dawn trickled through a dog-eared rip in the wagon's cover and worked its way under Elsbeth's eyelids. They fluttered open. Immediately she was aware of two things. Her back ached from hours spent leaning against the rigid side walls, and her shoulder muscles cramped under the weight of the youngster's sleep-heavy head.

With the return of Billy's rifle, a bond of trust had been forged and Cephas's tongue loosened. She knew the boy's name now. She knew his dull-witted candor. She knew of his alliance with Billy, his adoration of Tom, and she knew the remarkable tale of their ill-fated bonanza. Billy's injury worsened during their long trek into the city until fever and delirium made advance impossible and Cephas's lack of money made King Street their final option. After looking up and down Sacramento streets for Tom and not finding him, he'd retraced his steps and arrived in time to see Billy crawl into the back end of an unfamiliar wagon. He'd followed it at a safe distance, unsure what to do until his conscience got the best of him. He simply could not rest until he'd returned what was not rightfully his.

She and the boy talked long into the night while Billy thrashed about, wracked with fever. Elsbeth had lit a single candle and in the dim halo of its light prepared a medicinal brew, crushing Speedwell and chamomile leaves into a tin of tepid water.

"My mama's cure-all," she explained as she stirred.

While the mixture steeped, she handed Cephas a garment with instructions to tear off a few strips along the bottom. The boy's ears turned a bright red in embarrassment.

"Miz Elsbeth! These here are ladies' underthings."

"It's all I've got. Do as I say, Cephas. I think Billy might have a broken rib or two and I need to somehow hold it in place."

Once she applied a poultice and secured the wrap, she tested the herbal concoction and, as best she could, spooned it between Billy's lips while Cephas related Tom's fortuitous escape from the earthquake.

Elsbeth listened without interruption until Cephas said, "Mr. Tom always packed all his stuff into the supply cart 'fore he'd take off for town. That way he was never without his belongings."

Elsbeth glanced at the shirt with the red-patch sleeves which now adorned Billy Brooster. "All?" she asked.

"Yes 'am." Cephas nodded vigorously, then stopped to reconsider before adding, "Least the important stuff."

The look of pleasure from knowing Tom had almost certainly survived without injury disappeared from Elsbeth's face. The shirt which she had painstakingly mended had been left behind, cast off, flung away. Did her hard work mean so little to him? Worn out or not, she thought it should have been a cherished reminder of home.

From out of nowhere came an image from her past. A Sunday morning. After services Elsbeth and her brothers had ventured away from church where her father chatted with parishioners, past the garden gate, to a bare, windswept berm overlooking the river. There, in a crevice in the sandstone, a gray-green snake engaged in what appeared an exotic dance. It tangled and untangled its long, slender body before slithering away. In its wake, like a faded memory, lay a translucent, ghostly replica of itself.

The boys found a stick, impaled a coil of the sloughed-off skin, and dropped it at Elsbeth's feet. She remembered being both fascinated and repulsed by what she saw. What had once been a vital, living part of the snake's being was dead. No longer needed or wanted, the snake had merely shrugged it off and left it behind to crumble into powder, nothing more than the dust on which it lay. Was a shirt no different?

Cephas's voice entered her reminiscence and brought her back to the moment. He had not stopped talking while she daydreamed, and Elsbeth realized she had missed something about a broken wheel and a cantankerous mule. To cover her lapse of attention, she bent to the task of forcing more of her curative into Billy's mouth.

Cephas volunteered more. Tom had also carried a large pouch of gold dust filled from the pokes of a dozen others as shares toward the purchase of flour, beans and coffee, provisions to last them into September.

"That Mr. Tom shore was lucky," chuckled Cephas.

"Very lucky indeed." A thin layer of ice coated her words. "Tell me more."

The eager storyteller hardly needed encouragement.

191

He inched closer, lowered his voice.

"He'd always say, 'Ceph, I'm going back up North to a girl named Elsbeth.'" He tapped his finger on her sleeve. "That's you."

At once her features softened. Her heart swelled first with guilt then with tenderness for the man she had followed into California, and she forgave Tom yet another time.

"Yes, that's me," she said.

"Now he don't have no need to go back to Oregon. He's found you."

"Well, not quite."

"Sure thing, ma'am." Cephas poked at the prone figure on the floor. "He just don't know it yet."

"Billy? I thought you were talking about Tom?"

"Mr. Tom knows you too? Ain't that a corker."

Elsbeth bit her lower lip, quelling a flood of emotion. She refused to answer. Instead, she picked up a towel and dipped the corner into a bowl of warm barrel water and gently mopped at Billy's fevered brow.

Soon the candle burned to a stub, and the honey-sweet fragrance of beeswax filled the wagon. Cephas's head drooped and his breathing evened out. Nothing could lull Elsbeth into much-needed sleep. Desperate thoughts tormented her. If she occasionally dozed, it was only to wake with a start, new scenes of horror planted in her brain. The advent of morning seized her with the grim reality of the third day of Charlie's disappearance.

A dove cooed, its mournful plea reflecting her own mood. Elsbeth rubbed her eyes and shrugged Cephas's head from her shoulder. His mouth fell open. Animal-like snorts erupted. Other than that, he slept as peacefully as a newborn. Billy, too, seemed finally at ease. Neither stirred when she crawled over them to the driver's seat, threw off the brake, and took up the reins.

The oxen protested, having remained yoked together the entire night, but she refused the least delay and had herself not eaten, nor would she until Charlie was found. This she swore and snapped the whip.

The camp lights of the night before had wrought a cruel deception. The settlement was *not* close. Worse still, it seemed to move away as slowly and as steadily as she lumbered toward it. Elsbeth envied the birds the miracle of flight, for the squawking flock of crows, now directly overhead, were, within minutes, tiny black dots against the distant clouds. To ease the frustration of her own interminable pace, Elsbeth concocted a deception of her own. She concentrated on a narrow strip of grass immediately beyond the bobbing heads of her team and counted to fifty before looking up, hoping to be surprised at her progress. When there seemed to be none, she counted anew.

Gradually the faraway blur separated, and the bits of color took on shape. Some became women bending over washtubs filled with laundry. Others grew legs, trousers thrown over bushes to dry. These Elsbeth disregarded, focusing instead on the figures that darted here and there…the children. One chased a hoop. Others played with a dog. Occasionally the melody of their high-pitched laughter carried to her on the wind. Now she could not tear her eyes away from the camp. She sought the dark-haired youngsters among the towheads and carrot-tops. She thought she saw… No. Could that be…? No again.

Elsbeth sighed and leaned even farther forward, calling upon all her senses to help identify Charlie among the merrymakers of the camp.

"My dear little soldier," she said, not realizing she had spoken aloud, "are you here?"

Suddenly a voice close at hand replied, "Don't see no soldiers anywhere, ma'am."

While Elsbeth was intent on her single-minded mission, Cephas had awakened, joined her, and, though not comprehending what the object of his search was, mirrored her intensity in scouting the activity ahead.

"Mercy, Cephas," Elsbeth exclaimed, fumbling to retain a firm grip on the reins. "You startled me near to death."

"Pardon, ma'am." He hung his head until she reached over and patted his hand.

"It's not your fault. I didn't hear you climb out. I was looking so hard for Charlie."

"Who's Charlie?"

"Why Charlie's my little boy. He's lost and I'm so dreadfully worried about him. I searched Sacramento City, but he wasn't there."

"You found Mr. Billy."

"Yes, that I did. Now I think... I hope... I pray Charlie will be with this group of settlers."

"I can help." A broad grin spread over Cephas's face. He cupped his hands around his mouth and bellowed the name of Charlie. Two, three, four times. So loud the oxen tossed their heads and quickened their pace, a reaction Elsbeth had failed to achieve even with the sting of her whip.

"Cephas, I don't think..." But the boy would not be put off.

In the encampment, women stopped their scrubbing long enough to look up. Children dropped playthings. Even the menfolk set aside their tools to stare at the approach of a lone girl by whose side sat a youth, screaming at the top of his lungs.

Two men and a woman stepped forward, the outline

of their bodies forming a *bas-relief* against the tableau of awe-stricken settlers. Her search had narrowed to these last few yards, and she could stand the anticipation no longer. She leaped to the ground and rushed to close the gap between them. The gravity of the moment had its lighter side, though. Elsbeth smiled—first at Cephas's ingenuity in attracting attention and then at the sight she must have presented, her dress stained and torn, her hair in disarray. She wasted no time with introduction or apology.

"Have you picked up a small boy?" Although she spoke to the three adults, her eyes swept beyond them and scanned the faces of the assembled children. She no longer believed a word of Pierce's story about seeing Charlie take off with a young friend.

"Over two days ago," she continued, "my boy wandered off. In the hills, outside town." She waved a hand in the general direction of Sacramento. "I hoped he might have found shelter with your group. His name is Charlie."

A long moment passed while one of the men, his face frozen in a soured expression, scrutinized Elsbeth and glanced curiously at Cephas. His eyes revealed nothing. Finally, he dipped his hand below his waist to indicate a height of about forty inches from the ground.

"Little tyke? Brown hair, eyes?"

"Yes, yes. That's Charlie." Elsbeth clasped her hands to her breast, her excitement in tune to the rising tempo of her heartbeat. "He's here?"

"Not now. Might have been...for a day or so. Yours you say?"

The man lapsed into silence, whereupon the woman took up the story.

"We discovered him playing with the other boys. I lost sight of him for a while, in and out of the wagons those

195

lads were. By then it was evening and we had worked so dreadfully hard setting up camp, so we bedded him down for the night. Next day we sent Mr. Riggs—that's him over there, he's our cook—into the city to inquire. He needed to replenish his stores anyway. Mr. Riggs returned, reporting he'd left word everywhere of the lost boy and our whereabouts here. It wasn't much long after, a soldier rode in. Said he would take charge of the boy, return him to his parents."

Elsbeth blanched. "And you just handed him over to a stranger?"

The man roused from his self-imposed reverie, his demeanor now menacing. "He weren't no stranger. A soldier. An official of the government he was. We're law-abiding folk here."

The woman wrung her hands. "My brother-in-law... Please forgive. We've had a hard crossing. Circumstances have planted a bitter seed in his heart."

"I'm sorry for you, but you must tell me about this soldier?"

"We met him first in the mountains during our emigration. I believe he said his name was Sergeant Pierce."

"Oh, no! Pierce? Are you sure? Where did they go?"

"Why, my dear, I don't rightly know. Bound to be on toward town."

"Sacramento City?" To return there would require grueling hours, a test of endurance. All hope evaporated. Her throat tightened. Tears threatened. Even as she felt her knees become as India rubber, about to buckle under the strain of her predicament, an idea surfaced.

"You have horses." She had seen the small herd grazing in a nearby meadow. "I must have two horses."

To satisfy the doubtful look of the ill-humored man,

196

she added, "I'll pledge my wagon and team against their safe return."

He grunted but waved a hand at his sister-in-law which Elsbeth took for assent.

Preparations for departure ate up precious time. Elsbeth groused at the slowness of the man saddling the horses. To assuage her frustration at his pace, she rummaged around in the wagon, gathering a number of items to take with her including the gold dust in her earthenware crock which she carefully stuffed into a canvas pouch. Finally, she spread a blanket over Billy.

Cephas would ride with her. The community of settlers, drawn by curiosity, now drifted away to resume their chores. Only one small detail remained at loose ends. For this, Elsbeth drew the woman aside. Her oxen had been unyoked and turned out to appease their hunger, leaving Elsbeth's wagon stranded several hundred feet from the main body of the camp. She pointed.

"There's a man inside." She whispered to avoid drawing the attention and perhaps objection from the woman's companion. "He's ailing but on the mend. Would you be so kind as to look in on him from time to time?"

The woman also spoke in undertones. "I have a nephew...Chet. I'll send him now and again to check. Don't you worry."

The unspoken language of women, recognizing their role as caregivers, made further conversation unnecessary.

Anxious to be off, Elsbeth tucked up her skirts and mounted. When Cephas did not follow but stood instead, shifting from one foot to the other, she knew one more promise had yet to be made.

"Cephas," she said, as gently as her impatience would allow. "Get on that horse. We'll come back for Billy. He'll be

197

in good hands until then. Trust me."

The promise made, the boy swung onto the saddle. "Yes, ma'am," he roared and slapped his hat against the horse's flanks. As one they sprang forward. Startled, Elsbeth hurried to gather up her reins and catch up.

Hardly had the clatter of hooves died away when from behind the solitary wagon stepped a solemn-faced lad of six or seven. He shed his hiding place and hoisted himself up the tailgate where he peered inside just long enough for his eyes to adjust to the semi-darkness. Quickly he jumped down and bolted home.

"Pa," he called. "Pa, got somethin' to show ya."

"I'm terrible busy, Chet. Can't it wait?"

"Ya gotta come, pa." He yanked at his father's shirt and refused to let go until the man laid aside the harness he had been repairing.

For the second time that morning, Chester Holt interrupted his work and crossed the field toward Elsbeth's wagon. He picked up his shotgun along the way.

"This better be important, boy."

V

Tall deergrass and sunflowers near the height of a man batted Elsbeth's legs as she raced after the boy across the open meadow.

"Pull up, Cephas," she shouted above the drum of hooves. "Not so fast."

Seemingly oblivious to her cries to stop, Cephas continued to whip his mount. Elsbeth had no choice but to lash her own horse even harder. Slowly the gap between them closed. When Elsbeth finally came abreast of the boy, she reached out and grabbed the reins from his hands. One sharp tug and the pair of riders jarred to a halt.

"Too fast, Cephas, too fast." The horses snorted and wheezed. Elsbeth's own breath came in labored gasps. "We can't afford to lose these animals, Cephas. They aren't ours, and we mustn't waste them before we even get beyond those hills up yonder."

Cephas hung his head, letting only his eyes follow her pointing finger to the higher ground a short way ahead.

"Thought it best to hurry, ma'am," he mumbled.

"Yes, I know you did." For the second time that morning she extended a comforting hand and patted him lightly on the shoulder. "I want to get there too, but it won't do us any good to spend the animals and end up having to walk all the way to Sacramento City."

At her encouraging smile, the boy brightened and retrieved the reins. He bobbed his head. "Slow and easy, ma'am. I can do that."

"I know you can, Cephas."

Elsbeth sighed. She shifted in the saddle to look back along the line of their progress. The settlers' wagons appeared in the distance as tiny hand-carved toys, the children ants, the cattle round-backed beetles. Her own wagon stood apart, isolated from all the others. As she watched, a puff of smoke appeared near the back of the wagon. The muted report of a shotgun blast confirmed what she instinctively knew. For a brief moment fear for Billy Brooster nudged aside her deeper anxiety for Charlie. Cephas's head swiveled toward the sound.

"Someone's shootin' at Mr. Billy," he cried, giving voice to her own thoughts. Cephas jerked his horse's head in the direction of the camp, and Elsbeth sensed he would dig his heels into the horse's flanks and fly back down the valley.

She was tempted to do the same. The gravity of Billy Brooster's situation, however, receded almost immediately against the agonizing thought of her little boy in the hands of a man she considered beneath contempt.

"Cephas, no!" she called and lunged to regain control of his horse. She seized the cheek strap of the bridle and held on tight.

"We don't know what's happening. Could be someone's bagged a deer or quail. Could be that. It could."

His eyes argued against her logic. In reply she yanked more firmly on the bridle.

"We're not going back. Charlie needs me. I fear it'll take two to stand up to this Pierce fellow. And for that I need your help, do you understand me?"

"Ma used to say it's a man's duty to protect a lady."

"You'll be making your mama proud. That you will."

The young man's eyes watered, but Elsbeth's look left no room for argument. He allowed her to turn the horses and urge them toward the hills.

"Billy'll be all right," she assured him. "You take my word, he'll be just fine."

The horses set out at a brisk walk. Cephas remained sullen although a torrent of unspoken emotion worked the corners of his mouth. Elsbeth listened, straining to hear if a second shot would undo Cephas's tentative compliance. When no sound came, she bowed her head and privately uttered a word of thanks. For what, she wasn't exactly sure, for the silence could mean either of two things: her assurances to Cephas had been right or they had been terribly wrong. She didn't want to think of that now. What she did know beyond a doubt was Charlie was in danger. It took all her resolve not to thrash the horses into a headlong gallop.

As they gained the crest of the ridge, to Elsbeth's

delight, they happened on a well-worn horse path. It angled generally northward.

"We're in luck," she called to Cephas. "This ought to lead us right into Sacramento."

When the boy answered with only an incomprehensible grunt, Elsbeth fell silent too.

Cephas's on-again, off-again moods were tiresome and slowed their progress. At times he trailed behind, sulking. Minutes later he would bolt after a noise or movement in the grass. Before they had traveled very far, Elsbeth regretted bringing him along. When streams and rivulets began to crisscross their route, new problems arose. Cephas was easily distracted. At every fording the boy leaped off his horse and splashed through the water, collecting an assortment of rocks and stones—one for its smoothness, another for its unique shape, still others for their brightly-colored striations. He stuffed them into his pockets. Suspenders unaccustomed to the added weight strained, threatening at any moment to snap and send his drawers sliding past bony hips and landing in a heap around his ankles.

"Enough is enough," shouted Elsbeth, her temper flaring, when yet another channel of water sliced through the road. "Stay on that horse. We'll never get there if you don't stop holding us back." She slapped his mount on the rear and sent it flying. When she caught up to him on the other side of the stream, she sighed heavily at the sight of him. Water dribbled down his cheeks. Great blotches of wetness discolored the front of his shirt. She thought, but wasn't sure, there were tears in his eyes. She shook her head from side to side, disgusted at herself. She knew well the boy's limitations. How could she act in such a manner? What had this place done to her?

"Oh, Cephas, dear Cephas." Elsbeth dismounted and

ran back to the stream. She searched along its shallow bank, taking care not to soak her shoes, until she found a rock remarkable for its fiercely jagged edges and unique coloring of black and milky white. She plunged her hand into the water and returned with the stone as a peace offering.

"Here, Cephas. Look. Isn't this a pretty one? C'mon on, take it."

He hesitated but only for a second before his hand shot out and latched onto the weighty stone.

"It shore is pretty, Miz Elsbeth." He smiled. "It's gonna be my favorite."

Elsbeth felt forgiven, but she drew no comfort from that feeling.

Once again, they took to the road. Here and there other smaller paths intersected with theirs, widening the trail just as tributaries would spill into a river, relentlessly building a mighty waterway out of a trickle of melting snow. The dusty current of the road pulled them along.

Elsbeth slacked off on the reins, trusting the horse to keep to the trail without the need for her constant attention. This left her mind open to the tortures of her imagination.

Inside her head Pierce's face took on demonic proportions—his complexion darker, the lines of his mouth crueler. Scars plowed across his jaw. Elsbeth wasn't sure these even existed, yet she could not erase them from the images imprinted in her brain. She heard his laugh, and it mocked her. She smelled the stench of liquor emanating from his breath and clothes, and saliva filled her mouth. Mercifully no picture of Charlie formed to haunt her, but the certainty he was afraid and without his mother multiplied her torment.

Bent under the burden of her thoughts, Elsbeth hardly noticed the ever-changing terrain. Long ago they had left behind the higher country and followed the trail's gentle descent into the broad expanse of lowlands. They now entered an area thick with humidity and marked by patches of overgrown shrub and stands of pine. Nor had she registered the passing of the day. As the sun nudged past its zenith, Cephas edged his horse closer.

"'Scuse, ma'am," he said shyly in a voice made raspy by his lengthy silence. He pointed to where a mass of trees and thick underbrush hid the area just beyond the side of the road. "I hear voices."

Out of the blur of her private thoughts, Elsbeth forced her surroundings into sharper focus. She reined in sharply and placed a finger on her lips. "Shh. Let me listen."

Without the steady clomp of their horses' hooves to mask the sound, she heard it too. So far along their journey they had yet to encounter another living soul, leaving her to assume they traveled entirely alone, but Cephas was right. These were voices—human voices. Two of them.

A sudden catch in her throat was the unnerving reminder they were defenseless. Cephas had insisted on leaving Billy's rifle with its rightful owner, and she had not been able to talk him out of it.

The brush blunted the voices, though she could tell they were distinctly different. Not knowing what dangers other travelers might present sent a cold shiver down her arms. Her grip on the reins loosened and, unconstrained, her mount inched forward, but that little bit of distance was enough for the murmurings to separate into words.

"Shut your yap!"

Instantly, and with grave alarm, she recognized the gravelly slur of Clayton Pierce.

With uncharacteristic authority, and in a tone Elsbeth had not before heard him use, Cephas issued a challenge.

"Who's there? Who are you?"

203

Into this moment of high tension stepped Pierce who had until now been hidden amongst the foliage.

"Reckoned you'd be along sooner or later, Missy. Figured you'd give up on Sacramento and hightail it to that field where I found you the other day. Then you'd stumble onto that camp of travelers. Was right, wasn't I?"

"You've taken my child! Where is he?"

"Them folks were all too willing to be rid of him. I let them know I was heading back into town and would take responsibility for him. Nice of them to oblige and point you in this direction. I've been waitin'. Patiently, I might add."

"I demand—"

Elsbeth was interrupted by a sweet, dearly beloved voice which rent her heart with a single word, "Mommy!"

A tide of motherly longing swept over her, and she jumped to the ground and ran forward. Pierce barred the way.

"Not so fast, Missy."

She tried to push the man aside. When that failed, she attacked, slashing at his face with the only weapon she possessed...her fingernails.

"Get out of my way, you snake," she screamed. "Get away from my boy."

Pierce growled and shoved her with such force she fell to her knees. Cephas materialized at her side. She welcomed the boy's presence, but feared it would make no difference. Any command of the situation he'd previously shown had evaporated and his arm quivered uncontrollably against her own.

Clayton Pierce towered over them both. He removed his hat and fingered its dirty, lopsided crown then waved it over his shoulder at a huge chestnut-colored horse where Charlie sat astride. The child clung desperately to the saddle horn, sobs wracking his body. When Pierce finally spoke, it was directed at Elsbeth.

"You've got somethin' I want, and now I've got somethin' you want. Looks like we'll be bargaining on an even keel this time."

Elsbeth glared. Cephas looked from one to the other.

"Is he talking about the gold, Miz Elsbeth?"

This aroused Pierce's interest. "Gold, huh? You've got gold?"

"She shore does—enough to pay for the little 'un there." Elsbeth tried to make eye contact with Cephas—warn him into silence—but the damage had already been done.

Pierce chuckled without smiling. "The pot gets sweeter all the time," he said.

Trying to stall for time, Elsbeth said, "What is it you want?"

"I think you know, but here it is spelled out...Billy Brooster."

Never before had Elsbeth lied but she barely hesitated in answering. "Well, I'm afraid I can't help you. I don't know where he is." Pierce took a threatening step forward. "Actually," she continued, "he happened by my wagon on the outskirts of the city"—she nodded toward Sacramento—"and I told him I never wanted to see him—"

"Miz Elsbeth...?" Cephas interrupted, a puzzled look on his face.

Elsbeth ignored the boy.

"I told him to get out of my sight."

"Miz Elsbeth?" Now Cephas tugged vigorously at her sleeve. She shrugged him off and hurried on.

"He assured me he was heading back East...had enough of prospecting. That was days and days ago."

Cephas appeared ready to burst. Breathless, almost frantic, he protested, "No, no, Miz Elsbeth. Don't you

205

remember? We left Mr. Billy in your wagon up yonder by the camp. With all those people. The ones who loaned us the horses. You said Billy'd be all right and we'd go back to get him. Don't you remember?"

Pierce tipped his hat toward the boy. "Well, well, well. Thank ya, sonny." To Elsbeth he added, "Serves you right for bringing an imbecile along with you. That little deception will cost you." He eyed the satchel looped over the horn of her saddle. "You just forfeited your gold." He turned to Cephas. "Throw that bag over here, boy."

If Clayton Pierce's tone of voice was not enough to command obedience, the gun he drew from a holster at his side certainly was. Elsbeth had seen guns before, but never pointed straight at her. Up this close, Pierce's appeared to be the largest gun she'd ever seen. Cephas began to whimper. With his free hand Pierce roughly snatched Charlie from the saddle and thrust him at Elsbeth. She knelt and wrapped her arms around her son, kissed him over and over, called him her brave little soldier.

Then she turned to Cephas. "It's not your fault," she assured him, knowing full well he did not understand his role in placing them in this predicament.

She faced Pierce with a defiant look. "You've got what you came for. Take the gold and leave us alone."

"You seem to have forgotten the one part of the bargain that's missing. Thanks to the dummy here," he indicated Cephas, "Brooster'll be easy enough to find. I have only to turn these horses loose, and they'll head on home. All I have to do is follow. But how foolish would it be of me to leave three perfectly good witnesses behind." The man's eyes narrowed into slits. Furtively, he glanced up and down the road. "Next you'll want me to forfeit my horse so you can ride straight to the law. No. You tried to fool me. You refused your side of the bargain. You've earned three of my bullets, Missy, nothing less."

Petrified, her heart a war drum beating in her chest, Elsbeth saw the barrel of the gun rotate. She heard the click of the hammer. A mad man, she thought in horror. He'd kill an innocent child and not think twice about it. Struggling to her feet, she thrust her body in front of Charlie. Out of the corner of her eye, she spotted Cephas, grabbed onto his arm, and pulled him behind her too. Charlie clutched at her skirts. Cephas, however, twisted and turned. Be still, be still, she thought. No words passed her lips, but her mind shouted. Be still.

But Cephas would not. He broke her grasp and wriggled free. From the corner of her eye, she saw him sidestep from what little protection the fabric of her dress afforded. He wrested something from his pocket and hurled it. The object whizzed through the air, meeting its target with a dull, sickening thunk. In the same blink of an eye, a resounding boom shattered the afternoon.

Elsbeth gasped, unable to breathe. The blood drained from her face. A long second passed. Charlie's fingers dug deeper into her legs, and Cephas stared, open-mouthed. Another moment ticked away while comprehension settled in. She was not hurt. Nor Charlie. Nor Cephas. The shot had gone wild.

Only Clayton Pierce moved. He teetered forward. For a moment he seemed to hang in mid-air, suspended at a precarious angle like a marionette whose puppeteer has tangled the strings. Then his massive body crumpled to the ground. A crimson pool formed beneath a raw and ragged wound on his temple. The blood inched its way outward, crowning Pierce with a vibrant halo of red.

Elsbeth stared in disbelief. She looked for a rise and

fall of his chest but detected none.

"Dear Lord in Heaven," she whispered, steepling her shaking fingers. "What mortal sin is this?"

She looked at the man sprawled at her feet. He repulsed her, yet she felt riveted by the grizzly sight. A chill swept through her body. From out of a distant past her father's image arose. The Reverend Elsworth faced his congregation—righteous and sure—admonishing the flock to tread a narrow path, threatening wrongdoers with the fiery pits of hell. In other days Elsbeth would have cried "Amen!" as vigorously as her father denounced the sinner. Those days were gone. The last year and more of her life had stirred right and wrong together in a pot and served up a bubbling brew of doubt. Nothing was simple anymore. An imagined thwack of Bible against pulpit startled her back to the present. She repeated, "What mortal sin is this?"

In answer to her own question, Elsbeth spat on Clayton Pierce.

Gingerly she lifted her skirts above the ankle and stepped over his body to retrieve her satchel with its stash of gold. Nearby lay a rock…a black one, its surface rough and broken, exposing the white of its interior. She handed it back to Cephas.

"I told you this was gonna be my favorite," he said, nodding.

Carefully the boy wiped the stone on his trousers and dropped it into his pocket. He began to whistle then—cheerfully, up and down the scales. Without a backward glance, he folded Charlie's hand into his own and led the youngster toward the waiting mounts.

"Protectin' ladies," said Cephas into Charlie's ear, "is a man's job. You need to remember that, like I did."

Charlie heaved a sigh much too heavy for his tender

years. "He was a bad man. He hit me."

Cephas glanced over his shoulder at the prone figure of Pierce. "I reckon he won't be doing that anymore."

A shadow overhead caught Elsbeth's attention. Despite the warmth of the day, she shivered, for a formation of black, scavenging birds circled ominously against the white clouds.

Elsbeth gathered the reins of all three horses and stood in the middle of the road. She glanced northward toward the city. In her heart she knew this way would lead eventually to Tom. Here she saw her future. A home and family for Charlie and perhaps Cephas too. Yet when she looked south and envisioned her wagon and all it contained, she sensed loss, a gnawing emptiness she found difficult to describe.

She thought about life and the choices it offered. Along the way decisions were made. Some roads traveled, others rejected. Promises kept, promises broken. Which road would she take now? Which promise would she keep?

The two boys waited patiently.

Which road? she asked herself. Which road?

CHAPTER 10

The Road Taken

I

A yellowjacket sounded the first alarm. Straying from its mission among the poppies and clover, it flew in over a sleeping Billy Brooster. In a frantic but fruitless search for sweet nectar, it circled and swooped and buzzed relentlessly. Annoyed, Billy opened his eyes. His surroundings came slowly into focus and thought formed more clearly in his mind. He looked around, found himself comfortably bedded in a well-stocked wagon, a canopy of white shading out the sun. An herbal taste lingered on his tongue. A healing plaster warmed his back, and a cloth had been wrapped snugly around his ribcage. Save for a splitting headache and a catch with each breath, his physical condition had improved immeasurably. He tried to wring from his memory the circumstances that would bridge the gap between this place and the hellhole in which he had last closed his eyes.

He could not.

Soon other sounds intruded upon the humming of the bee—a nickering of horses, the lowing of cattle, a murmur of human voices. This last disturbed him most.

"Am I dreaming?" he wondered. Certain his mind had played a trick, he raised himself to an elbow and strained to listen. "That's Cephas's voice, but I swear I hear Elsbeth too. Where am I? In California or Oregon?"

Oregon seemed out of the question. But Elsbeth in California? How could that be? He had to know for sure.

He groped along the inside of the wagon until his fingers discovered a chink in the wall. He pressed one eye firmly to the hole and, by tightly closing the other, framed a small vignette of sunny meadow.

His effort was richly rewarded, for there stood Elsbeth. He couldn't believe his eyes. He recognized the same dress she wore when he bid her farewell at the edge of the Warner property. And hanging in this very wagon was the colored bonnet that framed her face when their paths crossed in Oregon City. It seemed forever ago. The sight of her was a soothing balm applied to a festering wound. But he also heard her voice. Two words—*Sacramento City*—found their way to his ears. While the sound was a comfort, its meaning confused him. Sacramento? Was she leaving? He struggled to stand, but his knees betrayed him. A shout emerged as no more than a croak. A dizzy spell overtook him. Pressing his forehead against the plank siding of the wagon, he used what strength he could muster to remain conscious, afraid if he succumbed to the demands of his body, he would later wake to find it had all been a dream.

The battle was lost. He slumped to the floor and closed his eyes. Whether he slept a minute or an hour he didn't know, only that new voices now demanded his attention. His eyes snapped open. He could not make out the individual words, other than to determine it was a man and a child who spoke them. He sensed danger. Lessons learned during his soldiering days set him instantly on guard. Once

211

again, he hauled himself to the narrow slit in the wagon bed, but the scene it opened onto had dramatically changed.

Cephas was gone. Elsbeth…gone. In their place two figures—one short, one tall, both recognizable. Chester Holt and his brat of a kid.

Scrabbling awkwardly, Billy crossed to the opposite end of the wagon. Leaning against the framework was his rifle. He grabbed it and, with great effort, climbed over the driver's seat and slid quietly to the ground. He longed to pause for the briefest of moments to let the pain for his effort subside, but urgency drove him on. He staggered to the cover of tall grasses and a bank of nearby trees.

A shotgun blast rent the air. Half crawling, half scrambling, Billy beat a path forward, pain be damned. The pliant grasses gave way, yielding before him and closing behind. As he ran, the swoosh of their stems echoed in his ears and tortured him with a single question: Who had given him away?

II

Hardened knobs of gnarled bark dug into Brooster's flesh as he leaned against the ancient oak for balance. The vein on his forehead throbbed, sending waves of pain to his eyes, neck, and shoulders. He fought to catch his breath.

The tree offered shade and support for his body, which was exhausted from the desperate effort to distance himself from Chester Holt. Its considerable girth assured concealment while he recovered a bit of strength. For that he was grateful.

A furtive glance around the tree trunk suggested his

escape had been successful. The field of grass, with seed pods swollen and nodding under the weight of their harvest, swayed gently. There was no sign he had passed through. The path of his flight from the settlers' camp and the refuge of Elsbeth's wagon had been obliterated by the resilience of the stalks and the action of the wind.

Once he entered the wooded area, shadow and the abundance of hiding places fanned the glimmer of hope. There had been no second discharge of a weapon. He cupped an ear, listening, trying to determine by other sounds if Holt was in pursuit. He heard only the pounding of his own heart.

Still, he worried for his life. The deeper forest lured him to seek a greater distance from the man he had robbed. It wasn't really robbery, he rationalized. He'd earned that money. But he also read Holt as a man with a long memory and an even longer will for revenge. Would he really shoot him over such a small stash of coins? Billy did not want to find out.

He pushed himself away from the tree and headed toward a ravine that promised even better cover. It proved not an easy route. He fell twice. It took minutes each time to recover from the jolt. And each time he blessed Elsbeth for the protection her bandages provided.

The ascent to the other side of the ravine was difficult and he arrived winded.

A moment, he told himself. That's all he needed. One moment's rest before trudging onward. His arm fell limply against his side. His grip on the rifle loosened, and once again he sagged against the tree.

"Ho there!"

At the sound, Brooster bolted straight, fumbled the gun to his shoulder, cocking it on the fly. His eyes darted here and there, straining to penetrate the half-light of the woods.

One spot loomed darker than the surrounding shadows. He aimed his weapon and ordered, "Don't move!"

"Not a muscle," came the answer.

"State your name."

"Sullivan. Patrick Sullivan."

Billy's voice lost its edge.

"Well, Patrick Sullivan. Move into the light...slowly."

A young man about Billy's age stepped forward. A ragged hat pushed far back on his head revealed a mop of curly hair. Wire-rimmed glasses magnified frightened eyes.

Billy relaxed. "Ho yourself," he called.

When first challenged, Sullivan had raised his hands above his head, palms out, to show he carried no weapon. Now stiffly and with his hands still high in the air, he ventured a second step forward.

Apologetic, Billy said, "Thought you were someone else."

"Well, I've the saints and me mother to thank I'm only poor Paddy Sullivan." With a wiggle of his finger he pointed to the gun.

"Sorry." Billy disengaged the hammer and tilted the barrel end of the rifle toward the ground.

Sullivan exhaled audibly and lowered his arms. "I've had better greetings from a swarm of angry hornets," he said.

"Bein' careful's all."

Sullivan pursed his lips. "Me mother always says prudence is a virtue. But if you had been any more prudent..." He shrugged away the remainder of the sentence.

"No hard feelings I trust." Billy moved to offer his hand, the gesture meant to convey the sincerity of his words, but at that moment a shiver passed through his body.

"You look a little under the weather," said Sullivan.

"Some."

"I can spare a bite or two from a sourdough loaf. It's not much, but…"

Billy didn't need to reply. His mouth dropped open at the mention of food. "I'd be most thankful."

"Grub's in my rig. Over there."

When Brooster followed Patrick's nod, he saw for the first time a small cart standing in among the trees. It seemed no more than a three-sided crate teetering on two rickety wheels. A heavy rope harnessed it to a dark gray burro who stood so still he could have been sketched in charcoal.

"You prospecting?"

"Oh, no. There's a fortune to be made in those foothills all right, but it's not in gold."

Billy wrinkled his brow.

"Mail," Patrick explained. "Letters, newspapers and such. Me mother always says a few words from home are worth their weight. And I've seen it with me own eyes. A single letter can pluck a man's spirits out of the depths and plant it on the mountaintops. Mail. I tote it in, I carry it out…for a fee, of course." He chuckled and aimed a knowing wink at Billy. "Sure beats pickin' and shovelin' all to hell and back."

The Irishman whirled about and strode to the cart. For such a small conveyance, it appeared overloaded. A blanket with ends securely tucked around covered a lopsided mound. What the bulky cargo might be, Billy could not guess. On top of it all lay a burlap mail pouch. Sullivan stuck his hand deep along the inside edge of the cart and rummaged around before extracting a square of linen carefully folded around a partial loaf of bread. Despite his hunger, the back of the wagon roused Billy's curiosity. He nodded toward the load.

"Quite a haul you've made. Mail business must be

215

good."

"Oh that…that's not mail at all."

Billy took a closer look. Only then did he notice the reddish-brown stain that marred the blanket and the few inches of trousers and a black leather boot which protruded.

"Reckon not," he said.

Sullivan ignored the suspicion imprinted on Billy's face. He calmly tore off a hunk of bread and handed it over. Just as calmly he explained finding a man alongside the higher road leading into Sacramento.

"You mean you're carting around a corpse?"

"Almost. In pretty bad shape…but not dead, not quite. Though, I must say, a passel of buzzards were getting mighty impatient for their next meal. It was me mother's voice I heard then…telling me to be a Good Samaritan. I know a doctor in town. I'll be takin' him there. If he dies, he dies, but it won't be on my conscience."

Sullivan then began to hum a lively tune. Without missing a beat, he yanked mightily on the burro's halter, wrenching the animal out of its inertia. Then he set off through the trees, calling over his shoulder, "If you're heading on into town, I wouldn't mind the company. This fella's not much of a talker."

Billy watched him go. The higher country beckoned. There he could lose himself in an endless maze of ravines and creek beds, become one more nameless, faceless soul in any of a hundred makeshift camps. Thus could he avoid the wrath of Chester Holt.

Yet despite the dangers of staying, Bill's feet refused to move. Something held him back. He remembered waking in a sun-lit wagon, his mind swimming with thoughts of Elsbeth. Her presence had been too strong, too real to be merely the product of a fevered mind stoked by the yearning

216

of a young man's fancy. The sudden appearance of Holt had surprised and frightened him. He had felt betrayed. But was Elsbeth to blame? Or was the whole incident just another piece of the unfortunate luck that seemed to dog his trail?

And Sacramento City, the two words spoken by Elsbeth, gave him a new goal.

"Wait!" he called to Patrick.

But Patrick had already halted, obviously amused at Billy's indecision. With a flourish of his hand, he patted his midsection and said, "Best to do whatever your belly's telling you. That gut feeling may not always take you in the direction you think it should, but it's usually the proper way to go."

"Is that something else your mother always says?"

"That it is, my friend. That it certainly is. C'mon, this day's aslidin' by."

As if released from a spell, Billy heaved a sigh, put his faith in the wisdom of Mrs. Sullivan's words, and limped over to Patrick for the long walk into town.

III

The sun dipped low toward the western horizon, generously splashing lavender and mauve across the face of an otherwise unremarkable building in the heart of Sacramento City. A wooden shingle tacked above the window identified the office and practice of Oswald Finster.

Billy scratched his head. "You sure about this?"

Patrick Sullivan brushed past him and knocked vigorously on the door. "This is it, all right. Doc's place. Open up," he shouted and pounded anew.

"Paddy, the sign says he's a dentist." Brooster jabbed

a thumb toward the mail wagon. "I think your friend's suffering from more than a toothache."

"Doctor...dentist. As me mother says, all one in the same."

Just then the door opened a notch, framing the pock-marked face and bushy eyebrows of Oswald Finster. A grunt of recognition followed. Patrick disappeared inside.

Left standing alone on the plank walkway, Billy paced restlessly...a few steps one way, the same few back. The approach of nightfall had brought a frenzy of activity. Shopkeepers secured their places of business. Traps and rigs rolled by as people ended the day and made for home. Others, for whom the evening meant the start rather than close of their day, migrated toward the raucous sounds and harsh yellow light emanating from a half dozen nearby saloons.

Although he had been in Sacramento before, nothing seemed familiar, but then, of course, he'd been near crazy with pain and fever. The bustle and noise pressed in from all sides. Billy wished he were anywhere else. He wished Patrick would hurry.

Why he even stuck around was a mystery, other than a morbid curiosity about the fate of the lump of human flesh in the back of Paddy's cart.

What was taking the kid so long?

Suddenly the hair on the nape of his neck stood at attention. A movement put him on guard. The burro, also on the alert, tossed its head and twitched its ears.

Billy raised his weapon and looked around. The blood-stained blanket shifted slightly, quivered, then settled once again into peaceful repose. Billy edged closer. At first glance nothing seemed amiss. The rumpled blanket still concealed the sack-of-potatoes shape of the stranger. The

218

leather boot still protruded. A more thorough inspection, however, revealed the man's arm had worked free and now hung limply over the side.

He chided himself for his case of nerves as he bent to return the arm to a less awkward position but stopped short. Adorning the third finger of the hand was a heavily embellished, silver ring.

"I know this ring," he gasped.

Unconsciously he lifted his hand to his cheek and probed a spot along his jawline. He could almost feel the imprint of this very ring burning on his skin, not once, not twice, but a brutal beating that seemed to go on forever. He grabbed the corner of the blanket and threw it aside. The man beneath lay still as death. Dried blood and purple blotches discolored his face. Swelling distorted the features, but his identity was unmistakable.

Billy recoiled. Fear and hatred coursed through him—first hot, then cold, then hot again.

When Patrick Sullivan reappeared at Finster's front door, he called cheerfully into the growing darkness. "Ho there. Wouldya mind lendin' a hand to lug this fella inside?"

When the expected response didn't come, the fellow peered around.

Billy Brooster was nowhere in sight.

IV

The darkening sky served to conceal Billy as he sprinted across the street and onto a crudely-constructed boardwalk. His frantic dash had little to do with any fear of the incapacitated man. Clearly Clayton Pierce could do him no harm in his present state. Would he even know it was Private Brooster who had lifted the cover from his body?

More likely Billy fled to save his soul, for his first wild impulse had been to finish the job someone or something else had started.

During his stint as a soldier at Ft. Kearny, he'd never killed, not in battle, neither an Indian nor rogue soldier, not even in self-defense. He wasn't about to start now no matter how patently he thought a brute like Pierce deserved to die.

He hastened along the boardwalk until he came upon a narrow alleyway that led behind buildings on the next street over.

Patrick's company on the way into town had been rehabilitating in both body and spirit. The walk had been leisurely, given the size of the burro and the size of the load it bore. Their conversation amounted to more of Mrs. Sullivan's pithy aphorisms which Patrick shared with free and easy laughter. The exertion of running a mere city block, though, left him lightheaded, winded and exasperated at this latest twist in his already tangled life. He came looking for Elsbeth but found trouble instead.

And Clayton Pierce was a heap of trouble.

Billy needed a refuge, some secluded out-of-the-way place to briefly hide while he gathered his wits.

A soft nickering placed him behind the livery stable where horses were fed and bedded while waiting to be sold or traded or temporarily boarded by their owners. Piled near a rear door was a shoulder-high mound of straw. It called to Billy's weary body. He collapsed on it, allowing a cascade of stalks to fall around him and conceal him on all sides.

Without concern for the ramifications of closing his eyes, he did. Immediately visions both nerve wracking and appealing appeared. For the moment he concentrated on the pleasant ones, the ones of Elsbeth. He tried to piece together how she had come back into his life in such a fortuitous, though puzzling, manner. On that account he failed, except for a few snippets of clarity which worked their way out of the murky corners of his memory: the helping hand pulling him to his feet, and the soft, encouraging words. There were the bandages around his aching chest, the ministrations of a caring person. He awoke in a wagon that was hers. He was sure of that, for he recognized the bonnet and, now that he thought of it, a reasonably new green shirt made to fit a child, one about the size of the little boy who clung to her outside the general store in Oregon City.

Soon other thoughts began to intrude, first like annoying gnats that refused to be batted away. They wouldn't stop, only grew in urgency until he could think of nothing else. No matter how far or how fast Billy ran, his past seemed like a pair of spurs, forever clinking malevolently at his heels. Unbelievably, Chester Holt had reentered his life. And now the hated soldier. He needed a plan.

Simply hoping Oswald Finster's skill was no match for whatever ailed Pierce was not a solution, but while he battled to come up with a better one, exhaustion won the fight.

V

How could he have fallen asleep? Worse yet, how could he have slept so soundly?

He had no recollection of when his mind shut down or when his body succumbed to the relative comfort of the straw. He knew only that the morning sun had crept in on felt-soled shoes and now jeered at him through the open side of the lean-to.

"Stupid!" he hissed. "Idiot!" With a furious kick of his boot, Billy scattered straw in a wide arc. From his hair rained a shower of chaff. He had lost precious hours to the night and had accomplished putting no more than a hundred yards distance between himself and Clayton Pierce. He grimaced at the thought he had spent the better part of yesterday walking within three feet of the man, but it was foolish to lament what couldn't be changed. Looking forward was his best shot If Finster were a better dentist than most and had acquired some skill at country doctoring, his patient might have made it through the night. How long would it take for Pierce to come to his senses and be ushered out the door? Twenty-four hours? Forty-eight? He allowed himself one day to comb the city for Elsbeth. Then he had no choice but to flee.

Although he would regret leaving Cephas behind, it couldn't be helped. As he had plainly seen up in the foothills, the boy was with Elsbeth. She was already caring for a child not her own. If he failed to find Elsbeth, Cephas would be in good hands.

Once the gears of an internal timepiece had been set in motion—a countdown ticking away—Brooster appreciated the need for haste. He moved off at a trot.

Sacramento was expanding at a breakneck pace. Each day hundreds of newcomers stepped off ships at the harbor or simply walked in over the mountains. In one way or another, all were there to exploit the rush for gold—no more or less obsessed with the myriad possibilities to accomplish that than Patrick Sullivan had been. For Billy, it made scouring the streets a daunting task. He scanned faces. He peered through doorwells. At each corner he paused and weighed the choices. Right or left? Forward or back?

222

At one particular intersection, Brooster hesitated longer than usual. He heard the scrunch of wagon wheels rolling along the street. A peg hinge creaked on the swinging door of a saloon he had just passed, and the tap-tap of footsteps behind him played along the outer edges of his awareness. Despite his heightened senses, he was not prepared for the gentle touch of a hand on his shoulder nor the soft whisper of a feminine voice in his ear.

"You looking for me?"

Billy froze. His head filled with a vision of Elsbeth—delicate figure, golden hair, eyes the color of a summer sky. For a moment, hope and excitement paralyzed his limbs, but he threw them off and spun around. It took a second for his mind to catch up to what his eyes recorded.

Her face was plain, somewhat broad and flat, with mousy hair braided into a knot at the back of her head. She wore a dress of bleached muslin. Its wide neckline scooped low in front and draped seductively to one side, exposing a milky white though somewhat plump shoulder. A bright blue feather boa snaked around her neck and down one arm.

She repeated her question.

"N-no," Billy stammered. "W-why would I be looking for you?"

She cocked her head and fluttered long, curving lashes, not boldly but with a shy desperation.

"For your amusement, sir."

Billy's eyes grew wide.

The girl persisted. "Are you meaning to take your pleasure here?"

She indicated a line of identical cubicles that formed a ragtag extension of the more solidly-constructed saloon. Each cubbyhole had been framed out in green wood over which stretched a tarp, topped by a peaked canvas roof. As Billy stared down the row, a fabric doorway flapped open and an obviously satisfied customer emerged, hitched up his britches, and swaggered away.

"No. No. I *am* looking for a girl but not a…not a…"

"Prostitute?"

"Her name is Elsbeth…but I've come to the wrong place."

"I see." The girl relaxed and the smile on her face became genuine. "That name's not familiar, but I've plenty of friends. I'd be happy to ask around for you, help you find her. If you'd like me to, that is."

Before Billy could answer, a red-haired woman, laced tightly in a gown of shocking green, swept out of the bar.

"Rosie!" she called. "Get back to work." A scowl darkened the woman's face.

Rosie cringed. "I am, ma'am. I am working."

The woman sized up Billy in one quick look. "So, you wish Rosie's services?"

"Later, ma'am. He's asking for later."

"That's right," interjected Billy, reading the plea clearly written on the girl's face. "Later…say about noon?"

"Yes, noon," said Rosie. "Let's make it noon."

The woman glanced from one to the other. "We'll expect you then," she snapped. She failed to see the exchange of winks as she roughly grasped the girl by the arm and led her away.

Billy turned the corner and carried on his search with a bit more optimism than he'd had before. Two making inquiries about Elsbeth were better than one, even if Rosie was a… He shoved that thought away and set his sights on a mercantile where a small clutch of people congregated outside. He waded into their midst.

The first thing he heard was *Tom*. This sparked his

224

interest. Were they talking about Warner? He tapped a neatly-dressed man on the shoulder.

"Excuse me, sir. Was that Tom Warner you were discussing?"

The man reacted first with a blank stare followed by a chuckle. He slapped his neighbor on the back while addressing the group as a whole. "Listen to this, fellows. A greenie." He pointed at Billy. "Doesn't know what a long tom is. Thinks it's a person."

The other joined him in laughter.

"Long tom…rocker," he went on, gesturing as if he were rocking a baby's cradle. "For shoveling out the gold faster than a simple pan. Four guys working in unison can wash out a hundred bucks worth a day."

That was the first Billy had heard of any such piece of equipment. The gang from Oregon City had never used anything other than their pans. Trying to cover his obvious lack of what was common knowledge, he pasted on a smile.

"Oh, yeah, *that* tom."

Now too embarrassed to ask about Elsbeth, Billy retreated, his head hung low, not only at his inadequacy in finding Elsbeth, but at the immensity of the task. He returned to the brothel empty-handed and dejected, brightening only slightly when Rosie slid her arm through his and led him into a tiny room off the side street.

"Hope you aren't in trouble over this morning?" he asked.

"Madam's been watching with an eagle eye, but no trouble, especially now you've returned."

She pulled closed the square of canvas that served as a door. The room was unbearably hot and scarcely large enough to accommodate the narrow cot and single wooden stand on which rested a basin of water. The straw mattress

225

crackled as Rosie sat down and patted the vacant space beside her.

Billy held up a hand. "Really, I didn't come for that. You said you might ask around about, you know, about Elsbeth."

When a shadow of fear passed over the girl's features, he hurried to add, "I'll pay anyway. For your time. No one'll be the wiser." He dug into his pocket and produced a coin.

Her smile returned but not for long. Rosie hung her head. "I'm sorry, but no one has heard of your Elsbeth."

Your Elsbeth. For a moment the full measure of what Rosie said was lost in the sound of those two words. *Your Elsbeth.*

"Sir?"

Billy's eyes regained their focus. "I'd best be going," he said and turned to leave. The girl leaped up and grabbed at a loose corner of his shirt.

"It's too soon. Madam will be suspicious."

"Then I'll wash up first." He stripped to the waist and splashed water over his neck and chest while Rosie looked on. Finding no towel, he wadded up his shirt and dabbed himself dry. Once dressed, he moved toward the exit. This time the girl did not intervene but rose and walked behind him through the opening. She apologized again.

"I *could* ask the owner of the saloon," she offered. "He usually takes his dinner there about this time when he's in town. Maybe Mr. Warner would know your friend."

Billy stopped so abruptly Rosie bumped into him.

"Did you say Warner?"

"Yes, Tom Warner. He owns this operation. Well, him and the madam."

"Might this be one of the days he's in town?"

"I should say so. Miss Kate is always in a growly

mood when he's not."

"Are you saying her performance this morning was a *good* mood?"

"As good as it gets." Rosie giggled. "I could go now and ask, seein' as you've paid."

Once again Billy dipped into his pocket and extracted a second coin. "That won't be necessary," he said slowly. "I'll take care of it. And thank you. You've helped me more than you know." He held the coin up in the light. "This is for you...and *only* you." He pressed the coin firmly into her hand and curled her fingers over it. As he did so, for the first time he smelled the lilac scent of Rosie's perfume and felt the warmth and pleasing texture of her skin. His hand lingered on hers.

Rosie took one look at her day's good fortune. With a squeal of delight, she broke free of Billy's grasp, threw her arms around his neck, and kissed him full on the mouth.

CHAPTER 11

All That Glitters

I

Elsbeth lay in the dark, eyes open and staring at a ceiling she could not see. Though she was exhausted, sleep would not come. The pendulum of her thoughts swung from profound relief at Charlie's safe return to confusion, doubt and despair.

Her head ached. She knew what Charlie wanted—a patch of ground with chickens to feed, not just today, but tomorrow and the day after that. God knew it was her dream too, but… But how to make it come to pass? She had no answer, and the question troubled her heart as mercilessly as the hard bed tortured her back. No sooner did she feel a moment of understanding within her grasp, than it was gone, vanished, a fine dusting of powder dispersed in a puff of air.

Charlie rolled over in bed. The rope springs barely protested as the little body settled into the curve of his mother's arm. Elsbeth hugged him close, not so hard as to waken the boy, but firmly enough to reassure herself he was there beside her.

It had been a long day.

As soon as she had turned her back on Clayton Pierce's body, she planted Charlie on the saddle directly in front of her and assigned Cephas the task of leading the third horse. When all were mounted, Elsbeth steered the meager caravan, not north to the city, rather south, along the same route that had brought them from the settlers' camp to this place of equal parts terror and joy. It was not a conscious decision to head in this direction. She just did it. Was it a sense of duty that guided her to the unfinished business of once again exchanging horses for her team? She would deal with explaining the third horse when the moment presented itself. Or was it the promise she'd made to Cephas? Perhaps it was something more.

They had traveled only a short distance when Charlie reached for her fingers and squeezed them in his own. His brown eyes, wide with trust, turned upward and burrowed deep into her soul.

"We find Papa now?" he asked.

Her voice stuck in her throat. It was a moment before she could speak. "Of course, my little soldier," she finally said. "Of course, we're going to find Papa. That's why we came to California. And I know just the place to start looking. I have a strong feeling he's gone on to Sacramento City. We'll just borrow these horses a little bit longer."

Not daring to face Cephas, she wheeled the horses in the opposite direction.

Cephas's protest amounted to a sputtered, "No, Miz Elsbeth! You're going the wrong way."

She pretended not to hear, while at the same time admitting to herself she had made a promise to him too. Eventually she would keep it, but not just yet. She was bound more firmly to her son's future happiness, so when Cephas stubbornly held his mount at bay, she again paid him no

229

heed.

This time, though, she listened carefully for a telltale sign as to what the lad intended to do. A clop of horses' hooves behind her, a sound constant rather than diminishing, meant he would journey with her into town.

Elsbeth was glad. She liked the boy. She liked his childish ways. She also owed him much for his strong throwing arm and eagle-eyed aim.

It didn't take long for him to catch up and pull alongside. Elsbeth flashed him a smile, not entirely surprised when he instantly returned one of his own.

"We'll be coming back this way for my wagon," she said.

"Yup. With Mr. Billy in it and everything will be okay."

His willing acceptance of that which was necessary came as a great relief. No wonder she liked the boy.

If Elsbeth expected a brisk ride into the city, it was not to be. Not only was Cephas easily distracted by pretty stones, but long pine needles and leafy twigs also captured his attention. She didn't have the heart to refuse him the simple pleasure of stopping to collect a sample or two, especially since he shared his booty with Charlie who squealed with delight at each offering.

At one point they encountered a stranger. It wasn't a pleasant meeting. At first sight, Cephas leaped off his horse and practically threw himself at the man, for he was standing at the roadside whipping his donkey with a leather strap.

"Stop that! Stop that!" yelled Cephas while he grabbed the offending arm.

"Get off me, you young cur. Can't you see I'm trying to get some cooperation from this ornery beast?"

Elsbeth too had dismounted, disgusted by the man's

behavior. As if a memory string had been plucked, and almost before she realized she was doing it, she flung a Bible verse learned under her father's tutelage.

"Numbers 22," she shouted. "Why have you struck your donkey? Your way is perverse before me."

Only after the words left her mouth did she consider she might not have correctly remembered the lines. No matter. The effect was exactly what she wanted. The man backed away from both donkey and Cephas.

The stranger apparently was not a student of God's words and misinterpreted what she said.

"You want to know why?" he countered. "I'll tell you. This jackass won't budge no matter how hard I try to talk him into it."

"I didn't hear much talking."

He lifted the strap and snapped it in the air. "There are more ways than one to get the point across."

While Elsbeth and the man debated the definition of *talk*, Cephas moved to the donkey's side and studied the load that had been piled on its back.

"This here animal's just trying to tell you somethin' in the only language he knows," he said.

"Really?" returned the man. "*You* understand donkey language?"

"You done packed him all wrong."

At that, Cephas began to untie the myriad knots lashing together a hodgepodge of bags and boxes, picks and shovels. One by one he laid everything on the ground. He rubbed the donkey's ears and hummed a little melody until the animal calmed. Rifling through the gear, he found a blanket and proceeded to lay it across the donkey's back.

"He's been rubbed raw in spots. This'll help."

"Hey! That's *my* blanket!"

231

"It still is," interjected Elsbeth, "only now it'll give some comfort to your companion."

The man humphed but remained rooted while Cephas methodically rearranged the articles into a more balanced burden. When finished, he resurrected some of the leaves he'd collected and fed them to the donkey. Charlie too gave up the hoard he'd stuffed into his pockets.

After stroking the animal's muzzle, Cephas climbed onto his saddle.

"Treat him nice and he'll treat you nice."

Words of wisdom, thought Elsbeth, her pride in the young man swelling. She too mounted, and off they went, leaving one befuddled man behind.

The incident left Elsbeth breathless, angry...and concerned. Cephas had acted heroically but impulsively. It was one thing to sympathize with the suffering of one of God's lesser creatures, but quite another to rush headlong into what could have led to a much different outcome.

The episode clearly upset Cephas, although Elsbeth doubted it was for the same reason that set her on edge. He lost interest in gathering stones and sticks. He lost his smile. Even pointing out a gurgling creek or a decaying log sprouting a cluster of unusual toadstools failed to restore his curious nature.

Charlie too was strangely quiet, so the remainder of their trip passed in somber silence.

As the weary trio reached their destination, remnants of a fading sun cast Sacramento's jagged skyline into a silhouette of flat and pitched roofs, vacant lots, and the skeletons of partially-framed construction.

They bedded the horses and ate the last scraps from the provisions Elsbeth had brought from the wagon. It was barely enough to appease their hunger.

"We've got to find shelter for the night," she said, frowning as the silver tones of dusk threatened to dissolve into total darkness.

Nearby stood a common hall. Rows of cots crowded its large, open room. For a price, one could buy the privilege of occupying a bed during one of three daily shifts. Elsbeth approached the owner. His gaze drifted over her shoulder, an unvoiced question written on his face. She read the look.

"No husband," she said. "But I can pay."

She sprinkled flakes of gold into the man's outstretched hand and waited until his face lit with pleasure. Finally, she prompted with, "The accommodations, sir?" and he led them to a far corner and a single bed. There he shrugged and said, "All I got left."

Elsbeth held her tongue, but her skin crawled at the pervasive smell of sweat and the cacophony of grunts, snores and noxious coughs.

The man disappeared. When he returned, he carried a length of material and a hammer. He tacked an end of the fabric to each wall, creating a curtain and affording them a small triangle of privacy. Elsbeth thanked him then pulled the blanket from the cot and spread it on the floor.

"Cephas, you're going to have to sleep there."

"Shore thing, Miz Elsbeth," he said. "I don't mind."

She ruffled his hair. "I know. You're a good boy."

Within seconds, Charlie fell asleep, and soon a steady wheezing rose from the floor. Cephas too had nodded off. Only Elsbeth lay awake.

What was she to do?

The hours passed, or was it minutes? A sudden movement at her side took her by surprise. The bed creaked and groaned. Just in time she stifled the scream forming in her throat, for the bony shoulder pressed against her arm

233

could only be that of Cephas. He curled close and sighed. She didn't have the heart to shove him away. Instead, she lay perfectly still and listened to the softly breathing boys on either side—one wrapped in the sleep of youth, the other deep in the slumber of innocence.

A second child under her wing, she thought. Two now to comfort and protect. She fought the crush of this added responsibility. "Impossible," she whispered.

Late in the night, just as her own heavy-lidded eyes drooped closed, Elsbeth saw her future. She knew what she had to do.

II

The clang of a cowbell rent the air, followed by the voice of a man bellowing, "Six o'clock, it is. Those of you wanting another shift, pay now!"

Elsbeth dragged her eyelids open, for the long hours of travel and worry had finally taken their toll. Orientation to her surroundings was slow in coming. A sheet of some sort, hanging from wall to wall, blocked out the rest of the establishment. Grunts and groans and the scuffling of boots on the ground from the other side of the fabric brought to mind the boarding house of the evening before. She added a groan of her own and roused the boys to face another day.

A basin of water on a well-worn stand stood next to the door. Early risers had apparently made use of it, for a brown scum blanketed the surface. Elsbeth swished the grime to one side and dipped her handkerchief, avoiding as best she could the dirt which had settled to the bottom. A good face-washing, she told herself, would be refreshing, perhaps even a lucky omen for the task of finding Tom.

She scrubbed Charlie as well, all around, under his chin, behind his ears. Cephas must have thought it was a game of imitation. He plunged his hands into the water and gaily splashed it over his face.

Stepping into the early morning was a relief. The pale light of a hopeful dawn colored the eastern sky. Gone were the wretched smells of the night before, replaced by the mouth-watering aroma of freshly baked bread. That lovely smell emanated from an outdoor oven a few shops away. It took no prodding at all to lead the boys in that direction. She purchased a loaf and shared it among them.

Once her hunger was appeased, Elsbeth asked herself the salient question: Where do I start looking for Tom? The answer was naturally "anywhere and everywhere." Since it didn't matter where she began, this very spot was as good a place as any.

The bakers appeared to be a hard-working team of husband and wife. She divided the dough and shaped up the loaves while he shoveled a batch of three into the oven.

"Pardon me," said Elsbeth. "Has someone by the name of Tom Warner come to purchase your bread? He's from up north in the Oregon Territory."

With barely a pause in her work, the woman said, "Sorry, honey. We don't ask names, only that they show their money first."

Elsbeth sighed. It was not an auspicious beginning, rather an indication of how difficult it was going to be finding Tom in a place where names seemed to have no meaning.

She corralled the boys and moved along.

The young ones were in high spirits now their bellies were full. Charlie giggled. The merry sound tinkled in the air, reminding Elsbeth of the glass chimes that hung in the church garden back home in Howardstown. The music made her smile. The memory brought her pain.

She shook her head and looked around. The boys trailed a few paces behind.

"Piggyback! Piggyback!" Charlie begged and Cephas obliged. Her son's arms now encircled the older boy's neck, and with his nose pressed close to Cephas's cheek, he whispered in his ear.

How easily they've taken to one another, Elsbeth thought. Brothers. It surprised her to realize this was not the first time the word *brothers* had crossed her mind.

She envied their playful conspiracy and longed to throw off her troubles and join in their game.

The search for Tom, however, was all-consuming.

A miracle would help, she thought. Once she'd had unquestioned faith in the power of miracles. *Ask, and it shall be given you.* How often had she heard that in a Sunday school lesson? So much had happened since she'd been sent away that her faith in anything had been rattled. Would God even find her out here in the West or was she lost to his hearing?

Oh, dear God, she prayed, help me. She only mouthed the words, for the boys were within earshot, and she was reluctant to have them overhear her desperate plea.

As the day wore on, her feet began to hurt. Her pace slowed, and her high expectations flagged. She might as well have been throwing seeds onto barren soil, for her efforts yielded nothing.

Cephas tired of carrying Charlie, so she took his little hand in hers, giving it an encouraging squeeze. She wanted to cover a few more streets, but a scuffling of boots on the nearby boardwalk distracted her.

A tall man dressed in black from head to foot burst through a doorway, ushering a pair of drunks out onto the street.

"Sober up, you two," the man hollered. "I see you in my jail one more time, and I'll personally kick your sorry asses all the way back to Missouri." He gave them a shove, sending both off the walk and one to his knees. The jolt failed to erase the drunk's cockeyed grin. He merely tottered to unsteady legs and batted the dirt from his pants. When he spotted Elsbeth, he blurted out, "Marnin' mum."

The men swayed uncomfortably close. Elsbeth felt her flesh go cold. In her mind she scribed a line in the sand several feet in front of her and prepared to fend off any advance the two might make in violation of that imaginary boundary.

For a moment no one spoke.

"A loverly sight you is," ventured one of the drunks.

His partner laughed, swept hat into hand and added, "Madam, you looks in need of a good man, and I could use me a wife." He spread his arms wide and hiccuped. "I'm yours for the takin'."

"Go on with you, Lucas," chided the first. "The missus back in St. Louey might be of a different mind."

"Taint aimin' on tellin' her."

"Well, maybe I am. Anyway, women is too scarce for you to be ahoggin' two."

The man named Lucas punched the other's arm, who responded by swatting him with his hat. In the heat of the quarrel, they apparently forgot Elsbeth altogether. Arguing loudly, they staggered off.

The breath whistled out of Elsbeth, but she continued to keep a close eye on the pair.

"Good boys them," said the man in black as he watched the two lurch away. "Leastways on those days they haven't scraped together enough for a few drinks. Fresh air'll

237

straighten 'em out in no time."

With the drunks at a safe distance, Elsbeth smoothed the folds of her skirt and gathered her thoughts.

The night had given her only fitful sleep and that had been filled with alarming bits and pieces of her year and a half odyssey across the land. She was tired beyond belief. What had kept her going? The answer lay a heartbeat away. On the scales of life, Charlie mattered. He would get the childhood he deserved.

She faced the man in black and asked, "Would you be the sheriff?"

He winked and tucked a thumb under his lapel, thrusting forward a silver star. "At your service, ma'am."

"Sir, I'm looking for a man."

In a glance the sheriff appeared to add one lone woman and two young boys and come up with, "I see. No good, desertin' husband, eh?"

Although the lawman remained on the boardwalk and she in the street, Elsbeth felt violated. Was she so pathetically obvious a total stranger could read the secret scribblings of her heart with the turn of a single page?

"Not my husband...my intended," she quickly corrected, then wondered why it seemed so important to make this distinction. "I suspect he's in Sacramento, but I don't know..."

Before she could finish and inquire about Tom, the strident clang of voices interrupted. Three Mexicans shouted at an equal number of Chinese. The group accosted the sheriff. Waves of sing-song nonsense and rapid-fire, tongue-rolling gibberish crashed upon the shore of law and order. The argument escalated into fisticuffs, and the sheriff dove into the fray.

Hunting down an absent *intended* now seemed

frivolous work for a man with a badge, even to Elsbeth. She retreated to the children and led them away.

"No help from that quarter, boys," she snapped, yet in the dark cellar of her heart, she heard whispered a tiny sigh of relief.

Not more than a stone's roll away a second man in black stepped onto the stage of Elsbeth's morning. He wrestled with two wooden beams, trying to lash them crosswise with a length of rope. The pieces slipped and clattered to the ground. Sweat stained his clerical collar. Elsbeth peered beyond his weary face to a congregation of deserted benches, vacant pulpit and silent bell.

Church empty, jail full, she thought. Such a sorry harvest from these fields of gold.

While she puzzled over why she even cared, a gentle voice asked, "May I help you, child?"

Words formed on Elsbeth's tongue but speech failed. Something about the sweep of this man's hair and the spidery maze of lines around his eyes reminded her of her father. She frowned and touched her lips with trembling fingers, agonizing over whether to answer him and accept his help or walk away. Would the simple act of acknowledging this lookalike transcend the miles and effect an armistice she neither felt nor wanted? She blinked away an unexpected tear.

"Foolish me," she murmured more to herself than to him.

"The Good Book says, 'Be not foolish but understand the will of the Lord.'"

"Ephesians," she responded almost without realizing it.

"Exactly. Chapter five. You know your Bible well."

"Perhaps too well."

The reverend raised his eyebrows, waiting for Elsbeth

to go on. When she didn't, he turned his attention back to the recalcitrant lumber and tried once again to force it into the shape of a cross. A second time it fumbled out of his grasp and landed at his feet. He kicked the boards soundly. He swore softly.

"Oh, let *me* help *you*." Elsbeth hurried to his side. "Put your hands here…and here."

Once the two pieces were in position, she looped the rope up and over, around and behind. "Hold it tight while I make a knot."

When all was secured, the reverend carefully leaned the cross against the crude wooden arch from which hung the church's bell and admired the handiwork.

"I believe I owe you a return for this favor," he said. "Perhaps something more in my line of work. Carpentry is obviously not my strong suit."

"I think that goes without saying." Elsbeth's expression softened into a smile.

"Aha! The cares of this world can't be too burdensome. You haven't lost the capacity to laugh."

He offered her a makeshift pew and settled beside her. The planks teetered precariously but held. From his pocket the reverend pulled a wrinkled handkerchief and mopped both brow and neck.

"When I answered the Lord's call, I envisioned a lifetime of guiding lost souls into the House of God. I never once suspected I'd have to actually build the accursed thing. And me all thumbs at that."

He rocked back on the seat and laughed at his own humor until the bench began to wobble.

At the sound of laughter, Charlie urged Cephas closer. The bell cord dangled within reach. Charlie grabbed it and pulled, delighted when the bell found its voice. Dong-

dong-dong.

"Charlie! You mustn't." Elsbeth jumped up, but the reverend only laughed the harder.

"Let the boy play. If he attracts some attention, so much the better. I confess, my humble church has gone rather unnoticed as of yet."

"You're not quite what one would expect of a man of God, are you?"

"Alas, my dear girl, the Bishop thought so too." He spread his arms to encompass the city lot over which he presided. "Hence my new parish."

"We must be kindred spirits then. 'Strangers and exiles on the earth' as it were."

"We don't have to be strangers." He offered his hand. "Reverend Ogle. Marcus actually. By the way, that was from Hebrews."

She grinned and nodded. "I'm Elsbeth..." Here she stopped. Her hesitation lengthened into an uncomfortable pause before she added, "...Elsworth." When the name brought no sign of recognition, her shoulders went slack. She relaxed, thankful the tight circle of religious fraternity had apparently bypassed this man. The past was past, exactly where she wanted to leave it.

"Well, Elsbeth. Strangers no more. That leaves only fellow exiles." Reverend Ogle eyed her warmly. "I have a reputation as a good listener if you care to talk. Remember, I've a favor to return."

The story spilled out then, not quite from the beginning but enough to explain her pilgrimage into California. She ended with, "Charlie depends on me. And now there's Cephas to consider."

True to his promise Reverend Ogle listened, even now when Elsbeth lapsed into silent reverie, her memories rewriting themselves on her face: a twitch of her cheeks, the set of her mouth, the look in her eyes—all told an ever-changing tale of love and hurt, hope and disappointment.

When she resumed her story, her voice was subdued and the reverend had to cup a hand behind his ear to hear.

"When I was a little girl, I had a dream. Nothing frightfully outlandish like running off to become an actress. Just meet a boy and settle down. I used to embroider linen squares with tiny blue flowers in the corner. Round and round in the shape of a wreath with my initial in the middle—'E.' I always left a little room to one side for a second letter. I'd lay the napkins in a row on my hope chest, close my eyes and wonder whose initial I'd one day stitch into that space.

"I had my life all planned, down to the last detail: neat little farmhouse, asters under the windows. I even knew how I'd arrange my cupboards. It was to be a simple life, Sundays with family and friends, a husband and babies. Not so special, you see, but quiet…workaday…safe."

Dong-dong-dong. The church bell came alive again under Charlie's persistent hand. Elsbeth looked up as one awakened from a gentle sleep and fast-fading dream. She hardly remembered she had spoken.

The minister patted her hand and said warmly, "And it's your belief all will be well once reunited with your young man—this Brooster chap."

Elsbeth started. "I didn't say that. Why no… It's Tom I must find—Tom Warner. I've promised Charlie, and my word is my word."

Ogle sucked in his breath and held it briefly before answering.

"Unfortunately, I find myself still in your debt. I can't help you. I know nothing of this Warner fellow."

He seemed so distraught in his helplessness Elsbeth

242

laid a hand on his shoulder and rubbed it gently.

"No matter," she said quietly. "You've been most kind, and somehow I feel better even if I'm no further along in my search."

She shooed the boys into the street. But before she had a chance to follow, the minister approached from behind. He cleared his throat and when he spoke, his voice was low, almost furtive.

"As a man of the cloth, I'm not one to steer my flock into perdition."

"Perdition! I should say not."

"And...and not that I know of such things, mind you...first hand, that is."

Elsbeth eyed him curiously.

"For word of one or the other of your fellows, you might just want to ask around at the cribs."

When Elsbeth's mouth dropped open, he hastened on, pointing reluctantly.

"Three blocks down...south of *Green-Eyed Kate's. Corner.* Side street."

He spun on his heels and marched back to his open-air church, moving so rapidly he brushed against the new-made cross and sent it tumbling to the ground.

"Oh my," Elsbeth declared. "The Lord indeed works in mysterious ways." She stared in breathless wonder at the reverend's coattails flapping wildly in his retreat, much like a giant black bird about to take flight. Slowly her gaze shifted, and she now looked down the stretch of three long blocks.

She looked but made no move. Her mouth filled with the taste of spoiled milk at the idea of making public—in of all places a whorehouse—that she needed to tramp up and down the coast in search of the man she was to marry. But that's not what kept her feet rooted to the ground. The reverend's initial misunderstanding held her back. How had he come to such a false conclusion? And why did she now feel poised at a crossroads, not knowing which way to turn?

Charlie had also heard the reverend's directions. Eyes and mouth agape, he too stared along the length of the street.

"Is that where Papa is?" he asked, his voice barely above a whisper.

"No, Charlie," said Elsbeth. "I don't think so. At least I hope not exactly there. It's only a good place to ask about him."

"Can we go ask?"

"We could. Or...maybe we should fetch our wagon first. Make sure everything's all right with...the wagon."

"Mr. Billy's there," piped in Cephas. "He'll look after things."

"Don't you remember? Billy was awful sick."

"Aw, Miz Elsbeth, don't you worry none about him." Cephas chuckled and his whole body shook with the effort. "He's shore the one for takin' good care of *hisself.*"

"C'mon, Mama. Don't you want to find Papa?"

Four eyes bore down on her. Outnumbered she took the first step.

"Of course, sweetheart," she answered. "But let's not get our hopes up."

The three blocks seemed to fly by, though Elsbeth had made no particular effort to hurry. Soon enough Cephas pointed out the saloon, and they stopped. A buzz of voices drifted over the swinging doors. In the background an accordion squeezed out a tune to the accompaniment of bottles clinking against glass.

Elsbeth had no desire to leave the boys standing at the side of the street, but there didn't seem to be much choice. Despite the feminine sound to its name, *Green-Eyed*

244

Kate's did not appear a place for children. She also had no idea what to expect once she made it to the corner and onto the dreaded side street. Tracing an "X" in the dirt with her heel, she pointed.

"Don't move from here until I get back."

Alone now, she peeked around the corner along a row of tentlike structures. If there was a correct way to approach a prostitute, Elsbeth was at a loss. She was loath to simply barge into one of the rooms. Even being this close to a brothel flooded her cheeks with color.

Just then a movement took her by surprise. Down the row a figure emerged, though Elsbeth could see only his back. A moment later a girl followed him out. She wore a flimsy dress and ridiculous feather scarf. The man grabbed her breast and squeezed, then pulled her into a rough embrace and kissed her.

Embarrassed and disgusted by the scene in front of her, Elsbeth began to turn away. Not soon enough. The man released his hold and stepped around. Instantly, recognition flashed across both his and Elsbeth's faces. He scowled, reached up and brushed the hair from his forehead, exposing a nasty, purplish welt.

Elsbeth grabbed her skirts and bolted, screaming, "Run, boys, run."

III

"Cephas. Over here. Quickly."

Despite the urgency in Elsbeth's voice, Cephas remained anchored to the mark plainly visible beneath his boots. His upper torso wrenched this way and that as if trying to overpower the lower half of his body which stubbornly obeyed Elsbeth's earlier mandate not to move. He held Charlie's hand in an iron grip.

Elsbeth wasted no time with an explanation. She grabbed Cephas by the collar and Charlie around the waist and propelled them toward the nearest hope for concealment—the saloon.

As one they lunged across the boardwalk. The bar's double doors swung inward, plunging them into the cool, dimly-lit interior.

The little group stopped short, rendered blind by the transition from bright light to relative darkness. Elsbeth crinkled her eyes shut. Even though she couldn't see, she knew they were the center of attention, for the hubbub of a moment ago died to an eerie hush. When she opened her eyes, the room came quickly into focus: a hodgepodge of tables, rowdy looking crowd, and a larger-than-life nude reclining within a lavish gilt frame above the bar. Of the dozens of eyes staring in her direction, she immediately recognized two.

Tom Warner sat at a table. In front of him lay a plate of food, a half-empty glass of beer held mid-air. Beside him sat a woman dressed in green, her red hair secured high on her head with fancy combs.

Elsbeth's world ground to a halt on an axis made of both relief and doubt. Finding Tom had consumed her for months, but where was her voice now? Where the well-practiced words of their reunion? Here he was, in the flesh, yet what sprang to her lips was this.

"Is there a rear door? We must get out of here at once."

Warner leaped to his feet, a stunned look on his face, but he asked no questions. Instead, he gestured them toward the bar. A single long stride brought him to her side, but still he said nothing. With a firm hand, he steered them one by one behind the bar, past a dumbstruck bartender and through a partially-concealed door.

The door led outside into a narrow lane, facing the rear exits of buildings lining the next street over. The alley was cluttered with barrels and boxes, but Warner guided them through the maze and up a flight of steps. Elsbeth hugged the wall, whispering words with no meaning to Charlie, praying the mere sound of her voice would calm him and keep him from squirming in her arms. The child was a heavy load and the stairs were steep.

In a moment they all crowded onto a very small landing and waited while Tom unlatched a door and ushered them inside.

In the corner stood a bed covered with a straw mattress and rumpled blanket. She deposited Charlie there with a stern warning not to make a sound. A small table and chair had been shoved against the outside wall where the room's solitary window made a valiant effort to emit light despite dirt and cobwebs layering its four small panes. On the floor lay a faded square of worn carpet. Tom threw aside a corner to expose a grate which, in the colder season, would draw up heat from the room below. Saloon noises funneled through it now.

Elsbeth stepped to the grate, mirroring Tom's hunched-over stance, and looked through the slats.

She gasped. The grate offered a clear view into the bar below. She needed nothing more than the top of his head to recognize the soldier who had taken Charlie.

"Where'd they go?" she heard him demand.

The bartender shrugged.

"Don't tell me you don't know," growled Pierce,

247

reaching for the man's throat. "You can see everything from here."

The man backstepped to the wall, jostling the nude. "I…I only serve the drinks. That's all."

A green-clad arm shot into Elsbeth's rectangle of vision and stayed the soldier's hand.

He spun toward her and hissed, "Keep outta this, lady. This ain't no business of yours."

"That's where you're wrong, stranger. This is very much my business. I'm Kate Malone."

"Th-that's green-eyed Kate," stammered the bartender, clawing at the fingers around his neck.

Pierce snarled at the man who broke free his grasp and scurried from sight.

"Where's the girl? I know she's hiding here somewhere."

"Now why would you want a girl when you could have a woman instead?"

More of the low-cut green dress came into view. A cap of red curls leaned close to the soldier. An arm snaked through his and hugged it close.

Elsbeth understood what the woman was doing. She secretly glanced at Tom, knowing Kate's assistance clearly wasn't for her benefit. While her head was turned, the sound of a chair being kicked and wood splintering filled the upstairs room. When Elsbeth looked again through the grate, the square below was empty, though a heavy tread of boots and the squeak-bang of the bar's swinging doors left no doubt Pierce had departed.

When the steady hum of conversation resumed, Tom hooked a toe under the rug and flipped it over the opening.

"Elsbeth! What in God's name are you doing here? And Charlie?" He glanced at Cephas. "And what's this one

248

doing with you?"

"You've no cause to abuse the Lord's name, Tom. I'm here because of you."

For a second time that morning Elsbeth recounted her story—the trip into California, the encounter with Clayton Pierce. She skimped on some of the specifics but concluded with, "He's pure evil. He took Charlie and would have killed us all if not for Cephas."

At the mention of the boys' names, the dam of silence burst. Squeals of delight poured forth, and the two young ones descended on Tom. He accepted the adulation, thumped Cephas on the back, returned Charlie's hugs.

"And all this because of who?" he asked Elsbeth when the boys' excitement died down.

"That soldier's looking for Billy, but I just know he means him harm."

"Billy?"

"Brooster. From Oregon City. One of the gold seekers who—"

"I know Brooster. Not a very sociable fellow, is he? A real loner."

"I'm afraid I wouldn't know about that."

"Question is...why would this Pierce assume *you* know where Brooster is?"

Irritation crept into Elsbeth's voice at the barrage of questions. "I'll explain that all later. But now it's your turn to answer a few—"

A light tap at the door cut her short. Without waiting to be acknowledged or invited, in walked green-eyed Kate.

"Tom," she said.

"Katherine."

Elsbeth wondered at the woman's boldness in entering the room and at the single-word exchange that ensued. The woman's name meant nothing, but the vivid hair and flamboyant attire tweaked at her memory.

The room was now cramped, the air charged with a friction that hadn't been there a moment ago. The silence lingered, stretched almost to the breaking point. The sun had dropped to the afternoon side of the building, and just as the woman moved closer to the window, a shaft of light pierced its grime and reflected off something on her garment.

A glitter of gold.

Elsbeth stared, all at once knowing where she had seen this Kate Malone before. What sparkled so brightly was a bead of gold worked into a delicate bow from which dangled a heart-shaped locket. The locket was inscribed with the letter "*E*."

The pin belonged to Elsbeth.

IV

Dust motes pirouetted in the sunlight, their animated dance a curious counterpoint to Elsbeth, whose rigid jaw and frosty stare betrayed her feelings. She couldn't take her eyes from the locket—*her* locket—pinned to this other woman's dress.

Kate Malone spoke first. "Tom?"

In answer he inclined his head ever so slightly. "Katherine."

Again, one word communicated much more than just a name, for Kate nodded in Elsbeth's direction, turned and slipped through the doorway.

"In the future it'd suit you to be a little more civil to my partner, Elsbeth."

"Your partner?"

"Well, you don't imagine for one minute I could actually afford a going concern like this? Took everything I was able to scrape out of that miserable mountain up there. Which wasn't much, mind you, even after a summer of bustin' my ass."

"Tom! The children."

"It's the godawful truth, Elsbeth. I didn't have enough until Katherine took a fancy to that little trinket of yours. It clinched the deal."

Here Tom broke into a broad grin and enveloped her in a bear hug.

"Looks like you've got yourself a stake in the business too."

Elsbeth choked as if the air had been sucked from the room.

"Me? Never."

She tore from his arms but immediately realized Charlie and Cephas watched from the bedside with rapt attention. She tempered her anger and lowered her voice.

"Tom, this is a saloon…and…and more."

"That's what brings in the most cash. Just wait. In a couple months when snow drives 'em all down into town, it'll bring in even more. A gen-u-ine bonanza."

Elsbeth thought of the precious snip of hair the locket had once held and the message it was supposed to convey: *Don't forget what you left behind.* She fought the emptiness Tom's words engendered, but Charlie was to be considered, and so she read into his next statement a certain amount of cheer.

"I'm saving every nickel too. By spring I ought to have enough money socked away."

She nodded, cautiously mimicking the spirit of his

enthusiasm. "Yes, Tom, that's it. Save this winter, and we can be back in time for the spring planting."

"Back? No, not back. Here in Sacramento. I've scouted another location. It's small but I'll add on. Make it real high class even."

He stopped talking then. Elsbeth studied his eyes. They revealed nothing but gazed off into a far corner. She twisted her neck around, seeking what he saw, knowing even as she did that Tom had stepped through an invisible door and into a time and place where she could not follow. She jumped when he suddenly punched a fist into his palm and swore.

"I'm not about to dig around in *any* kind of dirt again."

If he noticed her face collapse into a mask of despair, he gave no indication. Instead, he placed his hands on her shoulders and rambled on about faro tables, a dance stage and more. Elsbeth's would be the extra pair of hands he needed. "Even Cephas can be useful for cleaning up and the like," he murmured.

Elsbeth breathed in through tightly clenched teeth. She shoved his hands aside and issued an ultimatum of her own.

"I will not be a handmaiden to drunks and whores."

The words hung in the air, then settled with the dust. Charlie whimpered.

"Your place is beside me," Tom said firmly.

"My place?"

"A helpmate and all. I take care of you and you respect my calling."

"You have a *calling* to be a saloonkeeper?"

"You know what I mean. A man has his dreams, and he can't be held back. That's just the way it is."

Speechless, Elsbeth struggled to find the right words to point out his error, but all too quickly she realized Tom had spoken the truth. Hadn't her own mother stood by in silent surrender under the force of her father's injured pride? Hadn't the Emigrants' Road been paved with the blood and sorrow of submissive wives? And even the likes of Kate Malone, hadn't she gained independence only by forfeiting life, body and soul to the basest needs of men?

That's just the way it is.

Something bumped against the back of her legs. When she looked behind, there was Charlie, burying his face in the folds of her skirt, wetting it down with his tears. The weeping boy drew Tom's attention too. Together, he and Elsbeth bent to comfort the child. Their fingers touched.

"We can work this out."

The words echoed strangely, for each had come to the same conclusion, and they had spoken as one.

Tom gently tousled the boy's hair while Elsbeth stroked the backs of his hands. Soon the torrent dried into two salty tracks snaking down the youngster's face. They coaxed him onto the bed again. Though at Charlie's expense, the episode had served to unite Tom and Elsbeth in a common cause and blunt the jagged edge of anger. Warner ushered her to the only chair, dragging it away from the table so she could sit.

"We've got us a pretty sticky situation here," he said, leaning over her, yet seeming to speak more to himself.

"Certainly a little compromise would go a long way toward settling our differences."

Expecting a reply, she glanced up, but Tom pushed back from the table and paced a heavy-footed oval from window to door and back. Elsbeth pursed her lips and wondered if they were even talking about the same thing. She didn't have long to wait for an answer.

"Tell me where he is," he demanded.

"Where who is?"

"Brooster. Who else?"

She hesitated. "I…I don't know."

"That soldier downstairs sure thought you do. Don't you see, if we tell him where to find Brooster, we'll be rid of him…them. After all, it wouldn't do to have you and the boys hiding up here all the time."

"You can't just hand Billy over to a man like Pierce."

"From what you've told me, those two are nursing a grudge of some sort. But that has nothing to do with us." His eyebrows arched upward. "Or does it?"

Elsbeth ignored the innuendo. "You saw how Pierce was," she said. "He's a mad man. And remember I told you he was fully prepared to shoot me and Cephas and a two-year-old child. It's the devil he is."

Tom circled the chair, stopping behind her to brush his fingers along the nape of her neck. She hadn't remembered his hands being so coarse. She edged forward in the seat, away from his touch.

"Let's make a clean start of this. Where is he, Elsbeth?"

"Really, Tom, I don't know. A few days ago, but not now."

"It's for your own protection."

"I said I don't know."

She leaned her elbow on the table and placed her chin on her hand. The squeak of floorboards told her Tom retreated across the room. A moment later, squeals of delight suggested he wrestled playfully with Charlie. She was surprised to hear him say, "Tell you what, Elsbeth. First month our profit tops two hundred, I'll talk Katherine into

254

selling back that locket of yours. Doesn't that make you feel better?"

Although she had been furious he had so easily parted with her locket, the cherished possession seemed tarnished now. She bit her lip and pretended to stare out the window.

The view was of the side street. Although the glass was smudgy, a movement below caught her eye. An errant breeze ruffled the canvas sheets that served as rooftops to the row of cubicles adjacent to the building. They waved at her gaily—or was it maliciously?—for she knew without a doubt they hid a dirty little business of which she was now, however unwillingly, a part.

Her whole body sagged, senses numb. So, although her eyes remained trained on the street, at first she didn't notice the figure enter the scene. When she did, she started. The sun shaded the man's face. It was his clothing she recognized.

Elsbeth felt her heartbeat quicken. She stole a glance at Tom, fearful the pounding tha-dum, tha-dum had alerted him to her panic. He still played with Charlie, dropping an oversized hat onto the child's head, then yanking it off again. He paid her no mind.

She turned back to the window, straining for a better look, but this time the street was empty. Elsbeth rubbed her eyes. Had she seen him...Billy...or was her mind playing tricks? A second look. No clue. In a day filled with uncertainty, this was one question she would not allow to go unanswered.

Slowly she rose and crossed to the door.

The outside landing was not much wider than the steps leading up to it. The platform extended past the door, just barely. A post at each corner ran from ground level to the overhanging eave above, but there was no railing, and the lack of protection against a careless misstep unsettled her stomach. With infinitely more caution than she had exercised on the way up, Elsbeth began her descent. One hand lifted the hem of her dress to keep it from tangling her feet while the other slid along the outer wall of the saloon. In this way she maintained her balance and at the same time found an occasional fingerhold. Despite the precarious stairs, Elsbeth couldn't push from her mind the question, "Why am I doing this?" She had followed Tom into California, and she had found him. The nightmare that started with Billy would at last be over…with Tom.

End of story.

But step after step…against will and reason…she continued down.

"Ouch!"

She jerked her hand from the wall. A wood fragment, long and thin and ragged, protruded from the tip of her index finger. A droplet of blood obscured the entry point. Sight of the splinter mesmerized her as if it had materialized out of thin air and not the rough-cut timber to her left. She sank down onto the step, gingerly grasped the sliver and yanked it out. Glistening beads of red swelled and trailed along her finger. She shook her hand and they fell to the step below her feet. Her finger began to throb. She half-rose, driven by a desire to seek comfort in her mother's arms, but reality—a cold and heartless stranger—dashed in. Elsbeth sighed, raised her finger to her mouth, and stanched the flow of blood by sucking at the wound.

Then she was on her feet. Can't just sit here, she thought. I must at least warn him.

"Well, whadaya know, Missy? Fancy meeting you here."

Elsbeth grabbed for the wall to keep from stumbling on the last step.

"Surprise. Surprise. You didn't really think that little disappearing act of yours was gonna work, didja?"

Clayton Pierce ducked from behind a haphazard stack of packing crates. He leaned a hip against a wooden barrel in the crowded alleyway and crossed his arms loosely over his chest. Despite his relaxed stance, Elsbeth could see by the set of his feet he was ready to spring if she dared move. He wagged a finger back and forth between himself and Elsbeth. "You and me, Missy. We're gonna have a serious little chat."

"I have nothing to say to you." She thrust her chin forward, peering over his shoulder in an attempt to avoid his eyes. Despite an effort to remain aloof, her throat constricted and her palms began to sweat.

On the building behind Pierce a window cut into the wall mirrored activity taking place on the street fronting the saloon. The scene was apparently out of Pierce's line of vision, for he continued to glare at her, but the reflection afforded Elsbeth a view of what was happening near the cribs. The uneven surface of the glass yielded two figures that wavered with every movement. One was a girl. The other wore a familiar shirt with unmistakable elbow patches of red.

Her breath caught. Her face froze. She prayed she had checked her reaction in time. Deliberately she forced herself to look at the man in front of her. Purple flesh discolored one side of his face. A scab oozed yellow pus. Stubble blackened his jawline. His eyes were bloodshot. Mouth a thin, unreadable line.

Elsbeth shuddered. This must certainly be the look of Satan, she thought.

Suddenly Pierce tensed as if he read her mind and took exception to the comparison.

With all her heart Elsbeth wished to shout out, but to whom would she call? How many precious seconds would it take for Tom to hear and react and make it to her side? Pierce openly displayed a side holster strapped to his leg. The gun in it wasn't far from his hand.

Then there was Billy.

What if he responded to a call of distress and raced around the corner into a trap she herself had baited with a scream?

"Well, I'm waiting," she finally said. She crossed her own arms and tapped an impatient foot. "Ask what you will."

"You're all of a sudden mighty cooperative, Missy."

"If you're looking for Mr. Brooster, he's not here, not anywhere near here."

"My bones tell me different. I think you're lying."

"Then take your bones elsewhere. He's not in the city." Slowly Elsbeth cleared the bottom tread and sidestepped to the right, into the shadow of the overhead landing. When Pierce's eyes followed, his gaze drawn farther from the side street, she said, "Last I saw him, he was at that settler's camp down the valley aways. Ill he was." She nodded for emphasis. "Gravely ill. Probably dead by now. I doubt he could have survived. No…I'm sure."

Pierce's mouth twisted into a sneer.

"Whatever score you have to settle," she continued. "There's no one to settle it with. You might as well go back to wherever you came from."

She tossed her hair boldly as if to signal the end of their discussion. The gesture was a ruse. She felt no confidence, no courage. She wished only to cover up a second, clandestine glance at the windowpane. Once again she saw the patch of street with its squares of canvas flapping in the wind, but beyond that nothing. The couple had disappeared. Her breathing returned to normal.

Pierce shifted his weight and stroked the scruff on his chin. The faint scratch mingled with the drone of horseflies and the muted hum of the city.

"There's still the matter of a missing horse," he said. "My horse. Folks in these parts don't take lightly to such thievery."

"You'll find it properly bedded in a stable near the sleeping hall. I suggest you go get it."

"I'd surely enjoy the pleasure of your company."

"I made the mistake of going with you once. I'll not do it again."

In a single, sudden movement, Pierce closed the gap between them, the gun now grasped firmly in his hand.

"Actually, Missy, I insist."

CHAPTER 12

Tangled Webs

I

A man's thirst, among other appetites, could strike him at any hour, so morning, noon or night the saloon did a brisk business. Billy stood on the walkway outside, pondering his next move. A thin haze of tobacco smoke drifted out over the barroom doors when three strangers emerged and nodded to him.

"Afternoon, stranger," said one, touching the wide brim of his hat. Before the man could pass by, Billy blocked his way.

"'Scuse me, sir." He inclined his head toward the still-swinging doors. "Might you know if Tom Warner's in there?"

The man stroked his chin. "Lemme think. He was earlier. Can't say for certain now. Sorry."

He glanced at the man's companions, but they too shook their heads.

"Thanks anyway," said Billy as he stepped aside.

With a mixture of regret and anticipation, Brooster approached the entrance. A placard read *Green-Eyed Kate's.* Elsbeth's face flashed across his mind, and he decided his preference in eyes leaned heavily in favor of blue. Then he thought of Cephas. A confrontation with Tom lost much of its meaning without the lad. After all, it was the boy who had been taken advantage of, and the boy who needed to see Warner's true colors. Scenes from the earthquake rushed in— the terror and panic. Billy shivered as he relived the shake and roll of the ground beneath his feet and the desperate cries for help. When disaster struck, Tom Warner had abandoned not only Cephas but his partners and survived the ordeal with a grubstake that wasn't rightfully his.

Clammy palms warmed to newfound anger. Warner would pay all right—for a lot of things. On the other hand, if anyone knew where Elsbeth might be, it would be this same Tom Warner. He would have to be careful.

The swing of the batwing doors had ceased. Billy took a deep breath, grasped the shoulder-high rails and shoved.

The saloon was about half full, the patrons finishing up a midday meal or conversing at tables in twos and threes. Several men lined the bar, each with a knee cocked and foot propped on a shiny rail. A card game was in progress near the window. No one inside paid him much attention. He marched to the bar, pushed aside a pair of dirty glasses, and laid his rifle on the grimy surface.

"Be with ya in a minute," the bartender said.

Billy shifted position, now pressing his back to the bar. He scanned the room, first examining faces. No luck. He repeated his survey, this time looking at backs, sizing up build, age and hair color. He could make out no one who resembled Warner. A sole woman, none other than the one who had accosted him that morning, moved from table to table. She threw him a cursory glance, apparently satisfied he'd returned as promised, before continuing the circuit among her customers. No one else seemed to recognize him.

In this place he was just another Forty-Niner, an anonymous nobody in the brotherhood of eager hopefuls stopping off for a beer on the way to riches.

"What'll it be, mister?" asked the bartender.

Billy turned to face him. "Information's what I'm looking for."

At these words the bartender lost his smile. He had been bent congenially over the bar, but now he bolted upright, jostling the naked lady portrait and rattling bottles on the shelf behind him.

Billy eyed him curiously but continued. "I understand a Tom Warner from Oregon Territory is the owner here."

The bartender's brow glistened with sweat. His hand massaged his throat. "D-depends."

"On what? Either you know Warner or you don't."

While he waited for the man to dab his forehead with a bar cloth, Billy tuned his ear to sounds overhead. Ripples of laughter. A scuffle of feet. His glance swept upwards, scrutinizing the ceiling. Curls of sticky flypaper bobbed and twirled in the air current, their payloads a convincing endorsement of this newfangled device. Between the joists Billy noted a cut in the upstairs floorboards. A grate to circulate the heat had been fitted into the opening. The vent, however, was not empty but framed a face. Alert, inquisitive eyes stared down. A child's mouth formed a perfect "O."

"Charlie?" he whispered. This was the little boy he'd seen in Elsbeth's arms. And where the child was, so must be the child's mother.

Without waiting for the bartender to find his tongue, Billy turned abruptly and stalked out.

The front of the building offered no entry to the second floor, so Brooster rounded the corner, skirted the curtained cubicles of Kate's frontier-style bordello, and found the alley behind. A stairway there led to what appeared to be living quarters directly over the saloon. He hustled toward the steps and had mounted two when he stopped. A puzzled expression etched deep creases at the corners of his eyes. Several dark circles stained the lighter wood of the stair. He stooped and swiped his fingers over the spots. The circles smeared.

"Blood?"

Billy didn't think. He reacted. He bound up the steps and pounded on the door.

"Elsbeth! Elsbeth, are you all right? Let me in. Elsbeth, please!"

Even while he called out, he steeled his shoulder and heaved himself against the door. It flew open. The momentum hurtled him into the room. Just in time he checked his forward lunge, for another step would have thrown him against a startled Tom Warner. In a voice rimed in disgust, Billy spat out a single word.

"You."

Brooster glared while Warner staggered back a step, then two. Tom's leg caught the corner of the chair and he grabbed at it, saving himself from a fall but teetering awkwardly. With a curse on his lips, he dragged the chair between himself and Billy as if to fend off attack though none was threatened. "What do *you* want?"

Billy didn't answer, just raised his hand as if the sight of bloodied fingers explained it all.

It didn't and the standoff continued.

A rush of memories, none good, flooded in, feeding Billy's resentment of Tom. His face hardened. His cheeks turned red. He hardly noticed Cephas barge forward, bump the chair aside, and greet him with a crooked grin.

"Howdy, Mister Billy," he said and punched Brooster

263

playfully on the arm. "Come to your senses, did ya? I knew you would. Told Miz Elsbeth that. 'Billy can take care of hisself,' I said."

The mention of Elsbeth's name snapped Billy back to the moment. Firmly he gripped the boy's shoulder and looked straight into his eyes. "Where is she, Cephas? Where's Elsbeth?"

"Here with us." Cephas spread his arms in an all-encompassing sweep. Billy wondered if he meant their immediate surroundings or if the gesture included Sacramento City as well, if not all of California. He quickly glanced away and inspected the sparsely-furnished room. For the first time he saw Charlie, sitting cross legged on the floor and looking on the verge of tears.

"I mean now. Where is she right now?"

Before the boy could answer, Tom stepped forward and elbowed him away.

"Some answers first," he demanded. "What's your business with Elsbeth?" The two squared off again.

"No, you answer. Where is she?"

"She's safe with me."

"Safe? You call this safe?" Once more Billy held up his hand. The blood-stained fingers silenced Tom.

Cephas crept to Billy's side, straining for a glimpse of what caused the harsh exchange of words. At the sight of the blood, he gasped. His eyes opened wide, the irises clear blue islands in a sea of white.

"She only went outside," he whispered.

"She's not outside now."

Tom found his voice and, with an edge honed to his words, said, "Then she must have taken a walk. Perhaps she needed a breath of fresh air."

"The air right here seems perfectly fine. So maybe she

took a walk or maybe it was something else."

The Adam's apple in Tom's neck bobbed and he licked dry lips. "I wonder if...?" He hesitated and the pause dragged on.

"Out with it, Warner," Billy roared.

"There was someone here earlier looking for you. Mean son-of-a-bitch. Thought Elsbeth knew where you were."

Now it was Billy's turn not to answer.

"Soldier. Name of Pierce," Tom continued. "What do you know of him?"

"You called it right...a real SOB. Where is he?"

"Gone."

Billy snorted. "Gone, huh?" He started to pace the floor. Under his breath he said, "I doubt it."

"What?"

"That man has a knack for showing up where you least expect him."

"What are you saying?"

Billy stabbed a finger at Tom. "If Elsbeth's gone missing, that worm's involved and I hold you accountable."

"Me? Not so fast, Brooster. His beef is with you."

"She is out there alone, unprotected, thanks to you."

"I sure wouldn't place her in danger and, dammit, I want her found."

"No, *I* want her found."

Tom took a step, his advance matched by Billy's own, the two now nose to nose.

"Listen, Brooster. Stay outta my way. Elsbeth's my wife..."

"Your wife?"

"Well, almost."

Billy sucked in his breath. One corner of his lip

curled. *"Almost wife* or not, I intend to make damn sure Elsbeth's come to no harm."

Tom grabbed his arm, preventing his retreat. "Not so fast."

"I've wasted enough time yammerin' here with you," countered Billy. "Unless you're coming—and I mean right now—get a good look at my back 'cause that's all you're gonna see."

He flung off the restraining hand and made for the door.

"Wait a minute, Brooster. I like you less than poison, but we've got to work together."

With that Tom knelt beside the cot, shoved his arm into the space beneath and pulled out a Winchester. While still on his knees, he rapped sharply on the wooden vent and crooked a finger at someone down below. Shortly the click of footsteps mounting the stairs filled the room. Kate Malone appeared and hurried past Billy, raising an inquiring eyebrow at him as she did.

"I need someone to keep an eye on the little one," said Tom. "We have to leave. Shouldn't be long."

She nodded. "I'll get one of the girls."

"Appreciate it."

Barely an arm's length away, Charlie huddled against the wall. Tom bent and patted the child on the head. "We'll be back soon, son. Meantime, you stay here with Katherine…or whoever."

The boy's face dissolved in a look of terror. His eyes had been locked on Tom's, but now they traveled to the green dress and slowly upward to the green eyes. He let out a howl and clutched at Tom's sleeve, holding tight until Tom prized the boy's fingers away.

Billy forced a smile he didn't feel and stooped to child

266

level. "It'll be all right," he said softly. "Your Mama's lost but we're going to find her and bring her back."

A tiny frightened voice answered him. "Promise?"

"Promise."

The doorway proved to be another battleground with each jostling the other to exit first. Tom won. No sooner had Billy followed than Cephas was at his heels, wrestling with a canvas pouch. He tried to maneuver the strap over his head but managed instead to tangle it in the metal slide of his suspenders. His arms flailed in all directions until Billy yanked the strap free.

"It's Miz Elsbeth's," the boy explained. "She told me, 'Don't let this outta your sight.'"

Billy clapped him on the back and the door swung shut behind them.

The three made a curious trio walking the streets of Sacramento. Recognizing the urgent need for haste, yet not trusting Warner out of his sight, Billy constantly adjusted his pace. Too fast and Warner was behind him, impossible to watch or anticipate his next move. Too slow and Tom halted, apparently fearing the same, until Billy caught up. Stiffly and cautiously they traveled abreast with Cephas leading the way.

Without a clear goal in mind, Tom and Billy followed the lad. The route was haphazard. There were detours down side streets, across vacant squares of property, to the river and back. They described Pierce to total strangers to no avail. A woman in a frontier town was the exception rather than the rule, so that should have been easier. It wasn't. Even though time and again Billy provided details of Elsbeth's looks and dress, they had no success. Tom, however, scowled at Billy's apparent familiarity with the object of their search.

They swept through waist-high scrambles of weeds, poked behind woodpiles, even hoisted themselves up the sideboards of wagons left unattended in the street. They invaded saloons and gambling tents. No possible hiding place escaped their attention.

Suddenly Tom swore, for they found themselves in front of Kate's saloon. "Dammit, Cephas, you've trailed us back to where we started."

Weary of mind and almost ill at the thought of what their search might uncover, Billy hadn't noticed the familiar facade of *Green-Eyed Kate's* come into view up the street.

At the sharp words, Cephas cowered like a faithful pup who had been swatted for some misbehavior beyond its understanding.

"S-sorry," he whimpered. "You didn't tell me where to go."

"We don't *know* where to go, but even a blind fool wouldn't traipse us around in circles."

Billy interrupted. "Don't fret, Ceph. We're all worried about Elsbeth, and we're just trying to figure out where she might have gone."

"Is she going far?"

"What difference does that make?" erupted Tom.

"If I was goin' far, I'd want the horses."

The two men looked first at Cephas then at each other. Direction had come from the least likely source.

Although they still cast anxious, searching looks into darkened doorways and shadowed alleys, as well as exchanging furtive glances aimed at each other, the two walked swiftly, no longer jockeying for position. Their aim was now clear. They headed toward the heart of town where the blacksmith's shop doubled as a livery, Cephas tight on their heels.

Before reaching the stables, they ran into a dozen men or more who had gathered in a loose circle around a wagon stopped dead in the middle of the street. The commotion centered on the wagon's driver who shook a fist and hollered at someone hidden among the crowd. Off to the side, a youngster of about seven or eight lingered in front of a shop where barrelheads next to the entrance displayed an assortment of the store's wares. Shotgun shells and tin canteens shared space with sacks of meal and pyramids of fruit. The boy fingered a bright red apple at the back of the pile and out of the shopkeeper's view. Billy almost laughed at the impending act of petty thievery but sobered quickly when recognition dawned. He remembered the boy's eyes had been cold for one so young, unblinking too as he had watched Billy flee the wagon train and scurry into the mountains. It seemed so long ago and at the same time only yesterday. And was it really only yesterday he'd run for his life at the blast from a shotgun?

His attention was once again drawn to the loud disturbance. He didn't need to sort out the words or even distinguish the voice of the man clenching the reins of the wagon.

The boy's name was Chet. The angry driver, his father.

First Pierce, now Holt. His past was ganging up on him.

The fracas also interested Tom, and he hastened toward it. Billy, however, had no desire to rush headlong into his past in the form of Chester Holt. Making sure neither Tom nor Cephas were looking his way, he sidestepped into a field, along the side of a carpenter's workshop, and under the cover afforded by a shed propped against the building. He immediately tripped on a stack of rough boards but righted himself quickly and slid behind what looked like a finished cabinet or crate. He leaned his rifle against the wall, his mind whirling at this new set of circumstances. He needed a moment to think, to plan his next move, but his thoughts muddled when he gave the box a second look. He cringed, for the casket appeared to be just about his size.

Billy closed his eyes and willed himself to calm down. He inhaled long and slow, but before he could let the breath out, he was struck by a new awareness—another surprise in a day full of them.

He was not alone.

II

Thunder. She was certain the rumbling she heard was thunder, but the immediate threat came not from the weather, for the sky remained clear and blue.

"It won't be but a minute and I'll be missed." Elsbeth's voice rang strong despite the gun pointed at her chest.

"I'll do the talking, Missy. You keep your mouth shut."

"I will not."

In answer the soldier reached out and slapped her, almost knocking her off her feet. "You'll do as you're told."

Elsbeth decided to obey…at least for the moment.

As soon as they left the relative seclusion of the passageway behind the saloon, Pierce holstered his pistol. He snaked an arm around her waist and dug probing fingers into her side.

"We're just a happy couple out for a stroll." He snickered and wrested her closer, the hard outline of his gun bruising her hip.

Elsbeth struggled to gain some distance between them, but he would not relax his hold. Repeatedly her billowing skirt tangled in between his legs. When she gathered in a handful of material and attempted to pull it free, he hugged her tighter, sometimes lifting her clear off the ground.

And the man stank.

She tried not to gag and found the only relief from the foul odor of his unwashed body came when she held her breath...for as long as possible, until she feared fainting. Then she averted her head and inhaled through pursed lips. She did this three or four times before noticing that passing strangers—grizzled old men as well as lads boasting no more than chin fuzz—paused and stared. Not at the sight of such an unlikely pair, but at her.

What did their faces tell of them? Lovesick fool? Homesick child? Elsbeth recalled her morning encounter with the two drunks just out of jail. Women were scarce in California. Families had been left behind while the men quenched a thirst for adventure and fortune. Most likely, Elsbeth reminded them of a faraway wife, mother or sweetheart.

At once an idea took shape. To the next passerby Elsbeth flashed a brilliant smile. Immediately the young man stopped. Pierce snarled at the bold admirer, but his surliness failed to discourage the fellow who not only continued to gape at Elsbeth but actually approached. Silently Elsbeth prayed the young man's attentions would confuse Pierce and allow her to escape, but without warning Pierce stepped into the man's line of sight. He pulled Elsbeth into his arms and, crushing her against his chest, kissed her roughly on the mouth. Too startled to scream, Elsbeth choked and swiped the back of her hand across her lips. It did little to wipe away the vile taste he had left behind.

271

"The little bride," said Pierce to the stranger, but the squint of his eyes sent a different message, and the young man fled.

Elsbeth wilted. She needed a different tactic. A bigger distraction than a smile. A picture from her years in Ohio formed in her mind. It was a ploy used, not by her young friends but by the older girls. She had thought it a silly ruse, but the boys fell for it every time. And she was armed with the simple item required to carry it out...if only she could reach it.

This very morning she had used it to wash Charlie's face. Although it was still damp, she had tucked it up her sleeve where it was held in place by the cuff of her dress. The handkerchief wasn't terribly fancy. It had no lace, only a neat row of picot stitches crocheted along the border and her embroidered initial in a corner. It could not be mistaken for a discarded scrap of unwanted material.

The problem was it was in the wrong sleeve. To extract it, she would need to first free her arm from Pierce's iron grip. She attempted pulling away, but he reacted to her sudden movement by crushing her more firmly against him.

Elsbeth wasn't to be thwarted. She tried a different tactic, a manufactured sneeze, followed closely by a second so explosive as to double her over. This startled her captor, and he loosened his hold, just long enough for her to retrieve the handkerchief and dab it under her nose.

With a prayer in her heart, she let it slip from her fingers and drift to the ground. Within seconds shovels and pans clattered as three men dropped their gear and jumped to retrieve the dainty handkerchief.

The victor rushed forward, the prize in his hand.

"'Scuse me, ma'am. You've lost your handkerchief."

Pierce locked his arm tighter, but Elsbeth extended

her free hand, making sure her fingers brushed against those of her benefactor. Her eyes sought his. She smiled warmly.

The man blurted, "The very sight of a proper woman after so many months on the road lifts my heart. It does indeed."

His companions moved in closer and nodded their agreement while the first man continued. "Be much obliged to you, sir, for the honor of exchanging a few words with your lady. A bit of home, as it were, to take with me into the goldfields."

Pierce growled but Elsbeth spoke up.

"A small token," she said to the man while nodding toward Pierce, "might weigh in your favor. Offer him something and I'll be pleased to accompany you a short distance on your journey."

She cocked her head and lifted an elbow as if inviting an escort. In unison three hands dipped into three pockets and emerged as fists, clutching crinkled bills and silver coins. The men converged on Pierce. They bumped him. They jostled him, each eager to be the first to pay for the privilege of taking Elsbeth's arm. Thrown entirely off guard by the strangers, Pierce relinquished his hold.

Free, at last.

Elsbeth paused only a moment, just long enough to grab one of the three and reward the startled man with a whispered "thank you" and a kiss on the cheek.

Then she ran.

Around the nearest corner she raced. The first building on this street had a metal awning which threw its face into deep shade. Elsbeth rushed toward the sanctuary of darkness, elbowing her way through a snarl of pedestrians who filled the street. Her only thought was concealment, her goal the blue-black shadows.

Someone shouted. The voice rose above the crowd. Was she being berated by one whose feet she had trampled or was it the voice of her pursuer? She shook off the fear and sprinted the last few feet, before falling heavily against the storefront. She pulled her skirt tight around her legs lest a splash of color or flutter of fabric betray her hiding place. Over her mouth she clasped a shaking hand to muffle labored breathing that seemed to echo off the tin roof, the wall, the boardwalk, the air itself.

Only then did she chance a look behind. To her surprise the shuffling crowd, obstacles seconds before, provided a protective screen. It bought her time. She looked around.

The next structure, some fifty feet away, was nothing more than a canvas tarp stretched over upright poles. She could hear the clink of glass and ribald humor of men well on their way to drunkenness. In between her and the open air saloon, horses and burros had been tethered. Their hooves and appetites had rendered the patch of ground almost bare. The far end of the field was choked with thistle and beyond that she could see the new wood of shacks from the next street over.

Only one choice made sense.

She bolted for the horses. Their bodies would shield her from prying eyes. All too soon she realized her mistake. At her passing, the animals snorted loudly and pranced on restless legs. Neither soft word nor gentle touch would calm them.

"It's the stench of that man," she muttered under her breath. "His stink is all over me."

"Shush, shush," she begged but it did no good.

She fled the field before the horses gave her away, broke through a row of prickly weeds and sped toward a nearby shanty. It seemed to be a workshop of sorts. There were logs curing in the sun and piles of lumber cut into lengths lying about. More were stacked under an adjacent outdoor storage area. Elsbeth wriggled into a niche, well hidden in a dark triangle formed between the wall and the planks leaning against it.

She slumped to the ground and drew her knees to her chin. Though uncomfortable and cramped, the place seemed peaceful, a safe haven. Sawdust and curling paper-thin shavings gave off a pleasant smell. A spider's web hung above her head. On saner days she would have admired the delicate workmanship, but today was not sane.

Elsbeth watched with unnerving fascination as a fly lighted on the sticky threads. The more it struggled, the more entangled it became. Hadn't she too walked blindly into a trap? Why hadn't she stood her ground out there on the street? Surely someone would have dared confront Pierce. Instead, she ran. What a fool I was, she thought.

She dropped her forehead to her knees and shivered. At this moment she felt very much the fly.

III

Clamping her eyelids shut did little to ease the hollow ache of fear, for in this self-imposed darkness sound became the enemy. Benign street noises closed in to surround and threaten. Boots drumming the packed earth echoed all too near, and a merchant's innocent cry as he shouted up his goods mutated into the voice of Clayton Pierce.

Hands over ears solved nothing either, for through her fingers rushed wave after wave of panic, crashing against reason like storm surf upon a beach. The fatigue of recent days and events had clouded her thinking.

She bit her lip.

The air, used and reused in the confined space, became stale. The temperature rose. Elsbeth wasn't sure how long she crouched in the hideaway until a leg cramp made her aware of the passage of time. Perhaps she had eluded Pierce. Or he had given up. Or she had rated her importance to him too highly, and he had never pursued her at all.

This last thought, as unlikely as it seemed, brought a measure of comfort. She relaxed and considered shifting her position in order to stretch her legs. Before she could do so, a clatter and bang to her right put her on alert. She caught her breath and commanded her body into absolute stillness. A bead of resin dripped onto her hand. Another rattle and scrape of feet sounded almost at her side. A shower of sawdust drifted before her eyes and landed softly on her nose and cheeks. Shadows deepened. Elsbeth sensed the presence of another. Close. So very close.

Become smaller, she told herself. Invisible. Yes, invisible.

She hugged her arms tighter, but this slight movement triggered a tickle above her upper lip where a particle of sawdust remained. She tried to blow it away, but the urge to sneeze lingered, then grew and left her no choice but to reach up and brush at the torturing speck.

She didn't recall making any noise, but an utter silence settled in beside her. She knew then she had given herself away.

Hide! she thought. But how? Run! But where?

She stared at the wall of boards separating her from whatever lay on the other side. Suddenly a hand plunged into her hiding place and ripped away at the lumber. Elsbeth grappled around in the dim light but found no tool, no loose board, not a single article of use in her defense.

The smell of raw wood filled her nostrils as the last of her shelter tumbled to the ground. Hands encircled her wrists and pulled her to her feet. For a moment harsh sunlight silhouetted a figure, a man. Elsbeth tried to shove him away, but he held her fast.

Prepared for the worst, she heard, "Elsbeth? Is that you? Is it really you?"

She started at the voice. The black shape grayed into a familiar face.

"Billy?"

She felt his hands release their grip and trail up her sleeves to gently stroke her face. The rush of blood to her cheeks pulsated with the rhythm of her heart and drowned out the sounds of the world. A deep-seated fervor warmed her inside like a fire stoked to life on a winter's eve. Embarrassed, hoping she had not betrayed a feeling she had yet to fully reconcile within herself, Elsbeth abruptly turned aside.

"Praise the Lord, Billy. I feared it was someone else."

"Who?"

"A terrible, brutish, disgusting… You know he's after you?"

"Pierce." Billy growled. "Did he hurt you? I saw the blood, and we came searching right away."

"Blood?"

"On the steps outside the saloon."

"Oh, that. Just a sliver." She turned her hand over so he could see the gash on her finger. Elsbeth blushed a second time when Billy lowered his head and kissed the injured spot. His unshaven chin brushed her skin. She expected a weeks-old growth to be coarse and was surprised and pleased by its

277

baby-fineness.

"We," she said, reluctantly pulling back her hand and breaking their physical connection. "You said we."

"Ah, yes. Tom Warner and me. Cephas too. We've been up and down the streets."

"I managed to get free from…that man. I thought I'd found a good hiding place, but I guess I sorely misjudged it."

"No, Elsbeth. It *was* good. I never saw you."

"If you didn't see me, what were you doing in the woodpile?"

Billy's mouth drooped open. "Well, uh…" He rubbed the back of his hand against the nap of his whiskers, sighing audibly. "Circumstances arose making a slight detour necessary."

She frowned. "Meaning?"

"There's a man name of Chester Holt. He's here in town, up the street a piece."

"So?"

"Coming out from Missouri, I worked for him a spell."

"You didn't get along?"

"Passable well."

"You were mistreated?"

"Not so's you'd notice."

"Billy, don't make me drag this explanation out a syllable at a time. Why are you avoiding him?"

"For my work I was paid a fair wage…only Holt didn't exactly realize it at the time."

Elsbeth wrinkled her brow.

"I sort of took it."

"You stole from him?"

"Stole? Now that's mighty strong language. I earned that money."

"You're a thief, Billy? Is that what you're trying to tell me? And the good Lord above only knows why Clayton Pierce has been combing the countryside for you."

When Billy appeared on the verge of answering, Elsbeth raised her hands to stop him. She didn't want to hear. The pleasant glow she had felt on seeing him, alive and in good health, faded.

She pushed past him and raced toward the thistles. Billy followed.

Away from the carpenter's shop, she could hear the commotion Billy had mentioned, but for the moment she turned her back to it.

"Where's Charlie?"

"Tom left him in the care of a woman…the one from the saloon."

Elsbeth's lips hardened into a thin, straight line.

"And Cephas?"

"He's with Tom."

"And Tom?"

Billy pointed. "I reckon he's in the crowd up yonder."

Elsbeth looked where he indicated. Her fear of Pierce vanished. Tom would surely protect her. She had no doubt Billy too would keep her from harm's door. The first person to catch her eye was a lad standing at the fringe of onlookers. The boy bit into an apple while he stabbed at the ground with the battered tip of his shoe, sending dust clouds into the air. Next, she noted the lively harangue, not for its content, for the individual words didn't carry. It was the speaker's face that gave her pause. She recognized him—the sour old man from the settlers' camp. He sat atop a wagon seat and held tight the reins to a yoke of oxen—*her* wagon, *her* team.

"Chester Holt?" she asked.

Billy nodded.

Elsbeth remembered another time and place when she had left an ailing Billy in the care of this man's sister-in-law. Inadvertently, she had placed Billy at risk. She wouldn't do it again.

"You stay here. I'll go fetch Tom and Cephas. I owe this Mr. Holt his two horses in exchange for my rig. Maybe then he'll go away."

"He's my problem, Elsbeth. Something I've got to face, though I don't rightly know how to settle my tab with him just now. But I do know this. I won't let you go alone. What if Pierce is lurking about?"

"With all those people around, would he dare make a move?"

"Maybe not, but..." Billy lifted his rifle and examined it. "Short of murder, I don't know what will satisfy that man."

Elsbeth stared at the weapon in Billy's hand. "Then you mustn't go anywhere near him. Don't let false pride rule your reason, Billy, or you'll slam shut a door that might not open again." She stood on tiptoe and scanned the crowd. "Besides, Tom is there. I see him now." Her voice was dry and even. She didn't notice Billy's eyes grow cold.

Drawing in her breath, Elsbeth began to walk, all too aware of the crush of uncertain feelings when Billy fell into step at her side. Together they advanced.

Although the distance wasn't far, it seemed to take forever. Chester Holt's tirade continued unabated, evoking snickers and hoots from all around. He responded by damning the entire populace of Sacramento. He blamed anyone within earshot for not only a most recent test of his faith in humankind, but for his bad luck in general, for his misfortunate crossing, and even, it seemed, for the high price of potatoes. The only break in his stream of invectives came when he spied Billy and Elsbeth approach. At this he leaped

280

to his feet and aimed an accusing finger.

"The Devil's spawn," he screamed. "The both of them. Thieves and liars."

The press of miners and merchants parted like clods of dirt before a plowshare, leaving exposed the astonished couple, who stood transfixed by their new and unexpected role as center of attention.

Clambering from the wagon, Holt yelled again. "My horses! She cheated me out of my most excellent horses, cursing me with these worn-out, worthless creatures."

Elsbeth regained her wits and stepped forward, disregarding Billy's restraining arm, and spoke as calmly as she could. "Mr. Holt, you of all know better than that. The safe return of your horses was promised. My outfit was left only as collateral."

Reason fell on deaf ears. Holt's menacing eye impaled Billy. "Deny then that you hid this thievin' criminal under my nose to rob me even of these sorry animals the minute my back was turned."

"I do deny it…as the falsehood it is."

Red in the face, Holt scuffled in place, his hands fisted and white-knuckled.

Billy succeeded in pulling Elsbeth out of the way, then grabbed Holt by the lapel and shook him. Holt flailed his arms ineffectively. "Sheriff," he hollered. "Where's the sheriff? There's a murder in the making here!"

Billy threw him hard against the spokes of the wagon's wheel.

Elsbeth cut in. "Hush, you silly old fool. Your horses are at the stable being properly cared for."

At that instant Elsbeth spotted Tom and Cephas, although it was another man—one clad entirely in black— who extricated himself from the ever-increasing crowd and

281

tipped his hat toward Elsbeth. He was not a stranger. "Is that the solemn truth, ma'am?"

"It is indeed, sheriff," she replied. "Why else would I say so?"

The sheriff nodded toward Chester Holt. "Someone," he called out to the crowd, "go round up the horses in question. We'll wait."

The presence of the law bolstered Holt's churlish demeanor. "We'll do just that. And in the between time, there's another matter needs to be set aright. This scoundrel, Brooster, stole from the cache of coins in my wagon. A hundred dollars worth."

"That so, son?"

Billy had no answer. He hung his head.

"'Fraid I have no choice then but to arrest you."

Elsbeth faced the sheriff. "What if the sum were repaid? Would that discharge the debt and keep Billy out of your jail?"

"Sounds like an expeditious solution to me, ma'am."

Under his breath Billy confided to Elsbeth. "I have no money."

"But I do," she whispered back.

"No," sputtered Holt. "He's got to be punished. Punished, I say."

"Case dismissed," answered the sheriff.

Elsbeth beckoned to Cephas. When the boy sheepishly entered the open space, she relieved him of the pouch slung over his shoulder.

"Thank you for guarding this so carefully for me, Cephas." He blushed even as a wide grin spread across his face.

From the satchel Elsbeth pulled a white crock with a protruding stopper. She uncorked the jar and from it poured a mound of shiny flakes into her palm. Billy murmured, "Elsbeth, no," but she had already made up her mind. She held out the amount for the sheriff to inspect. He nodded approval, and she deposited the gold into Holt's outstretched hand. He quickly stuffed it into his pocket, though even as he did, he muttered "unfair" and "they're all agin me."

At the periphery of her vision, Elsbeth saw Tom crane his neck for a better view of the transaction, his face screwed up in curious interest. Then she saw him approach.

"This is a bit rash of you, Elsbeth, to part so readily with a good deal of gold. Brooster has admitted his guilt. The crime is his. How is it you're so willing to pay his debts?"

"Not pay, Tom. It's only a loan."

"Hmm." Tom put his arm around her shoulders and smiled. "We'll call it an investment then. No harm in seeking a good return."

"No, Tom," she replied, keeping her gaze on Billy. "There'll be no interest charged."

"It's just we have to be careful with our resources. Finding claims with paydirt is no more than a lottery…lucky only for some."

"I'm sure I can manage temporarily without this little bit."

Tom's smile dimmed, though the possessive clutch of his embrace never faltered.

The sight of the gold seemed to remind the onlookers of the real reason they had traveled so many grueling miles to California, and it wasn't for entertainment in the streets of Sacramento. The crowd exhaled as one. Those with mining gear or other supplies hoisted it to their shoulders. Others began to disperse. An eerie silence befell the scene. It lasted barely a breath, for just then Chester Holt looked up and over the heads of the remaining bystanders.

"You people need proof there's a conspiracy afoot against me? There it is."

He pointed wildly, and as one the crowd pivoted toward Clayton Pierce, who was at that moment attempting to negotiate his own mount away from the shuffling crowd while he led two additional horses tied securely to a stout rope.

"Those are *my* horses."

Holt's accusation carried above the hubbub, stopping everyone in his tracks, including Clayton Pierce.

"He's in cahoots with the girl."

Pierce growled. "Shut up, old man."

"No. This was all planned, a distraction so's I wouldn't notice them makin' off with what's rightfully mine."

Sunlight flashed on the steel barrel of Pierce's revolver. No one had seen him draw it, but now he aimed it at Holt. "I said shut up. I got business with that girl but not about horses."

Billy too had been quick. He emerged from the scrambling crowd of miners, rifle cocked and leveled at the horseman.

"This has nothing to do with Elsbeth. Leave her alone. You're looking for me, and now you've found me."

Behind rough, black whiskers and lingering bruise, Pierce's color rose. His eyes narrowed to slits, his mouth became a crooked sneer.

"Well, well. Face to face," he snarled.

"Drop the gun and get down," said Billy.

The sheriff moved in slowly, his own weapon steady in his hand. "That would be advisable, leastways till I've sorted through this whole affair."

With a thunk Pierce's weapon dropped to the ground, though he remained seated.

284

"You, too, son," added the sheriff and removed the rifle from Billy's grasp.

Pierce reached behind him and unknotted the rope leading Holt's horses. The animals skittered a few feet away, and the man jerked his head at Billy. "There's your horsethief, sheriff," said Pierce. "Not these two nags. One of Uncle's Sam's own. A deserter too. I'm gonna haul his ass back East...dead or alive."

He still made no move to dismount but shifted in his saddle. Elsbeth watched him closely, especially his hands. She saw the right one drift slowly but deliberately downward to a place hidden from the sheriff's view. In a saddle holster the butt of a small gun was clearly visible.

Elsbeth's throat constricted. Whether from the shock and pain of the surprising new charges against Billy or from a final, sudden rush of Pierce's hand, she had no time to determine. She looked quickly at Tom. He, too, wore a pistol, tucked under his belt. She snatched it away and slid into view.

"'All the sinners of my people shall die by the sword,'" she said and raised the gun at Pierce. "Amos 9:10."

In that same instant a blinding light streaked from the sky. A deafening boom shattered the afternoon and rolled and rumbled through the city before spending itself across the flat Sacramento plain. A few drops of rain puckered the dust at their feet, but all eyes focused on four wisps of smoke that hung lifeless in the air.

A whimpering Chester Holt staggered against the startled oxen. He caressed the tip of his ear. Blood oozed along his fingers. Clayton Pierce tumbled from his horse and lay motionless on the ground, a pearl-handled gun still gripped in his hand, a smoky vapor wafting from its barrel.

Elsbeth teetered off balance, recoiling from the kick of the weapon she held. A third cloud of smoke wreathed the

285

sheriff's face, and from behind the fourth stepped the Reverend Ogle.

Tom rushed to Elsbeth's side and drew her close. He whispered into her ear and stroked her hair. In turn, she sagged noticeably into his arms and allowed him to rock her back and forth. Over his shoulder Elsbeth watched the reverend dab a handkerchief on Chester Holt's wound while a small boy looked on. The sheriff nudged the prone body of Clayton Pierce, shrugged and walked away.

Elsbeth pushed herself free and asked, "Is he truly dead this time?" The jagged wound in the man's chest left no need for an answer.

"Is what he said the truth? Desertion? Government property?" she asked. But when she turned to where he had stood, Billy Brooster, like so many times before, was nowhere in sight.

She felt a hand slip into hers. "Gosh amighty, Miz Elsbeth," said Cephas. "Sure got quiet around here."

CHAPTER 13

"We Gather This Day..."

I

"Mmm."

Elsbeth had almost forgotten how good hot water could feel. And soap. Real, foaming, sweet-scented soap. She sank lower into the copper tub. It wasn't much larger than a wash basin, but she could sit down in it, let the sudsy water caress her body, and try not to dwell on the fact this was Kate Malone's room and her tub and her soap.

"Mmm," she said again.

When the water gave up its warmth, Elsbeth reluctantly rose and stepped out, wrapping a blanket around her.

The morning sun filtered through lacy curtains and mottled her feet with patterns of shadow and light. She wiggled her toes on the woolen rug then crossed to Kate's dressing table. There she ran her finger wistfully over the smooth alabaster handle of a hairbrush. She picked up a hand mirror and studied her face. The previous nineteen months had indeed altered the childish innocence of this minister's daughter. But into what? she asked herself. Not harder, not bitter, not even unattractive, just somehow different—the only word to come to mind. She returned the mirror to the dresser, careful to replace it exactly as she found it.

On a peg nearby hung a dress. It fell in graceful folds, its soft cambric neither stained nor ripped.

Kate's dress.

Elsbeth edged closer, almost touched it.

Tom had relayed the offer. "Wear it. Katherine doesn't mind."

But Elsbeth minded.

She donned her own clothes instead—a dark blue skirt and gray blouse with leg-of-mutton sleeves and a white collar. It was worn but not noticeably so. She had retrieved it from her trunk in the wagon.

A scratch at the door urged her to hurry. After she had hooked the last of the buttons, she opened the door.

"There's my little soldier," she said.

Charlie flung himself into her arms. He had been scrubbed clean and his hair combed. A span of wrist peeked between his cuff and hand, reminding Elsbeth how much he, too, had changed.

"Mama, let's go. Let's go."

Elsbeth hugged him close, but it was like trying to capture a whirlwind. He spun from her grasp and danced around the room. In a blink he was back in her embrace. He raked his fingers through her still-wet hair then traced her mouth, pressing and molding her lips into a smile.

"Everyone's waiting for you, Mama."

The door from Kate's room emptied to the alley behind the tavern. Tom and Cephas waited just outside. They marched back and forth like sentries pacing out their watches. She thought how handsome Tom looked in frock coat and necktie. Cephas had grown, or so it seemed, from boy into young man. Hurriedly she tucked a wayward tendril of hair behind her ear and went outside.

Tom greeted her with a frown. "I thought you were going to wear…?" He stopped mid-sentence and smiled. "Doesn't matter. You look lovely, Elsbeth."

He escorted her along the alley to a borrowed springboard wagon and helped her aboard. He gestured Cephas to climb into the bed behind and swung Charlie in beside the boy. The toddler, however, scrambled over the seat and nestled in between Tom and Elsbeth, opening a gap between the two. Neither objected.

Yesterday's unexpected storm had cooled the air and muddied the streets, but it had passed with the night. Today the sun shone brightly. It reflected off puddles, glistened on windowpanes, sparkled like diamonds on the damp grass.

It was just the sort of day every girl dreamed about for a wedding day.

Within minutes they arrived at Reverend Ogle's church-without-walls. He waited, Bible in hand. Elsbeth noted the wooden cross behind him, planted firmly though somewhat atilt. He offered his hand and steadied her as she alighted the wagon.

"It's good to see you again, Reverend," she said.

"And unarmed no less." He threw open his coat as if to prove it true.

"Reverend Ogle, you continue to amaze me…and amuse me." Elsbeth joined in his laughter.

"But now to the business at hand." With a flourish he stationed Elsbeth center aisle. "The bride," he whispered, gifting her with a look of fatherly love though his now-sober expression also hinted of apprehension and unspoken concern. Then he left her to busy himself with the others.

Elsbeth watched as he assigned places to each of Tom

and the boys. She waited calmly, only marginally aware that Ogle had apparently changed his mind and now shuffled them again and yet again, almost as if reluctant to begin. She studied her clasped hands. Empty. They should be holding a nosegay, she thought, or posies. It *is* my wedding, after all. But the only one to ever give her flowers was not among them.

Suddenly her skin prickled as if touched by an unseen hand. In response she lifted her eyes and scanned the street and the buildings lining it. Other than the traffic of strangers, what was she expecting to see? Whom was she expecting to see?

The answer was nothing...no one.

The events of the previous afternoon remained vivid in her mind. It had all happened so fast—the lightning and crash of thunder, the explosion of gunfire. When she had recovered from the noise and confusion and had asked Billy to explain himself and the new charges leveled against him, his absence spoke for him—and loudly.

The crowd had thinned, and Tom ushered her away from the body sprawled at their feet.

"First I must speak with that man," said Elsbeth and headed toward the one remaining drama of the afternoon.

Chester Holt's string of curses had subsided under the ministrations of Marcus Ogle though, by no means, had he given up his protest. When the minister retreated, Holt moaned to anyone who would listen, "Brooster should pay. He made me out the fool and he should pay for that."

"You've *been* paid, Mr. Holt," said Elsbeth. "You've a pocket full of gold, and your horses are safe and within view. I'm reclaiming my wagon. I regret you've been hurt, but I hope never to lay eyes upon you again."

While the injured man sputtered and gasped, groping

for an appropriate retort, Elsbeth stalked away. She found Tom engaged in conversation with the reverend.

"So, young man, you say you're in need of a preacher's services?"

"That's right, sir. And soon." When Elsbeth approached, his arm encircled her waist. "Elsbeth and me," he continued. "The two of us."

Ogle looked from one to the other. He nodded at Elsbeth and to Tom said, "Then you must be...?"

"Tom Warner."

"Tom Warner. I've heard of you from several quarters."

"Uh...about the...?"

"Wedding."

"Yes sir. A lady needs someone to take responsibility for decisions and the like. I promised her we'd be married. That right, Elsbeth? No excuse to wait any longer."

"And what do you say, Elsbeth?"

"It *was* our intent...is, I mean."

"Settled then," said Tom as he took Elsbeth's hand in his, an expectant look on his face.

"Not now, my boy," said Ogle. "We're in for some weather. Now won't do at all."

As if on cue dark clouds roiled overhead and bloated droplets of rain spattered the ground, sending even the most curious of bystanders scurrying for cover. Tom ran for the wagon, pulling Elsbeth along with him.

"Let's get sheltered for now. I'm sure Charlie's missing you."

Tom urged the team of oxen into motion while Elsbeth sat beside him, the rain washing her face. From time to time she peered around the canvas cover and along the rain-soaked, deserted streets.

No one had stepped forward then, and no one stepped forward now.

Tom was still at her side, only a day had passed and so many things had changed.

"Elsbeth, you may join hands with Mr. Warner." Ogle's words brought her back to the present.

"Yes, of course."

Abandoning her thoughts, she extended a hand to Tom, but it was Charlie who ran forward and caught it up. The boy also grabbed Tom's and hung on to them both, seeming to understand intuitively he was the link that held together this chain. Despite a disapproving glance from the reverend, he held on tight.

"It's all right," said Elsbeth. "He's part of this." She sighed and weakly returned Tom's smile.

Ogle nodded and cleared his throat. "Dearly beloved, we have gathered here today..."

His words penetrated Elsbeth's mind in spurts, for she was more attuned to the relentless pressure on her fingers from the eager child at her side.

"...it becometh those who enter into marriage to weigh with reverent minds..."

She had weighed it all, hadn't she?

"Husbands, love your wives. Wives, submit yourselves unto your husbands."

Husbands love, she thought, wives submit. The way it's been throughout the ages. The way the Bible teaches.

"Into this holy estate, this man and this woman come now to be united."

Before her eyes flashed scenes from the long road she'd traveled to this end.

"Thomas, do you take—"

"'Scuse me for interrupting, Reverend. It's Amos. My

292

name is Amos Warner. Tom's only my middle name. Want everything right and proper, you know."

"Yes. Well then, Amos, do you take Elsbeth as your wife? Will you love her and comfort her? Will you keep her in sickness and in health? Will you forsake all others so long as you shall live?"

"I will. Yes sir, I will."

Moved by his sincerity, Elsbeth looked at Tom anew. In him she saw a family for Charlie. A home. Someone to provide. She had followed him into California for these very things, and he had just promised them all. Wasn't this what mattered? All she'd ever wanted? Her dream?

"Elsbeth, do you forsake all others?"

Caught by surprise at the sound of her name, Elsbeth realized she had missed Ogle's recitation of her vows. The reverend stared at her curiously.

"For as long as you live?" He raised an eyebrow.

Charlie's hand quivered with anticipation. Tom seemed ready to burst. Without turning around she knew the ceremony also touched Cephas, for he sniffled audibly from a bench behind them.

With Ogle's question still hanging in the air, the answer to her own quite suddenly became clear. She raised her chin and opened her mouth to reply.

"Yes! Yes! Yes!" Charlie bubbled over with excitement. "Say yes, Mama. Say yes."

Elsbeth looked down at the child. Slowly she sank to her knees and touched a fingertip to his lips.

"My dear Charlie," she said quietly. "I can't imagine what you must think life is all about. The people you love disappoint you and let you down. Like your first Ma and Pa, they go away and you can't fathom where or why. I know you don't understand any of it.

293

"Maybe I can explain it this way. Life's a long, long road, like the one that brought us here to California. Sometimes the path is clear and other times we lose our way. The going is rough, then smooth, then oh so hard again. Sometimes we even find ourselves on a road where we never thought we'd be. But to get where we want to go, we have to keep on following the road...and the right way isn't always the easiest.

"Mama's doing an awful lot of talking, isn't she? All along you've been my good little soldier, Charlie. Now you're going to have to be brave for me one more time."

She picked him up. Tom still held the child's other hand, but Charlie wrested free and clung to Elsbeth with both arms and a strength far beyond his meager years. Entwined as one, they faced the minister.

"Reverend Ogle, you've been so kind to me and troubled yourself to put aside your church building to prepare for this service. But the truth is, I can't allow you to go on. My answer is no."

A secret smile flickered at the reverend's mouth but died when Tom spoke up.

"Hold on there. It's too late. You can't stop now. We're almost married. *I* agreed to it. *I* said yes."

"But I didn't and I won't."

"I think you owe me an explanation."

"I owe you nothing other than to say it wasn't meant to be. If I owe anyone, it's your father—for his kindness and acceptance Any other debt I may owe will have to remain in my heart."

"What about our plans to build a business in Sacramento?"

"You mean run a saloon...full of shameless women? Those were your plans, Tom."

294

"What about the boy? I've developed a great fondness for the boy."

"I know. That weighs heavy on my heart, but you've also developed a great fondness for my gold. And I think your eagerness to bind us in a marriage contract is tainted by something that seems to concern you much more than me or Charlie."

"What could that possibly be?"

"Yourself, Tom. Yourself."

Tom's voice took on a razor's edge. "It's that Brooster fellow, isn't it?"

"No, Tom."

"I say it is. Every time I turn around, he's there. First up north, then trailing along to the diggings, and now here in Sacramento."

"Billy has nothing to do with my decision."

"You're a foolish woman, Elsbeth."

"Perhaps the future will bear that out, but for now it's the choice I've made."

Tom's face clouded, but he had run out of words.

Elsbeth shifted Charlie on her hip. "Charlie and I have a different road to follow—with Cephas if he chooses to join us."

With that she glanced toward Cephas. For a few seconds the young man rocked nervously on the wooden seat, then rose and stood by her side. When Tom made no move, Elsbeth turned and left.

As they departed, threatening words rang out from behind. "This isn't the end of it. I'll have the last word, Elsbeth. I swear I will."

A quick glance around shocked Elsbeth. The man she had at one time agreed to spend her life with stood indignant and red-faced, the Reverend Ogle's restraining hand clamped firmly on his shoulder.

"Good-bye, Tom," she murmured, surprising herself how little she cared whether he heard or not.

She and the two boys walked a full block before the warmth of the sun soothed her anguish and eased the knots in her neck and shoulders. She studied the shadows thrown out before them—three well-defined heads, one united body.

It was Cephas, however, who voiced her thoughts.

"We'll be gettin' along just fine, Miz Elsbeth."

She caught up his arm and gave it a squeeze.

"Yes, Cephas, God willing, we will."

II

From where he sat Billy Brooster could see the sheriff. The lawman balanced his chair on two legs while his body bridged the walk outside the office—his back against the wall, feet crossed over the hitchrail, eyes shut. He appeared to doze, but Billy knew the man was not sleeping on the job.

Abruptly the chair tipped forward, the front legs scraping sharply as they landed. The sheriff cursed out loud. Only then did Billy hear a scuff of boots and realize someone approached.

"Sheriff, I need to discuss some business with you."

The lawman didn't rise nor did he lower his legs which blocked the newcomer's advance and held him out of view. But Billy recognized the voice, and he shrank deeper into the shadows of his cell.

"Perhaps we could better handle this in your office," said Tom Warner.

"It's a fine day, young man. We can talk right here."

"It has to do with Brooster."

The sheriff ran a fingernail between his two front teeth.

"The cause of that commotion on the street the other day," continued Tom.

"I'm listening."

"That Brooster is trouble. Army deserter, you know."

"So's half the miners tearing up the streambeds around Sutter's and on up the Feather."

"He stole a horse from the United States government. That's a serious offense."

When Tom received only a lethargic nod for an answer, he dug into his pants pocket and thrust a number of coins into the sheriff's hand.

"Here's two hundred dollars to put up as reward to whoever finds him and lands him in jail where he belongs."

"Patriotic cuss, ain't you?"

"Some things are only right."

The sheriff lined up the coins in the palm of his hand. "See what I can do," he said.

"I'm counting on you."

"Bet you are."

The footsteps died away. The sheriff lumbered to his feet and walked inside, throwing his hat on the desk. The coins jingled each time he bounced them in the palm of his hand. Finally, he faced the room's one cell with its wall of iron strips latticed like the top of a cherry pie.

"You heard?" he asked.

Billy Brooster stepped into the light. "I heard, yes. But I don't understand."

"Seems there's a load of revenge he needs to shed."

"On me obviously. I still don't get it. There's nothing

297

here for me now. He's gone and married Elsbeth. I only want to get on with gettin' on."

"Ah…puzzle solved. Not married."

"Who's not married?"

The sheriff jerked his head toward the open door.

"You're mistaken. I saw them." Billy started to pace. "I hid near the mercantile across from the church. Saw them stand up in front of that minister. I didn't like it one bit, so I left." His whole body sagged, but he continued on, though his voice was low, as if talking only to himself. "Everything they said about me is true. What would I have to offer her?" He chuckled without mirth and rapped his fist on the ironwork separating himself and the lawman.

"She didn't make it to the 'I do.'"

In answer to Billy's questioning frown, the sheriff explained. "That minister as you call him—Marcus Ogle—likes to stop by on occasion—share a nip or two. Seems to think it's not fitting for a man of the cloth to imbibe in a public tavern, so he comes here. We shoot the bull some." He shook his head. "Damnedest minister I ever saw."

"So? Go on."

"Turns out the young lady walked out on the nuptials."

Billy groaned and retreated to the far corner of the cell where he kicked straw around the floor while the sheriff opened a strongbox under his desk. Tom's money disappeared inside and the padlock snapped shut.

"Best we get going, son."

The cell door clanked open. It hadn't been locked. After gathering his few possessions, Billy exited the confined space and waited while the sheriff tidied his desktop. Beside him heavy leg irons and handcuffs hung from a hook on the wall. Billy's stomach soured when he looked at them.

"Seeing as how you came along freely, and admit your guilt, and I know you had nothing to do with the demise of one Clayton Pierce, I reckon there's no need for the hardware," said the lawman, gesturing at the manacles. "C'mon on, let's not miss that steamer."

"Who actually did kill Pierce?" asked Billy.

"Now, why you wantin' to know that?"

"From what I witnessed, four shots rang out. One was aimed at me." His voice almost a whisper now, Billy continued, "Elsbeth fired too."

"Not likely Pierce intended doin' himself in, and that little gal couldn't hit the broad side of a barn if she tried. She's clean in my book."

"Then..."

"Then there's Marcus and me. I'm not about to be accusing a man of God, and I consider myself a pretty darn good shot, so let's leave it at that."

It appeared they had used up their conversation. Neither man spoke as they made their way through the commercial district, crossing first to J Street then angling west on Front until they reached the wharf. Here activity increased as ships disgorged both men and supplies.

"Greenies," remarked Billy. "Every last one."

He scanned the eager faces and felt much older than his years. His brief experience in the goldfields had hardened his outlook and taught him lessons about mind-numbing labor, disappointment and loss. But these new Argonauts had traveled too far to want to hear the truth.

Billy sighed. "They wouldn't be smiling so grandly if they knew what lay ahead."

"Not all gold and glory, huh?"

"No, sir. I helped bury six good men in the diggings."

"Sickness?"

299

"Earthquake."

"You were lucky then."

"Not as lucky as Tom Warner."

"How so?"

Reluctantly Billy relived those terrible hours. One by one he recited the names of the dead. He wouldn't have called them friends, but comrades surely, and the recollection of their lonely graves darkened his face.

"Tom Warner likely watched it all from the bluff. With an extra hand we might have found and saved one or two, but he took off."

"No law against being a coward."

"It was just mighty handy he had everyone's share of the provisions with him in the camp wagon. Don't seem fair to those men's families."

The sheriff stroked his chin. "And now this same Tom Warner is part-owner in Kate Malone's place."

"That's right."

"Hmm."

They fell into silence again while all around the bustle of commerce continued. Despite the numbers jamming the dock and marketplace, a sameness manifested itself in the heavy boots, the sturdy trousers, checked shirts and slouch hats of this singular fraternity of adventurers. The Army uniforms, therefore, contrasted sharply, and Billy spotted them immediately.

"You're doing the right thing," said the sheriff as he hailed the two soldiers. "Eight and a half months' duty at the garrison in Sonoma. Coulda been worse."

Billy nodded. The soldiers fell into place beside him, one on the left, one on the right.

"Do your time," the sheriff continued. "Clear your conscience. Wipe the slate clean." He laughed out loud then and slapped his knee. "Darned if I'm not starting to sound like ol' Marcus."

The soldiers prepared to escort Billy toward a waiting ship but were still within earshot when the sheriff added, "By the way, Brooster. That reward money. Shame for it to go to waste, and since the terms dictated by its generous donor seem to point to you as the rightful recipient, it'll be waiting here if you decide to return."

Billy couldn't help but appreciate the irony.

III

A playful wind blew across the valley, transforming the canvas of spring flowers into a living thing. Elsbeth was glad to be rid of the depressing winter rains. Although hungry miners would soon be lining up at her wagon, she paused in her work to breathe in the fragrant air and enjoy the riot of color. The breeze lapped at the linen cloth she had spread over the long plank table and threatened to sail it away along with the assortment of bowls and plates she had used to anchor it. But it was too nice a day to mind. Humming a lively tune, she collected two sizable rocks from under the wagon and placed them among the dishes. The sun was almost straight up, a good indication hungry men would be arriving at any moment.

"Interesting sign."

Elsbeth waved as Reverend Ogle strode rapidly toward her.

"Cephas painted it," she said.

For a moment they both regarded the large whitewashed poster propped against the wagon's tongue.

"CHEPE MEELS" it read. They burst out laughing.

"We mustn't laugh," warned Elsbeth. She swallowed hard before facing him with hard-won composure. "It was a labor of the heart. That's all that matters."

"Ah, yes indeed."

"Besides, I hear there's talk of statehood for California. That'll mean schools for my boys. Until then, the men who eat my meals don't care a fig how it's spelled."

"Your kitchen has a fine reputation, Elsbeth."

"It's carried us through the winter and that terrible flood. Without my wagon, I wouldn't have been able to move everything so easily to this location. I might have suffered as badly as the townspeople. Anyway, I have a surprise."

She took his arm and walked him behind the wagon which occupied the front third of her recently-purchased lot. She led him past a beehive-shaped clay oven partnered with a firepit and huge, cast iron stewpot to where a picket fence was taking shape. Ox-eye daisies and pale purple violets bloomed in orderly beds near the rails and uprights, framing an opening that lacked only a gate. Here she stopped and pointed. Four stakes tied with strips of red fabric had been driven into the ground. Lengths of string stretched between them and formed a perfect rectangle.

"My very own house, Reverend."

"You'll not return East?"

"No. My future is here. Beyond this fence, inside this gate…a new life, Reverend Ogle, the thing of my dreams." A rosy glow of pride colored her face as she gazed out at the sticks, for here indeed was her dream. When she thought about it, she hardly recognized it from the dream of her youth. It had evolved just as she had and taken on a different shape and hue. But it was hers nonetheless. "A canvas tarp is not a roof," she explained. "A crowded wagon is not a home.

302

Charlie and Cephas deserve more. And me. I want it, too."

Ogle eagerly offered to help her build and his easy friendship brought comfort, but Elsbeth pictured his still half-finished church and contemplated his questionable skill at carpentry. Perhaps he entertained the same thoughts, for the moment they looked at one another they broke out laughing again.

"I have news, too," said the clergyman as he dabbed at his eyes with a handkerchief. "The sheriff has put a lock on *Green-Eyed Kate's*."

The reference to Tom's saloon sobered them both.

"I heard it had been damaged in the flood."

"No, no, Elsbeth. This is something new. A question of how Warner came upon his original stake in the place. The sheriff uncovered claims to that money from other miners and the families of some who'd died. The interruption to business got up Kate Malone's Irish dander and she sent Tom packing."

"Tom's gone?"

"Headed north to Oregon Territory, day before last."

IV

"Show me again, Mama."

"Charlie, if I keep showing you, I'll never get the work done."

"One more time, please."

Elsbeth dropped the hammer she'd been using to nail a wooden plank to an upright post. She took the child's hand and followed him inside the beginnings of their new home. Although the walls were only two courses high and mother

303

and child could easily have stepped over, they walked around and entered through the gap that would become the front door. Neat rows of stones lying along the dirt floor defined future rooms. She pointed as she spoke.

"The fireplace will be built there. A big braided rug will cover the floor where we're standing. The table will go over there."

"That's for eating supper at, right?"

"And for doing your lessons. My bed will be in that little room."

"And here's my bed." Charlie jumped into the center of the second small room and threw his arms wide.

"Yes, Charlie. Unless I can manage a loft above. Then you and Cephas will sleep up there." Their eyes lifted toward an invisible upper floor but saw only the California sky, plum-colored now with the approach of dusk. Elsbeth took a deep breath. "That's someday, Charlie. But we do have our fence. All done, all around."

She whirled in circles, her skirt fluttering wildly as the spun.

"Mama, who's that?"

The serious tone in Charlie's voice brought her to a standstill. A darkened figure waited outside the new swing gate. Elsbeth shaded her eyes, but the setting sun cast the visitor as a silhouette and she couldn't make out who it was.

"Yes?" she called.

No response.

She left Charlie, slowly made her way toward the man, and was almost upon him when he removed his hat and thrust into her hand an offering of a single white-petaled daisy with buttonlike center of yellow.

"A beautiful flower for a beautiful lady," he said.

She recognized the gift—a product of her own

garden—and she recognized at last that no stranger had come to call. Her mouth went dry.

"Billy." An uninvited blush flashed across her cheeks. She hoped he wouldn't notice. "I was sure we had seen the last of you."

He chewed on his lower lip while he explained where he had been. "I have only one more wrong to right…my debt to you. I've come into the sum of two hundred dollars. Legally," he added.

"And then what?"

"I'll look for work." He glanced over her shoulder. "Maybe try my hand at house-building if I can find someone in need of such a service."

"And then what?"

He reached over the gate and gently stroked her hand. "Settle down…if someone will have me."

Elsbeth studied his face, examined his eyes and read his soul…then opened the gate and, just as she had done so many months before, invited him in.

Made in the USA
Coppell, TX
26 May 2023

17361451R00184